NOT ANOTHER
Love Song

NOT ANOTHER
Love Song

Olivia Wildenstein

Swoon READS
New York

A Swoon Reads Book
An Imprint of Feiwel and Friends and Macmillan Publishing Group, LLC
120 Broadway, New York, NY 10271

Our books may be purchased in bulk for promotional, educational, or business use. Please
contact your local bookseller or the Macmillan Corporate and Premium Sales Department at
(800) 221-7945 ext. 5442 or by email at MacmillanSpecialMarkets@macmillan.com.

Library of Congress Control Number: 2019948818
ISBN 9781250224644 (hardcover) / ISBN 9781250224637 (ebook)

Book design by Mike Burroughs

First edition, 2020

10 9 8 7 6 5 4 3 2 1

swoonreads.com

To all the young dreamers who dare to want something out of reach.

A-Side
Ten

1

One Strange Cookie

A *short stranger will come into your life this year.*

"That's specific." I wave the paper at my mother, who's sitting across the table from me in our favorite Chinese haunt.

Golden Dragon is not the best or trendiest restaurant in Nashville, but we've been going to it since before I could wield chopsticks. I'm still not a pro. Half the time my dumplings slither out and plop into the sauce bowl, spraying the salmon-colored tablecloth with brown spots.

Mom tucks a short strand of blonde hair behind her ear. Her pixie cut makes her look like a rock star, but decorating houses for people in the music industry and paying for my music classes are as far as her involvement in *that world* goes. She prays I'll grow out of my aspirations, but music is my life.

"You don't have any plans to make me a grandma, right?"

"Ew." I wrinkle my nose. "Definitely not. Besides, I want a career."

With or without my mom's blessing, I'm going to be the next Mona Stone. Sometimes I think Mom doesn't want me to become a musician because Dad was a musician, and even though she must've loved him at some point—the point when I was conceived—she no longer harbors fuzzy feelings for him. Anytime I listen to one of his songs, her lips thin. He's not even alive anymore, but whatever went wrong between them has endured beyond the grave.

"What does yours say?" I ask.

She cracks her fortune cookie open and extricates the tiny white scroll. "*Your shoes will make you happy today.*"

"No way." I snatch the paper from her fingers. Sure enough, that's the message. "So? Do they make you happy?"

She stretches out one of her legs and scrutinizes her brown suede bootie. "You know what? I *am* feelin' mighty happy right now."

"And here I thought sharing spring rolls with your lovely daughter was the source of your happiness."

"Nah." She winks. "It's the shoes."

I fake pout.

Although she smiles, it doesn't reach her eyes. "I'm gonna miss these weekly dinners next year."

"Mom—"

"I want you to get out of this town and see more of the world." In other words, she wants to send me away from the music scene. It's funny that she thinks my passion is geographically induced. I simply take advantage of what my town has to offer.

Sometimes—especially when Mom wants to shove me out of Nashville—I wish I'd been born to Mona Stone. Like Mom, my idol's self-made, but where Mom contented herself with settling among the stars, Mona conquered the freaking moon.

I want the moon, too.

Mom signals for the check and digs out her wallet. "I got one of my customers to write you a recommendation letter for Cornell. I'll email it to you when we get home."

I sit on my hands. "Not all singers become train wrecks."

Her mouth flattens, then: "Angie . . ."

"Look at Mona Stone. She never got into drugs *or* alcohol, and she started at eighteen."

"Mona Stone shouldn't be your idol."

"Why not?"

"Because."

"Because what?"

Miss Ting slides a plastic tray with our bill over one of the brown sauce spots. When I was younger, Mom and I played a game: if I could eat a meal at Golden Dragon without dirtying the table linen, I got to play DJ in her car the entire week. If I lost—which was the usual outcome—I was stuck listening to Mom's favorite satellite preset: Classic FM. I don't dislike Vivaldi, but I have a preference for songs with lyrics.

Mom drops two twenties in the small tray, then stands and hoists her fringe bag over her shoulder.

I stand up and follow her to the glass door. "Why do you dislike her so much?"

"Because she chose her career over her family!" Mom's voice booms out of her and rings through the parking lot.

I clench my fingers around my phone. "The choice wasn't hers!"

Mom folds her arms. "Really? Whose choice was it, then?"

"Her husband's. *He* left *her*."

Mom shakes her head, and her dangling gold coin earrings jingle and gleam. "Angie, I'm glad you're driven *and* stubborn, but don't be naive. Mona's husband left her because the woman cared more about her fans than she cared about their kids." Her grip on her biceps turns white-knuckled. "Same way your daddy cared more about his guitar than he did about us." She adds this in such a low voice it barely registers.

But it does.

It's never been a secret that Dad was passionate about music, but this is the first time I realize how wildly jealous my mother was of his passion. Maybe Mona reminds her of Dad. Maybe that's the fatal flaw in my trajectory to stardom—idolizing someone who hits too close to home. Maybe if I worshipped a singer with a stable family life, she'd be supportive.

"I'll never do that, Mom. I'll never abandon you."

"Me?" Mom croaks. "Oh, baby, I'm not worried about you abandoning me, 'cause that's simply impossible. You couldn't get rid of me if you tried. I love you too darn much. But I really want you to see what else is out there. You're only seventeen. Gosh, at seventeen, I had no clue what I wanted to do."

But I do. I've known since I was a kid.

No good has ever come of cornering Mom into conversations she doesn't want to have, so I back away from it, from her. She might think I'm naive, but I'm not.

I stare at the sun dipping on the horizon, swathing my hometown in pastels. "I promised Rae I'd stop by her place tonight."

It's our ritual. Every year, on the eve of the new school year, I hang out with my best friend. We don't braid each other's hair or anything, but we make a list of things we want from the year to come, then stick our lists into her metallic-pink piggy bank and check them over on the last day of school to see how much we've accomplished.

"You want me to drop you off?" Mom asks, beeping open her silver Volvo SUV.

"No, I'll bike there. And I promise, I'll be home by nine."

Mom nods.

As we drive away, I fiddle with the radio dial until I catch the tail end of a Lady Antebellum song. I'm about to tune in to another station when the radio host mentions Mona Stone's sitting next to him and has an announcement.

I side-eye Mom, wait for her to tell me to change the station, but I don't think she's even listening.

"Hi, Mona."

"Hi, Ned. Thanks for having me on your set."

"So I heard you had some big news for your fans."

"I certainly do." Her speaking voice is honeyed and melodic, exactly like her singing voice. "First off, I'd like to thank y'all for the outpouring of kindness for my latest album. I'm so honored by your love and devotion."

"It's a fantastic album."

"Aw, Ned, you're sweet." She laughs. She has such a great laugh. "Anyway, I was invited here today so I could speak about a little contest I'm hostin'."

I sit up and sneak a glance at Mom again. She still hasn't looked my way or changed the station, which is a miracle.

"This is for every aspiring songwriter out there. If you've written a song, send it my way. It could become the title track on my next album. All the details are up on my websi—"

Drake's voice blasts out of the radio.

"Mom—"

She keeps spinning the dial, as though trying to find the bandwidth furthest from the one Mona spoke on. "Don't even think about it."

I plant my elbow on the armrest and glare out my window.

"I can hear you thinkin' about it, Angie."

Finally Mom turns the radio off, and the silence is so loud I wish she'd just tune in to her classical station already.

"Don't you see this is a calculated move to get her hands on other people's talent?"

I don't retort that maybe Mona genuinely wants to help a person, because Mom won't hear me. She's deaf and blind to all of Mona's good qualities.

In complete silence, we drive past the Belle Meade Plantation, take a couple of turns, then veer down a road lined with massive houses.

"Mom, I told you I'll bike over to Rae's."

"I'm not dropping you off." Her tone is slightly more supple than earlier. There's still an edge to it, but I can tell she's fighting to calm down. She'll probably go into cleaning mode the second we get home. That's her favorite pastime when she has steam to blow off. *Dust bunnies, beware.*

"Okay." I sigh. "So where are we going?"

"I wanted to show you my new project."

She glides the car in front of a mammoth wrought-iron gate, then powers my window down and leans over me.

"This?" I gape at the gray stone mansion with its white-framed bow windows overlooking a sloping, manicured lawn planted with cedars and sharp hedges. "Whoa. It's huge."

I shouldn't be surprised, really. Since the feature she landed in *Architectural Digest* last spring, everyone with money and four big walls calls to hire her.

"Who bought it?"

"A man called Jeff Dylan."

"What does he do?"

"He's an entertainment lawyer."

I gather my wavy shoulder-length hair and lift it off my neck, then coil it into a topknot. Even without an elastic, it holds. "Is he, by any chance, hot and single?"

"This is a job, Angie, not a first date. Besides, I'm not looking for a boyfriend."

This is one of the reasons I believe she must've loved Dad . . . she's never replaced him.

After a couple more seconds of ogling her new project, she pulls the car back into the street. "I saw Jasper the other night."

"Yeah?"

"You two used to be such good friends."

My hackles rise, because I sense what she's getting at. Mom and Jasper's mom are best friends and they secretly—okay, they're totally not subtle about it—wish that Jasper and I get together someday. That'll *never* happen, though. He's a jock. I don't date jocks. I don't date anyone, for that matter. I don't need any distractions.

"Is he still at the top of your 'Hot List'?"

I whip my neck to the left so fast it cracks. "Mom!"

"What?" she asks, all innocent.

"How do you know about that list? Did you go through my things?"

"My biggest pet peeve is a messy room. You want to keep me out? Clean it up."

"It's *my* bedroom. Mine. Not yours. Besides, I like my mess." I hook my finger into the switch to power up my window. I tug so hard I half expect it to pop right off. "And it's not *that* messy."

It sort of is. I call it organized chaos.

"I didn't mean to look at the list. It fell out when I was evening out the stack of LPs you use as your nightstand."

I glance at her, still irritated. "And you just *had* to read it?"

"I like to know what's going on in my little girl's life. Would you rather us be Snapchat friends?"

My eyes go vinyl-wide. "No way."

"You don't have to tell me everything, Angie, but don't shut me out either, okay?"

I relax in my seat. "I wrote that list when I was a freshman. Jasper's more in love with his biceps than he is with any girlfriend. Plus, he's dated nearly every girl in our grade."

"Glad to know my daughter doesn't date players."

Amusement trumps irritation. "According to Rae, my standards are too high."

"That, you got from me."

"So Aidan was exceptional?"

I don't bring up my father every day, but whenever I get an opening, I'll throw in a question—or three—and hope she says something sweet about him. He couldn't have been all bad.

She grips the steering wheel tighter.

Could he?

2

The Boy with the Princess Band-Aids

After I pull on a pair of cutoffs and a white tank top, I holler to Mom, who's vacuuming every surface of our two-story house, that I'm off. I power the garage door up and hop onto my electric bicycle. All my friends applied for driver's licenses the second they turned sixteen; not me. Dad passed away in a head-on collision, which has made me petrified of operating large vehicles.

I turn the motor on medium so I don't arrive panting and sweating, and pedal to Rae's with my earbuds blasting Mona Stone's first album. Even though she's released eight more, her first record remains my favorite.

At a traffic light, I tap my fingers against the handlebar to the beat of the percussions and drums. When the light turns green, I swing onto Rae's street. Adrenaline spikes through me when I come wheel to bumper with an enormous black SUV. The vehicle screeches to a halt, but still nicks my bike and sends me flying off the saddle. I yelp as my palms and knees connect with the asphalt. Thankfully the impact isn't too violent, so my helmeted head is spared.

Hazard lights flash, and then neon-blue sneakers race toward me. I press myself into a sitting position. Both of my knees are bleeding, and bits of gravel cling to my scraped palms.

With trembling fingers, I unlatch my helmet and dust off the grit.

"Shit." The backlit driver squats down next to me.

"I'm okay," I say, even though I'm wobbling all over as though I were made of Jell-O.

"Did your head—"

"My head's fine." I blink, then squint to try and make out the still-crouched person.

Although the stranger's voice is deep and his jaw is coated in stubble, his face still has a boyish roundness. College-aged, I suspect.

"I have water and Band-Aids in the car." He walks back to his SUV and grabs a Walmart bag from the backseat, then crouches in front of me and squirts water over my knees. With a handful of tissues, he blots the watery blood.

I notice his hands—I always notice people's hands. His are large with long, elegant fingers—pianist hands.

Pianist hands that are still all over my knees.

Suddenly self-conscious, I shift my legs out of his reach. "Really. It's okay. Just scratches."

His mouth twists as he lifts the pinked tissue and inspects my torn skin. My injuries are only skin deep, but they'll probably still leave marks. Not that I'm worried about scars. Unlike Rae, whose plastic surgeon father made her so fearful of imperfect skin that she learned to apply sunscreen before she was even potty-trained.

"I didn't peg you for a Disney princess enthusiast," I say, as the boy breaks out a pack of girlie Band-Aids from his shopping bag.

"They're my sister's."

I frown at his lack of humor, then peer past him into the car, but it's empty. He peels the backs off two bandages, then tapes them to my skinned knees.

Afterward, he tosses his arsenal back into the shopping bag and checks his bulky metal watch, which is so crammed with dials and arrows it's a miracle he can read the time.

I wonder if he's on his way to meet a date. A boy this good-looking must have a girlfriend.

He grabs my phone and earbuds, which still leak Mona Stone's heady voice, and his lips contort. "Here." He all but shoves them at me. Frowning at his sudden animosity—not that he was Mr. Sunshine before—I unglue my gaze from his face and transfer it to my phone. I grumble when I realize my screen is shattered. "Does your insurance cover phone repairs?"

His eyebrows pop up. "How do I know it wasn't broken before?"

Jerk. I don't say it out loud, but I must think it real loud, because he rises from his crouch and stalks back to his car. I presume he's going to drive away, but instead he keeps the door open and leans over the armrest.

A couple of seconds later, he trudges back, a store receipt flapping in his hand. "Here."

I blink as I take it from him. "You want me to pay you back for the Band-Aids and the water?"

A nerve twitches in his jaw. "My phone number's on the back. Check your bike, and tell me how much I owe you."

Although it looks painful for him, he offers me his hand. I don't take it. Wouldn't want to subject him to any more agony.

The heels of my palms smart as I push myself up, but at least they're not bleeding. I grab my helmet and bag and right my bike. Besides a crooked spoke and scuffs on the glossy black frame, it seems fine. I turn the motor off, because my legs are shaking too much to cycle.

Hand resting on the frame of his open car door, he watches me for a moment. I watch him back, but then that turns awkward, so I lower my eyes to his T-shirt, which reads BEAST MODE ACTIVATED.

"You need a ride somewhere?" he asks.

I jerk my gaze back up to his face.

His eyes, which look golden in the rapidly setting sun, are guarded and reticent.

I shake my head. "I'm not going far."

He climbs into his car fast, as though worried I might change my mind. I start walking my bike down the sidewalk, straining to hear his car tires screech. Either he has the quietest car, or he hasn't driven away. I cast a glance over my shoulder. Even though the hazard lights are off, his car isn't moving. He's probably just as shaken up as I am by the collision. He honks, and it makes me jump. I spin my head around just in time to avoid knocking into a streetlamp.

Is that why he honked? To warn me?

Ugh. He must think I'm a total klutz, which isn't going to help my case about my cracked cell phone screen. The store receipt with his phone number feels as though it's burning a hole in the back pocket of my cutoffs. Maybe *I* have insurance for the screen. I hope so, because I don't want to contact him. He'd probably ask me to prove my phone wasn't damaged before, and I really don't feel like having to prove myself to anyone.

Except to Mona Stone.

I quicken my strides, buoyed by the desire to look up everything about the contest on Rae's computer.

3

Rules Are Meant to Be Broken

For the past hour, I've been poring over Mona Stone's website, reading every line of fine print about the music competition.

"Mom will never consent to this," I grumble to my best friend, who's lacquering her nails the same bright hue as her cell phone case.

Hot pink is Rae's favorite color. Even her bedspread, on which we're both lounging, is dotted with pink swirls. When we were kids and had to draw self-portraits for school, she'd always paint herself with pink eyes instead of brown. She even sported pink contacts when we were twelve, but they made her look like a bloodthirsty vampire.

She holds up her fingers and blows on her nails. "Maybe Mona will launch another one next year. Once you're eighteen—"

"Rae!" I say, horrified.

She jerks her face toward me, the movement creating a ripple in her very straight, very long, and very blonde hair. "What?"

"I can't wait that long. Besides, what if this is a once-in-a-lifetime thing?"

Rae studies me a moment, then studies the shot of Mona midperformance that graces her laptop screen. "How 'bout you write a song first? Then once it's written, you play it for your momma, and since it'll obviously be fan-freakin'-tastic, Jade will have to sign on the dotted line."

I flip onto my back. "You really think she'd change her mind? She hates Mona." I pull my bottom lip into my mouth. "We had another fight about her after dinner, which, weirdly enough, led to talking about Dad. The way she speaks about him, you'd think he was a monster." I turn my head to look at my friend, who's started applying polish to her toes. "Has she ever told your mom anything about him?"

"Not that I know of, but I can ask."

I sigh. "I'd appreciate it."

"Ready to make our senior-year bucket list?" Before I can say yes, Rae leaps off her bed and grabs a pad of paper from her desk. It's pink and scented and has her name embossed at the top.

She tosses me a pen and a sheet of paper, then plops back on the bed and begins jotting down bullet point after bullet point of things that range from getting accepted into her dream college (Stanford, for their premed program; Rae's wanted to be a heart surgeon since we dissected a frog in middle school) and never dating another jock (her ex was one, and it didn't end well) to graduating valedictorian and getting elected prom queen.

Someone who doesn't know Rae might deem her delusional, but I have no doubt she'll be ticking each one of those boxes. She's the most gorgeous and popular nerd who's ever walked the hallways of Reedwood High.

As her pen loops and flows over her paper, I finally write down my ambitions for this school year. Or rather, my *single* ambition.

"Um, why's there only one item on your paper?" she says, cocking a perfectly plucked eyebrow.

"Because that's all I want."

"Come on, hon. What about getting a boyfriend? Or—"

I grunt.

"What?"

"I need to focus. Boys are a distraction."

"What you need is to live a little."

"And I will, but first"—I tap one unpolished nail against my sheet of paper—"I want to win this contest."

"It's nationwide."

"So?"

"So it's a little like winning the lottery."

"No it's not. The lottery is all luck; Mona's contest requires talent."

"Which you have, but which a lot of people have too." Rae leans toward me and wraps one hand around mine. "I admire you, hon. I've always admired you. But what if it doesn't work out? You're sensitive, and—"

"Thanks for the vote of confidence," I grumble, snatching my hand out of hers. I scoot off the bed and stride toward the door, eyes prickling with heat.

Before I reach it, Rae says, "This is what I'm talkin' about. You're about to cry."

I rest my hand on the doorknob but don't turn it. "I'm not."

"Angie . . ." Rae's suddenly at my side, her pretty pink nails circling my forearm. "Don't put all your eggs in the same basket. Spread them into different baskets. *Find* different baskets."

"I don't want different baskets."

Rae sighs real loudly. "Fine, but you're not allowed to whine and cry if you lose."

"Fine." I'm still staring at her hand, which finally comes away from my arm. Her fingertips have blurred a little.

"And just so we're clear, I do believe in you."

I finally look back up at her. She's a couple of inches taller than I am, but not so many that I have to tilt my head back.

She gives me a one-armed hug. "Now let's call the beast who knocked you over."

That's how I entered the driver of the large black SUV's information on my phone—under *Beast*, for the T-shirt he was sporting. Yes, my phone still works, but the cracks make it difficult to read the screen, plus

I almost sliced my finger. I ended up winding a piece of tape around the bottom to keep the cracked glass in place.

"We're not calling him," I say.

"You said he was hot."

"Rae, he gave me his phone number so I could tell him how much it'll cost to fix my bike. Running into me wasn't some creepy pickup scheme or anything."

Rae fake pouts, but then moves on to discussing the possibilities of there being new kids in Reedwood High this term. Every year, there's a handful of them. Talking about them gets Rae as excited as I become when my favorite artists drop a new single.

Funny what gets people's pulses pounding.

4

The Beast in Tennessee

I spend the night dreaming with my eyes open, Mona's contest electrifying my brain. By two a.m., I come up with a melody that I think is good until I play it on our baby grand before heading to school. It sounds so awful that I glower at the black and ivory keys a solid ten minutes before plunking them in an attempt to make something better rise.

Nothing better rises.

Well, besides my mother. She walks into the living room dressed and made-up, asking why I'm not ready yet. I cover the keys and lug my tired and annoyed self back up the stairs and then over to school.

After hooking up my bike to the rack in the parking lot, I speed up the flagstone path and into the grand redbrick building. Classroom doors are still clicking shut in the hallway lined with sunshine-yellow lockers. The color is supposed to be soothing and energizing, or so says our principal, who's a great believer in everything feng shui and holistic. She had a Buddhist monk rearrange the classrooms last year. In some of them, the desks fan out around the whiteboards like sunrays.

"Angie!"

I spin around to see Rae pulling open a classroom door.

"Tell me you have first-period history with Mr. Renfrew."

"I didn't get my schedule yet."

I'm starting to walk away when I almost bump into a wall of tanned skin covered in fruity body lotion.

Melody Barnett smirks at my knees. In my haste to leave, I forgot to replace the princess Band-Aids with flesh-colored ones. "Took the training wheels off your bike?" She says this low enough so that Rae doesn't hear.

Mel adulates Rae—like most everyone in school—and dislikes me—like most everyone in school. People don't get our friendship.

"Bite me," I say, pushing past her.

In a pair of high-wedged espadrilles that make her legs look longer than my entire body, Melody toddles toward Rae, flapping her schedule as though it were Willy Wonka's golden ticket. "I have history too, RaeRae."

Ugh. Even the sound of her voice is grating, high-pitched and nasal, which makes her first name quite unfortunate.

Mel loops her arm through Rae's and tugs her into the classroom.

"I'll save you a seat," Rae says to me.

Once they're gone, I start toward the registrar's department, a modern wing made entirely of glass that houses the administrative desks and the principal's office. Only one other person is waiting for their schedule this late.

Jasper leans against the secretary's desk. "If it isn't my all-time favorite singer," he says to me.

I roll my eyes. "You've never even heard me sing."

"That's not for lack of tryin'." He rakes his fingers through his side-swept golden bangs.

"I don't sing in public."

"You're aware that if you want to be a singer someday, Conrad, you'll have to sing in front of people?"

"I'm not ready yet."

He shoots me a sly smile. "Can I get a private showcase when you *are* ready?"

"I don't do private showcases."

"You wouldn't even have to sing," he says in a low voice.

My pulse trips.

The secretary hands him a sheet of yellow paper, then asks for my name. The enormous printer behind her roars to life and spits out another piece of yellow paper.

Jasper skims his schedule, then stuffs it in the pocket of his khakis. "What class do you have?"

"Calculus with Mrs. Dabbs. You?"

"History."

"Rae and Mel have history too."

"I'd rather *you* had history."

I blink at him, then blink down at my schedule, because I'm not sure what to do with that comment. Jasper and I have been friends for almost as long as Rae and I. Granted, we're not as close, but still . . . I fold and refold my schedule until it's no larger than a mosaic tile.

"Angela, Jasper." Principal Larue chirps our names.

I turn, ready to apologize for being late, but the words stick to my tongue. Next to her stands the beast who ran me over.

Okay, he didn't run me over, but it was a close call.

The principal smiles up at him. "I'd like you to meet our newest student."

"Welcome to Reedwood, dude," Jasper says.

The beast nods, rolling his white button-down's sleeves to the elbows, revealing tanned forearms with ropy lean muscle. I bet the rest of his body is just as nice . . . Not that I'm interested in the rest of his body. Or anyone else's body, for that matter.

I zip my gaze off him and set it on the principal, who's traded in her signature permed hair for a funky new hairstyle—a short Afro adorned with a silk scarf that makes her look a decade younger.

"Would you be so kind as to show Tennessee to his classroom, Angela?"

"Me?" Since I forgot to replenish my depleted supply of oxygen, it comes out as a squeak.

Nice.

The beast . . . I mean, *Tennessee*, presses his lips together so tightly that his stubble-coated jaw tics. I still can't get over the fact that he goes to my school. Let alone to *high* school.

"I can show him to his classroom, Mrs. Larue," Jasper proposes.

When Tennessee's gaze dips to my knees, to the Band-Aids I haven't removed, Jasper steps closer to me and angles his body as though to shield me from the beast's piercing golden eyes.

"If I'm not mistaken, you have history, Jasper"—she taps his forearm—"and Angela has calculus."

She's not mistaken. Mrs. Larue lives and breathes for her school and students. She knows everyone's names, allergies, and grade point average. Once, she even asked how I'd enjoyed the Fleetwood Mac album I'd bought at the PTA winter market. Even though I'd mumbled something about "Dreams" being one of my favorite songs, what I'd really wanted to say was, "Do you secretly work for the CIA?"

"Let me get you three tardy slips so Mrs. Dabbs and Mr. Renfrew don't penalize you." Her heels click on the smoke-gray floorboards as she walks over to her secretary's desk and grabs the slips. She jots down our names, then hands the slips to us. "You will never have this day again, so make it count."

Tennessee arches a thick eyebrow.

"Run off now, my children."

Once we're back in the quiet hallway, Jasper slings an arm around my shoulders. It feels incredibly heavy, and not because of his bulky muscles. "What brings you to Tennessee, Tennessee?" Jasper asks.

Tennessee hikes his black backpack higher on his shoulder. A silver bracelet glints on his wrist. There's an engraving on it, but I can't make it out.

"Ten. Just Ten." Instead of answering Jasper's question, he asks, "Is the principal always this . . . *cheery?*"

I shrug out from under Jasper's arm. "Always."

"Every morning, she spouts some philosophical crap over the PA system," Jasper says, which is true. Principal Larue reads us a quote every morning. "But she's a chill lady."

Through the frosted glass window of Mr. Renfrew's classroom, I spy Rae and Mel sitting together at a collaborative desk. So much for saving me a seat . . .

"Take good care of my girl, now, Ten." Jasper winks at me before entering the classroom.

Once the door shuts behind him, I say, "Our classroom's three doors down," at the same time as Ten says, "Your boyfriend's friendly."

"He sure is."

Why I don't correct him is beyond me. Maybe it's because I want him to think I'm more popular than I am. Or maybe it's so he stops eyeing me as though I were some pitiful hick.

5

A Tall Order of Insufferable

Tennessee and I have three classes together—calculus, art, and English.

In calculus, where there's assigned seating, we're stuck next to each other—a consequence of turning up late on the first day. Rae doesn't get why I'm so glum about having to sit next to Ten. She, along with most of the female student body, thinks he's a God-given gift to the girls of Reedwood High.

I don't get it. Sure, he's hands down the most handsome guy at Reedwood, but his surly attitude is *such* a turnoff. All week, he ate lunch by himself and couldn't get into his car fast enough after school let out. Not that I was keeping tabs on him. He's just so tall that he's hard to overlook. Plus he wears his brown hair spiky instead of floppy like ninety-nine percent of his peers, which adds a solid inch.

"I wish he'd mauled *me* with his car," Rae says dreamily, glancing over at Ten, who's already seated at our double desk.

He stares out the window at the middle school half a mile away. Unlike our brick building, its design is modern—brushed concrete striated with long strips of windows that reflect the late-morning brightness.

"The second bell has rung, Miss Conrad. Please take your seat," Mrs. Dabbs says, pushing up the sleeves of her crimson tunic, which she's paired with wide-legged pants in the same shade. Combined with her frizzy red hair and streaky blush, she resembles a candied apple.

She should take makeup tips from Mona Stone, who's always put together so perfectly. My dance teacher, who used to be one of Mona's backup dancers, told me my idol does her own makeup because she doesn't like anyone poking at her face. The second she shared this with me, I spent hours watching tutorials to learn how to line my eyes and dust sparkly powder over my cheekbones. I don't wear more than mascara and concealer to school, but if I had to go onstage to accept a Grammy, I could glam myself up real quick.

A couple of minutes into the class, Mrs. Dabbs quizzes me on parabolas, and I scramble to locate the answer between the lyrics and musical notes I scribble in the margins of my math textbook.

She poises her felt-tip pen against the whiteboard. "So, Miss Conrad, what is the difference between a parabola and a hyperbola?"

Sweat beads on my upper lip, and I lick it away, flipping through the book in desperation. I hate being put on the spot. How will I ever succeed as an artist if I can't stand to be the center of attention, though? Did Mona ever get flustered in high school? Probably not.

"Hyperbolas have two curves that mirror each other and open in opposing sides. Parabolas only have one curve." It's Ten who answers.

Mrs. Dabbs shoots him a smile as white as the board behind her. "Thank you, Mr. Dylan." She turns to me. "Miss Conrad, may I suggest you use the weekend to study for my class since you are clearly too distracted by your doodling"—she sweeps her arm in my direction, making all the blood in my body converge in my face—"to pay attention to my lesson?"

I untuck my wavy brown hair from behind my ears to curtain off my glow-in-the-dark complexion, then spend the rest of class with my head bent over my book, attempting to memorize equations, which clearly won't serve me considering my choice of career.

The second the bell rings, I toss my stuff into my fabric tote, impatient to escape this torture session.

"You're really into music, huh?" Ten asks, halting my escape. He's reading the flowy lyrics I inked on my bag—the chorus from my favorite Mona Stone song.

Startled he talked to me, I don't immediately answer. Finally, I say, "It's my life."

He puts away his books slowly, as though trying to drag out the moment. He's probably waiting for the classroom to empty so he doesn't have to chat with anyone else on his way to the cafeteria.

For some reason, I follow up my comment with, "The quote under my picture in last year's yearbook said: *Angie Conrad likes music more than she likes people.*"

A corner of his mouth quirks up, and I blink, because the beast is smiling. Ten hasn't smiled once since arriving at Reedwood. At least, not at me.

I stand up, hoisting my tote onto my shoulder. "Do *you* like music?"

He evens out his already neat stack of textbooks. "No."

My head jerks back. "How can you not?"

He slides his books into his backpack and zips it up. "Do you enjoy the sound of a car alarm?"

Sets my teeth on edge. "Does anyone?"

"My point exactly."

He's standing now, so I have to crane my neck to look at him.

"Are you seriously comparing music to a car alarm?"

"Maybe."

He tumbles several notches down in my esteem, not that he was that far up to begin with.

"Wow." I shake my head and start walking toward the door of the now deserted classroom, but because I can't leave well enough alone, I wheel around. "You can't possibly dislike every type of music."

He lifts his hands and starts ticking off his fingers. "Rap, country, classical, and jazz suck. Ballads and soft rock are tacky. And don't get me started on pop, hard rock, or R&B. Oh, and disco should be outlawed."

I hoist my bag farther up my shoulder, fingers clenched so hard around the fabric handles they'll probably tear.

He smirks, as though he gets a kick out of being a total jerk. "You seem really upset by this."

"I am!"

He stops right in front of me. "Why?"

"Because . . . because . . ." I release my bag's handles and drag my fingers through my hair a little roughly. Why am I trying to reason with this guy? "You know what, forget it. To each their own, right?"

I turn around and take the high road—or at least the one that leads away from Ten.

6

Crushes and Crushing Comments

I meet up with Rae by her locker, which is plastered with pictures of boy band members with swooping bangs, dazzling white teeth, and hard lines of muscles. I bet Ten abhors boy bands too.

"How was calc?" She waggles her brows.

"Awful."

Tennessee strolls by us, his gait even and so damn self-assured. The child in me wants to trip him. Not that I've ever tripped anyone. But if I had to trip someone, Ten would be that someone.

Rae shuts her locker. "Want to come over and watch a movie tonight? It's book club night."

Our mothers founded this very exclusive book club where they drink way more than they read. Jasper's mom is also a member, along with a bunch of other Reedwoodian mothers. They meet every first Thursday of the month, but talk about it *all* month.

I tell her I'm in, but regret it at lunch when she asks Melody to come too. Of course Mel says yes, and then she asks if Laney can tag along since they were supposed to hang out, and Rae says the more the merrier. I'm bummed she's invited Mel and Laney, but it's Rae. Rae wouldn't be Rae if she weren't surrounded by her court at all times. In a way, I'm glad she has them in her life since music takes up such a huge chunk of mine.

While I sip apple juice, Jasper trots over to our table. He spins the free chair next to mine and straddles it. "Did I hear y'all mention a movie night?"

Melody flips her chin-length hair. "Hey, Jasper."

On his way toward the jocks' corner of the cafeteria, Brad, Jasper's best friend, stops by our table. Laney's black eyes dart to his ultra-pale blue ones that play hide-and-seek underneath his shaggy brown hair. He and Laney use to be an item, but they split up last spring. From what Rae told me, it didn't end well.

"Yo, J-man, some sophomorian chicks just asked me if you were single." A smug grin laps against Brad's fuzzy face. I think he's trying to grow facial hair, but *trying* is the key word.

"That's not even a word, Brad," Rae says, rolling her eyes at him.

Jasper eyes me as he says, "Not interested."

The last time Jasper paid me this much attention was when we played Guitar Hero back in middle school and I beat him by a million points.

Brad turns but halts midspin. "By the way, Conrad, I approve."

"What do you approve of?" I take a long swallow of my juice.

He points to my shirt, which is stretched a little tight. "Rae's daddy's work. Looks very natural."

I choke on my apple juice.

Rae narrows her eyes at him. "I noticed you were scheduled for a ball lift in Daddy's agenda, or was it a testicular implant? You have just the one, right?"

Brad flips her the finger, but I can tell by his reddening jaw that her comment hit hard. He glares at Laney, whose lips begin to tremble.

"Screw you." I'm not sure if Brad says this to Rae or Laney.

Once he's stormed off, Laney jumps out of her seat, tears streaming down her narrow, pale face. "How could you, Rae?"

Mel stands up. "That was cold, Rae."

"He insulted Angie!"

Mel glowers at me as though this were *my* fault, before running after Laney.

Jasper chuckles. "I dig girl fights."

"Shut up." Rae jabs at her vanilla pudding. "Brad's such a prick. Why are you even friends with him?"

Jasper grins.

"And why are you still here, Jasper?" she adds.

He stops rocking his chair back and forth. "I was tryin' to score an invite to your chick night."

"We don't invite boys to *chick* nights."

"You should. We'd liven it up."

"Oh, please." Rae rolls her eyes.

"What if I brought Tennessee?"

Rae plants her elbows on the table and leans forward. "I'm listenin'."

"Please no. He's so obnoxious," I say.

Jasper's gaze surfs toward the table Ten is occupying with a potted palm. I wonder why he still sits alone. I've seen him hanging out in the hallway with a couple of kids, all from the track team. I assume he must run track, unless he just enjoys discussing electrolytes and speed intervals.

"If he comes," Rae says, "you can come."

Jasper's out of his chair in under a second. He jogs over to Ten. I watch them talk. When Ten's gaze bangs into mine, my fingers tighten around the juice box, and it squirts into my face. I snatch a paper napkin off my tray and blot my eye, which has already started to water.

A minute later, Jasper plops his palms against our table and leans over. "Mission was a bust, RaeRae, but I might've heard our new QB has the hots for a certain leggy blonde."

Rae glances over at Jasper's section of the cafeteria, the VIP area. It's not cordoned off or anything but might as well be considering the string of jocks and cheerleaders wedged together. If it weren't for me, Rae would be sitting there too.

Rae returns her gaze to Jasper. "I'm not into jocks."

"Since when?"

"Since last year," I say softly.

"Oh." He palms his hair. "Right. Not my brother's finest hour."

Jasper had a front-row seat to that debacle, what with Rae's ex being none other than his older brother.

Rae squashes her bottle of water until it's no thicker than a compact disc. She's probably imagining it's *the boy we no longer talk about*'s soul. He graduated last year, but that's not the reason we don't talk about him. We don't talk about him because he cheated on Rae and shattered her heart. It took months of late-night commiseration over tubs of ice cream and popcorn to get Rae out of her funk.

"Besides, I favor intellect over brawn now," she adds.

Even though Jasper's close with his brother, he doesn't leap to his defense. "Shouldn't personality factor in?"

"Just because Ten keeps to himself doesn't mean there's something off about him. In my opinion, it makes him sort of intriguing."

Like a serial killer is intriguing.

Jasper grunts as he pushes away from the table. Before returning to his section of the cafeteria, he asks, "So, is that a negative on chick night?"

"Yes." Once he's out of earshot, Rae asks, "Did you want me to invite him?"

"Who? Jasper?"

"Yes, Jasper. He's totally into you."

"We're just friends, Rae."

"But you did pick up on all those flirty vibes, right?"

"That's just Jasper. He flirts with every girl."

"Uh-huh." She gives me a look, one eye a little more shut than the other.

"He does. Anyway, I'm not interested."

"You used to be."

"Back when I was a freshman. That ship has sailed." I finger the silver arrow speared through the cartilage of my ear. Rae and I were supposed to get matching piercings, but she chickened out at the last minute, claiming her parents would have a fit.

"I saw your mom chatting with Ten's dad this morning. He's cute. For an old man, that is."

I release my earring so fast my hand smacks into the table. "Mom knows Ten's dad?"

She hikes up an eyebrow. "Duh. Your mom's redoing his house."

"Mom's re—" My mouth rounds in a perfect O.

Rae shakes her head. "Sometimes, I think you live on a different planet from us mere mortals." She pats my hand, but I don't feel her touch.

I can't believe Mom's working on Ten's house.

I stand, and then I'm walking over and sliding into the chair in front of him.

"Did you know I was your interior decorator's daughter?"

He uncaps his water bottle and takes a slow swallow. "Jade might've mentioned you and I attended the same school." A ray of sunshine cuts through the palm fronds and across his face, making his eyes shimmer like the surface of Richland Creek at sunset.

I rake my hair back. "You're on a first-name basis with my mom?"

He dips his chin to his neck and studies me from over the rim of his bottle. "I assumed you knew."

"I didn't."

Rae's walking over now, my bag swinging from her fingers. She hooks it over the back of my chair, then takes a seat next to me. "Hiya, neighbor."

Ten shuts the book he was reading and leans back in his chair. Rae asks him something, which I miss because my phone starts chirping Mona Stone's newest chart-topping single, "Legs Like These."

I dig my phone out of my tote and squint to make out the caller's name on the cracked screen. I think it says *Mom*, which would be ironic since we were just talking about her. I swipe my finger over the screen to pick up the call. It doesn't work the first time. Or the second time. By attempt number four, I manage to pick up, but it's too late. A notification for a voice mail pops up soon after. Miraculously, I manage to listen to it.

"Hey, baby. A client's flying me out to Salt Lake City to visit their new property. I'll be home in the morning. I arranged with Nora that you sleep over at their place tonight. Call me when you get out of school, okay? Love you."

As I lower my phone, I tell Rae, "I'm sleeping over at yours."

"Whoop." Then: "You really need to get your phone fixed." Since Rae's aware of how my phone was destroyed, I understand her message is intended for Ten.

"Hey, RaeRae, come over here a sec!" Jasper bellows from across the cafeteria.

She lets out a sigh but gets up. "He's probably going to ask me how to win you over."

I gape at her, then blush.

"Don't worry, I won't tell him that the way to your heart is Mona Stone." She taps my shoulder, then whirls around, her straight hair fanning out like in a shampoo commercial.

"Win you over?" Ten asks. "Isn't Jasper your boyfriend?"

"My boyfriend? I don't have a boyfriend."

He cocks an eyebrow.

Right . . . "I never said he was. You just assumed it, and I didn't deny it." I grab my bag and hook it over my shoulder. "Anyway—"

"You never sent me the bill for your bike repairs."

"Because it's fine. The frame's a little scratched, and I fixed the crooked spokes with pliers." I start to turn away, then add, "As for the phone, my mom said she was going to check if our insurance plan covered the screen repair." It must've slipped her mind, though, because she hasn't come back to me with an answer. "Seems like your family's been keeping her too busy to remember her own."

I don't mean to sound jealous, but as I walk off, I realize it came out that way, which is weird, because I've never been jealous of Mom's clients. Then again, Mom's never kept secrets about them from me before. Why didn't she warn me Ten went to my school?

7

InSinkErating My Dream

On Fridays after school, I hang out with my vocal coach, who doubles as my piano teacher.

Mom found Lynn after I told her that if she didn't sign me up for singing classes, I'd buy a Rottweiler with my allowance. My threat—which wasn't a total bluff since I really did want a dog—worked. The day I turned thirteen, she took me to Lynn's house for a singing lesson.

And then she signed me up for Lynn's summer music camp, which was where I learned to dance—and I don't mean the discombobulated swaying I used to perform in front of my mirror, clutching my hairbrush in lieu of a microphone.

Lynn had hired Steffi, one of Mona Stone's backup dancers, to cover the dancing part of her camp. She's the one who taught me how to use my muscles and absorb rhythm.

It was the best month of my life. It must also have been the best month of Lynn's and Steffi's lives since that's how they met.

To this day, their wedding has remained one of my all-time favorite events. First, because Lynn and Steffi put on a show with stage lights, sparkling outfits, and fog machines. And second, because most of Steffi's friends still worked for Mona Stone, so I got tons of gossip on my idol.

Lynn stops playing midnote. "DO-EE-DO, not DO-A-DO. You're not concentrating, Angie."

"Sorry."

"From the top. And this time, relax your jaw and open your mouth wider. I want to see your tonsils."

I open my mouth so wide my lips feel like elastics about to snap. Lynn nods in rhythm to the keys she presses, her head acting like a metronome. My lungs expand, and my throat clenches and unclenches as I release notes I wasn't able to reach a year ago.

After the lesson, I take a seat on the bench next to Lynn and let my fingers trail over the keys in no particular sequence or rhythm. Once she deems me warmed up, she places sheet music in front of me.

"You mind if I play you something I wrote?" I ask.

"You wrote a song?"

I nod. "Mona Stone's holding a songwriting competition."

"Of course you heard about that." Lynn is very aware of my obsession. Unlike Mom, she doesn't condemn it.

"It could be my lucky break."

Lynn shoots me a pained look.

I shrug. "I know, I know. Thousands of people are going to submit something, but a girl can dream, right?"

"Let's hear it." Lynn walks over to the window and sits on the edge of the teal chaise Steffi scored at a flea market. Mom *loves* that sofa chair.

Inhaling a deep breath, I press my fingers against the piano keys and let my creation pour out of me. The melody starts out slow and quiet, but then quickens and turns louder, the beat pounding and churning, slicking the parlor in fluorescent pinks and yellows, brightening the very air. By the time the last note peters out, Lynn is no longer sitting on the chaise. She's standing behind me, watching my fingers intently.

I pull my hands into my lap and wring them. "So? What do you think?"

Lynn bobs her head, as though the melody's still playing out in her head. "It has a *ton* of potential."

I sit there dazed because Lynn doesn't dole out compliments easily, but then reality knocks into me as hard as Ten's Range Rover. "You're not just saying that because you're my music coach and you adore me?"

"I do love you to bits, but that right there"—she wags her finger at the piano—"made me proud to be your teacher."

My eyes prickle.

"Let me hear the lyrics now," she says, settling down on the bench next to me.

"Those still need work." *A lot* of work.

"When's the deadline?"

"Halloween."

"Better get cracking, then."

"You think I have a chance?"

She levels her gaze on mine. "Did your mom okay it?"

"Not yet."

She squeezes my shoulder. "Well, I hope she does." She nods to the sheet music in front of me. "Now, practice this piece."

I dip my chin and start playing it, wishing that every beat of the day were accompanied by a melody—a soundtrack to life. Music would spill from the sky, curl from the grass, and seep out of the asphalt.

Ten would hate it.

I falter and hit a wrong note.

Why did *he* have to creep into my mind? Of all people . . .

Right before my hour's up, Lynn asks me to perform my song again, so I do, and she studies the way my fingers move over the keys and spread to reach chords. She's memorizing it. After I'm done, she scoots next to me on the bench and gives it a go. Lynn's amazing like that—she can flawlessly play back anything she sees or hears.

"Okay, so now listen and think of the story you want to tell," she says.

I sit up straighter. As my melody spirals through the room, an image begins to form in my mind, faint and shiny at the edges. Smears of yellow and deep red bloom. And then a slash of lime green and thick dabs of steel black. Melodies always appear to me in Technicolor.

"Anything?" she asks.

"A girl running. Gazing at the sun."

"And?"

"Stepping out of shadows or pushing them away?"

"Good . . ."

She tucks a lock of traffic-cone-orange hair behind her ear. When I met her four years ago, her hair was yellow—and I don't mean blonde, I mean corn-on-the-cob yellow. The following year, it was pink, then blue, which earned her the nickname of Skittles.

Long after my song comes to an end, the notes keep swirling in the air like dust motes. Silver and gold. Shiny. Cheerful. Hopeful.

"You should make your mother listen to it," she says.

I tense up. What if Mom asks me why I wrote it? I'm not ready to have my dreams ground up like food waste in our InSinkErator.

"Ask her what the music makes her feel. It might help you with the lyrics." Lynn checks the wall clock mounted over the shelves that sag from the weight of binders filled with sheet music and dusty rows of CDs. "You better go before Steffi marches up here to claim you."

I smile, because Steffi's done that quite often. Lynn and I get lost in music and forget how much time has passed. Thus, the clock. There was no clock my first year. Steffi nailed it to the wall after my repeated tardiness.

"See you next Friday." I grab my bag and denim jacket from the chaise and dash down to the basement.

Transforming the cluttered gray space into a dance studio was my mother's wedding present to Lynn and Steffi. She lined the walls with floor-to-ceiling mirrors, hung heavy beige drapes to conceal electrical wiring and pipes, screwed a barre into the mirror, and covered the cement floor with hardwood planks. But it's the lighting that really makes the place spectacular, the mix of large, color-changing stage lights and tiny spotlights scattered like faraway constellations.

"I was beginning to think you'd forgotten about me," Steffi says, her torso folded over one stretched-out leg.

"Never."

"Did Skittles wear you out?" She unhooks her foot from the barre.

"She tried. Only you ever succeed."

Her large dark eyes, which are the same shade as her buzzed hair, crinkle with a grin.

"Try not to kill me too much," I add.

She laughs. "Why? Do you have a hot date tonight?"

"Yes." When her eyes spark with intrigue, I add, "With Mom and the TV."

"You lead an exciting life."

I'm aware my Friday night could be a tad more exciting, but once I make it big, I'll be out on the road or at parties all the time. The thought catches me by such surprise that I drop my bag and jacket on the floor instead of on the bench.

Where's this confidence when I need it?

8

Even Lawyers Have Pinterest Boards

When I get home, Mom's sitting at the round table, sipping a glass of wine while flipping through a fabric sampler. She runs her fingers over a piece of violet raw silk. "Hey, baby. How were your lessons?"

"Great." I grab an ice-cold bottle of water from the fridge, then walk over to her and sit, stubbing my toe against the fossilized tree-trunk base. I always stub my toe against it even though we've had the same table for over ten years now. "Why didn't you tell me Mr. Mansion's son goes to my school?"

"Mr. Mansion?"

"Jeff Dylan."

"Oh." She runs the tip of her finger down the stem of her glass. "Jeff didn't want me talking about his family."

"Why? He's an entertainment lawyer, not a movie star."

"Does that mean he's not allowed privacy?"

I frown. "I just meant that a heads-up would've been nice."

She returns her attention to the fabric sampler.

"Does he represent anyone famous in the music industry?" I ask, before guzzling down some water.

"I didn't ask."

"I bet he does." Considering his new mansion, he must have some serious heavyweights in his roster of clients.

"Angie . . ."

Even though Mom doesn't finish her sentence, she doesn't have to. I understand her the same way she understands me—she doesn't want me to pester him *or* his son. Not that I ever would. Even though a connection would be nice, I'd rather make my own way in the world.

"So? Does he have a clue about what he wants?"

"Believe it or not, he doesn't just have a clue. He has an entire Pinterest board."

"Whoa. Does he have good taste?"

She slides her tablet between us, taps in her security code, and brings up the Pinterest app. She types his name, and his home decor board materializes.

I scroll through it, surprised. "Is he really going to put a swing over his swimming pool?"

"His daughter would like him to."

"What's his budget?"

"He can afford to put a swing over the pool, and he can afford me." Mom runs her index finger against a taupe velvet that matches the color of her skinny jeans. Like Mona, Mom has great taste in fashion.

As she tips her wineglass to her mouth, I almost tell her about the contest, but chicken out. Instead, I remind her of my phone's dire state.

"I thought . . ." She leans back in her chair and shoots me the strangest look. "Didn't you just get a new phone?"

"It wasn't *that* new."

She frowns. "It's still in the box."

"What box?"

"Over there." She points to the white marble console table by our front door that looks like a roll of toilet paper flew off the holder and unspooled—but prettier. On top of it lies a small box.

I stride over to the table and pick up the box. "Where did you get this?"

"It was in our mailbox."

Ten's face pops into my mind. Did he get me a new phone?

"Next time, please warn me before making such a big purchase, okay?" she says.

"I didn't buy it."

"Then where did it come from?"

"I, uh, have no clue." I pause. "Actually, maybe I do."

Her eyebrows almost converge on her forehead. "Okay . . ."

"I should go set it up." I head up the stairs and into my bedroom to get out of Mom's line of sight while I check the accuracy of my hunch. I dig the phone out of the box, plug my chip inside it, then power it on. After I finish setting it up, I stroke the pristine screen that feels like velvet under my thumb.

ME: Did you get me a phone?

A couple of seconds later, a message pops up: *Who's this?*

ME: Angie.

BEAST: I owed you one, didn't I?

ME: You owed me a new screen. Not a new phone!!

BEAST: Costs the same.

ME: No it doesn't.

Pulse drumming, I text: *I can't accept it.*

For a long moment, he doesn't answer. But then the word *Beast* flashes on my screen. I bite my lip. Texting him is one thing, but talking to him . . . that's something else. I suck in some courage and answer.

"Did you take it out of the box?" he asks.

Shoot. I hadn't thought about that.

"I'll pay you back, then, but it's going to take me a couple of months to get you the whole amount. My allowance—"

"Angie, keep the phone. And keep your money."

"But—"

"Look, someone gave it to me, but I already had one. I didn't need it. You did."

I bite my lower lip. "I don't like owing people."

"Consider it a thank-you gift for not pressing charges."

41

"Charges! I would never." I fold my legs underneath me and sink onto my comforter. "Maybe your little sister wants a new phone."

"My little sister's phone is brand-new."

I gnaw on the inside of my cheek so hard I almost draw blood. "Well, thanks." I hesitate to hang up, but decide to be courteous. After all, he gave me a brand-new phone. *And* my mom's working for his dad. "Where did you live before here?"

A pause. Then: "New York."

"You liked it there?"

"I did. Better than here."

"Why?"

"Because New York isn't obsessed with country music."

Why am I talking with him again? *Right.* The phone . . .

I think of Rae, of her telling me that she tried to talk Ten into hanging out with her over the weekend, but he acted about as excited as her grandma during Sunday Mass, and she's *always* dozing off.

"Do you have a girlfriend back in New York?" I blurt out, then wince.

"No." After a beat, he asks, "What's with the cross-examination?"

"I'm just trying to figure you out . . . You're not exactly forthcoming. But then you patch up my knees and give me a phone, so"—I drum my fingers against the wrinkled white duvet cover—"so I assume you're not completely insensitive." I look at Mona's poster, which hangs next to my full-length mirror. "Mom took me to New York when I was little. It was very . . . *overwhelming*. And loud. I was completely terrified of getting hit by a cab."

"Did you?"

"Nope." I smile. "I've only gotten hit once, and that was in my home state, by an SUV."

I hear the sound of springs. I wonder if he's lying on his bed. I wonder what his room looks like. Is it a disaster zone, or has Mom finished decorating it?

"What does your father do?" he asks.

What made him think of my father?

I tuck my hair behind my ears, but my willful strands rush straight back around my jaw. "He was the lead guitarist of the Derelicts."

"Was?"

"Passed away when I was three. Car crash."

"Shit," he murmurs.

"Yeah." I'm about to ask if he's heard of the Derelicts when I remember he hates music. "What about your mom? What does she do?"

"My mother's dead, too."

I gasp softly. "Oh. I'm sorry, Ten."

"It's fine. She died a long time ago. Heart cancer."

"*Heart* cancer?"

"Did I say cancer? I meant heart attack. She had a bad heart."

I'm a little stumped at how detached he sounds about her death, but then assume he wasn't very close to her. Unless aloofness is his way of coping with loss. "So it's just you, your dad, and your little sister?"

"Yeah."

"How old is your sister?"

"Twelve." A breath whooshes through the phone. "You ask a lot of questions, Angie."

My spine jams up tight. "I was just trying to be friendly."

"Is that the only reason you're interested in my home life?"

I bristle, because I wasn't the only one asking questions. "You think I'm trying to suck up to you because your dad's an entertainment lawyer? Get over yourself."

Instead of acting mature, I hang up, feeling a strong urge to toss the phone he gave me at the wall.

So much for trying to be courteous.

9

Defrosting More than Freezers

I spend all of Saturday attempting to come up with lyrics.

I thought it would be easy matching words to my melody, but it's not. I toss my notebook aside and listen to my Discover Weekly selection from Spotify for inspiration. When that doesn't help, I put on running shoes and sprint out the front door. I don't run far or long, just far and long enough to get rid of my writer's block.

Dad apparently used to go on runs when he was working through his music. It's one of the few things Mom has told me about him.

When I get home, I forgo a shower and make a beeline to the piano. I play the melody, stopping and starting a hundred times to scribble down new lyrics, and then I rearrange the chords until the little black dots are swimming around on the staffs.

"Angie, I'm home!" Mom yells.

The sky outside has turned an electric shade of blue.

I massage my temples and get up from the bench. Stretching my arms over my head, I walk to the kitchen, where Mom slides two brown paper bags onto the emerald granite island.

As I help her put the groceries away, I ask, "What are we having for dinner?"

"Butternut mac 'n' cheese. Want to help make it?"

"No. But I'll watch and play DJ."

"Why don't you ever want to cook?"

"Because I suck at it, Mom. I either burn everything or measure things wrong. Remember when you asked me to make glazed carrots for Thanksgiving, and I added a quarter cup of salt instead of sugar?"

She smiles. "Still don't understand how you could add that much salt without thinking it was too much seasoning."

"My point exactly." I scroll through my phone for my current playlist and synchronize it with the kitchen's wireless speakers. As music spills into the room, I fill a glass with soda water and settle on one of the cowhide barstools tucked underneath the island.

Mom peels the squash, slices it in half, scoops the mushy insides into the InSinkErator, and then dices the hard flesh. As she fills a large pot with water, thyme, and other stuff, I toy with the idea of playing her my song.

Before I can cop out, I say, "I wrote a song today."

I don't mention the Mona Stone contest. I'll have to bring it up soon but don't feel brave enough today.

She glides the cubed squash into the simmering broth. "Can I hear it?"

I nod, and she trails me out into the living room and takes a seat on our cream-colored couch. I roll my head, and my neck cracks, and then I stretch my fingers and place them on the keys, which are still warm. I don't peek at Mom while I perform my song, scared of what I might see on her face.

I don't look her way once I'm done either.

At least not for a long moment.

When her silence becomes too oppressive, I rub my clammy hands on my leggings and spin around. "What did you think?"

"I thought it was"—she runs a finger over one of the decorative patches on her army-green blouse—"good." She offers me a smile that doesn't reach her eyes.

I feel like she's trying to be polite, which is weird, because she's my mom. She doesn't need to be polite; she needs to be honest.

I look up at the cove lighting, which is buzzing. Or maybe the buzzing's inside my head.

"I—I need to go check on the pasta," she says. If she's trying to destroy my drive, she's doing an awesome job.

I turn back toward the piano. "Do you mind if I keep practicing? I need to work on the chorus."

"Sure. Take your time."

I punch a couple of keys as the floorboards creak beneath her retreating footfalls.

I play my song again, and the notes color my bleak mood.

What does my mother know about music anyway? *Nothing.* My father was the one who understood harmonies. He might not have gushed about my musical prowess, but at least he would've offered constructive advice, unlike Mom's total disinterest.

As I run through my song again, I create a note on my phone and dictate the lyrics. When I finish, the silence sounds louder than my song. I stop playing and scroll through what I wrote, change a word here and there, and then I take it from the top and match the new lyrics to the chorus's melody. I make a few adjustments, then play the entire song again, singing the lyrics softly.

Like my fingers, my heart holds incredibly still, because this time everything fits. I close my eyes briefly, relishing this tiny, perfect moment. I wish I weren't savoring it alone, but it beats sharing it with someone who detests music.

On legs that feel like fragments of clouds, I drift back into the kitchen, sit on the barstool, and sip my soda water that's no longer chilled or bubbly.

Mom's stabbing at our freezer with a metal pick. A huge slab of ice cracks off and thuds at her feet. She wipes her flushed brow on her forearm, then crouches, scoops up the ice, and chucks it into the sink. "Dinner'll be ready in thirty minutes."

For once, I'm not hungry, but I don't tell her that. I simply watch her hack at our poor freezer again.

Guilt swarms me, because I think my music did that. Made her stressed and angry. "Do I sound like Dad? Is that why you hate it?"

She flinches. Even her arm that's suspended in midair shudders. "Can you set the table?"

She can't even answer me. Heaving a sigh, I do as I'm told.

She rinses the icepick, then sets it on the drying rack and wipes her hands on her jeans. Although she didn't use it on me, my heart hurts as though it's been de-iced too.

We eat in silence. At some point, she tucks a lock of hair that's escaped from my ponytail behind my ear. I think it's her way of apologizing for not being more supportive. And I forgive her because I love her.

That's how love works. If you can't forgive someone, then you don't love them enough.

10

The Voice

On Monday, I don't say hi to Ten during calc. I don't even glance his way. Or at least I try not to. But as he jots something down in his notebook, the sun bounces off his bracelet and blinds me. When he rests his forearms on the desk, I catch the inscription on his bracelet: I ROCK.

Seriously, *I rock*?

He's obviously not referring to music considering his distaste for it. How big is this guy's ego?

Class drags by. The only thing remotely interesting about it is Mrs. Dabbs's outfit—she wears all green today, which lends her a startling resemblance to a tulip. Where does she get her style cues from? *House & Garden*?

As we study derivatives, I stretch my neck from side to side. Every Sunday, before our usual dumpling and spring roll feast at Golden Dragon, Mom and I go to a power yoga class. Yesterday's was particularly strenuous, but at least it took my mind off the chorus I can't nail and the infuriating boy with the stupid bracelet.

"No questions for me today?" he asks as I gather my things after class.

I eye him. "Nope. I know all I need to know about you."

He inclines his head to the side as though he doesn't quite believe me. "I'm going to get my old phone fixed, so—"

"Angie, please stop with the phone. I don't want it back." He lines up his books before sticking them into his backpack.

But I don't want it either. Instead of bringing it up again—I'll just give it back to him, and that'll be that—I shoot out of my chair and stride out of the classroom. I'm so concentrated on putting distance between Ten and myself that I smack into a hard chest. Hands come around my biceps to steady me.

I lift my eyes and meet bright-blue ones.

"Hey there, Conrad." Jasper's breaths hit my forehead in bursts, as though he's been sprinting through the hallway to reach me.

"Hi."

"I was coming to find you." His jaw's a little flushed, which reinforces my suspicion that he ran.

"Yeah?"

He lets me go, then rubs his neck. My bag slides down my arm, so I hoist it back up.

"Want to hang sometime this week?" He sends the words flying at me as fast as one of his footballs.

"Um."

People shuffle past, knocking me into Jasper. I'm so close I can see his pupils pulse in anticipation.

"We could go to a movie or something," he says.

"Um. Sure?" He breaks out into a grin that freezes when I add, "Let me ask Rae—"

"Rae?" His smile falls. "I meant you and me."

Oh. Oh . . . "Like a date?"

He rubs his neck so hard I wonder if he has a crick in it. "Yeah."

Whoa. "I can't."

"Why?"

"Because Mel likes you," I blurt out. "She's my friend. I can't do that to her."

Jasper doesn't question that Mel and I are friends, which strengthens my resolve not to get involved with him. If he really liked me, he'd know who my friends are—*is*—and see right through my lie.

"Anyway, I need to get to class." As I sidestep away from Jasper, I bump into another male body. I look up and find Ten staring down at me. "Sorry," I mumble, before hurrying to my next class, alert so as not to knock into yet another person.

I want to tell Rae about Jasper asking me out, but she's too busy discussing homecoming with the committee she's invited to have lunch at our table.

After school, although I planned to go straight to Lynn's house to ask her for input on my song, Rae coerces me into grabbing frozen yogurt. Since I can never say no to food or to Rae, I end up at the Dairy Fairy with an extra-large serving of rocky road.

"RaeRae!" Melody waves at us from the line of customers.

Rae gestures her over, which leads me to guess they made up. From the way Laney, who's standing next to Mel, glares at the refrigerated display, I'm deducing she and Rae didn't.

"I'll grab two more seats," Rae says, which gets Laney's attention. Rae hooks her foot around the leg of an unoccupied chair and drags it over. "Can you grab that one, Angie?" She tips her head to the empty chair behind me.

I grab it and spin it around just as the girls make their way over to our table.

"Who wants to go dress shopping for homecoming with me this weekend?" Rae asks.

Laney's black eyes taper on Rae. Unlike Mel, she doesn't sit.

"I'm real sorry about the Brad thing, Laney," Rae says. "I hope he didn't retaliate or anything."

Laney's lids hike up in surprise at Rae's concern. Or maybe it's the apology that has her baffled. "He didn't."

I find Brad's nonretaliation surprising. Maybe he's not as big a jerk as he seems to be.

"So, shopping?" Rae repeats.

"I'm in. I saw this gray dress at the mall that I'm dying to try on," Mel says.

"Laney?" Rae asks.

As she sits, Laney bobs her head. And just like that, the hatchet is buried.

Laney's only been in Reedwood for a year, so I don't know her well, but I assumed she was the type to hold grudges because of how reserved she is. Which is silly, of course. Personality isn't determined by how vocal you are.

Rae glances at me. "Angie?"

"I do need a dress."

Rae rolls her eyes. "Don't sound *so* enthusiastic," she says, which makes Mel snort and Laney sort of smile.

Mel sucks on her spoon, then points it at me. "Did you ask Ten to homecoming, Angie?"

"Ten? No." I shake my head. "Why?"

"I was just curious. You two seem close."

"What?" I sound like someone's strangling me.

Rae's cheeks grow as fluorescent pink as her nails. "Why don't we all go dateless?"

"Cool with me." Mel scrapes the bottom of her frozen yogurt cup. "Laney?"

Laney sighs. "Sure."

As we discuss hairstyles and makeup, Rae's skin tone settles back to its normal hue.

After we part ways, I bike over to Lynn's house, rehearsing my lyrics softly. The more I ruminate on them, the more ambivalent I feel. I desperately need Lynn's opinion. By the time I reach my coach's house, my stomach is as knotted as my windblown hair.

I roll my bike down the paved pathway and hook it to the porch rail, then pull off my helmet and finger-comb my locks as I ring the doorbell.

What if Lynn hates the lyrics? Would she even tell me?

Finally, the door opens. "Hey, Angie," Lynn says. "Did we have a lesson today?"

"I wrote the song. I mean, *a* song. I wanted to run it past you and maybe work on it. If you have time." I was so intent on getting her opinion I didn't stop to consider if she was busy.

"Um. I'm free in a half hour. Can you come back then?"

I'm taken aback. *Come back?* "Can't I wait inside?"

Her left eye spasms. "Um." She glances behind her, at the door of the piano parlor.

"Or I can wait out here?" I say.

She releases a breath. "Okay."

After she closes the door, I flop down on the porch swing. My history notebook peeks out from my bag, which I take as a sign. I grab it, along with my notebook, and read about the Vietnam War, jotting down important facts, but soon wisps of the piano lesson inside distract me. Like drifts of pollen, the voice trickles through the drywall and coils in front of me.

I sit up straighter, as though adjusting my posture will somehow make the voice clearer. It doesn't. I need to get closer. I find myself creeping around the house, toward the window of the piano parlor.

Like the rumble of thunder, the voice grows louder, deeper, strengthening until it overpowers the birds chirping in the magnolia tree. I stand with my back against the wall, my fingers tapping the rhythm against the rough surface. When Lynn plays the treble clef, hitting higher notes, the voice splinters, and the music stops.

My fingers still. I hold my breath, afraid Lynn and her student will hear me breathing.

Lynn starts up again, this time on the bass clef, and the voice takes on a roundness, a depth, a raspiness that pitches me into a velvet chasm of sound. I hope the singer doesn't smoke, because it would damage her throat. Vocal folds like hers shouldn't be exposed to nicotine. They should be sealed off from any pollutant. I close my eyes, hanging on every note. The voice morphs into a tangible, fluid thing that undulates and bends and bursts with deep colors. Scarlet, violet, navy.

Lynn reaches the next low octave, and still the voice throbs and sways, braiding with the instrument until they fuse and become indistinguishable. A part of me is jealous, but another part is awestruck.

Lynn once told me to treat singing like a sport: to become good at it requires building muscle; to stay good at it requires practice. Yes, some people have musicality and can match pitch, but most lack power and texture. Those two elements separate the *greats* from the *goods*. The voice I'm hearing right now is definitely a great.

I finally peek through the window. The haunting, eddying tune halts so suddenly my body feels as though it's been spit out of a vortex. I stare at the girl—who's really only a child—and she stares back. Her mouth rounds, and then she tilts her head down, and her face vanishes behind the bill of a pink baseball cap.

Lynn leaps off the piano bench and marches toward the window, livid. I jump backward, half expecting her to fling the window open and throttle me. Instead, she pulls the heavy drapes closed.

I dash back to the front porch. All I did was look, so why do I feel like I've just murdered someone? My fingers scrabble over my history notebook just as Lynn bursts through the front door.

"What were you thinking?" she hisses.

"I'm . . . I'm sorry."

Loose sheets of paper flutter like feathers on the gray floorboards. I bend over to retrieve them and try to line them up, crumpling the sides. They don't line up. I sandwich them into my history book and stuff everything in my bag.

"What are you doing?" she asks.

"Leaving." I crouch, and after several attempts, manage to get my U-lock open. My fingers tremble as I toss my bag into the basket.

"I'm sorry I yelled, Angie." Her voice has lost some of its sternness.

Without turning, I jerk my head in a nod.

"She's just shy," Lynn adds.

"I understand," I say, even though I don't. I don't understand much of anything right now. I don't understand why I'm fleeing, or why Lynn hissed at me, or why I feel so wicked.

How could someone with such an extraordinary voice be shy?

"She has an incredible voice, doesn't she?" Lynn calls out as I begin pedaling away.

Something edges her voice. *Sadness?* Why would she feel sad about her student being gifted? Does she think I'm jealous?

I turn a corner and almost ram into a big black car. The car honks, brakes screeching. I swerve to miss it and end up on the wrong side of the road. I pedal quickly back to the right side, wheels grazing the raised curb, then I brake. My pulse is all over the place. Pressing one hand against my heart, I wait for it to even out.

Once the punching in my rib cage lessens, I look over my shoulder, itching to go back, but I don't want to seem like some psycho stalker, so I make my way back home.

11

Long, Boring Conversations

Soft rain pelts the windows of the classroom while the steel-gray light of the rain clouds turns the manicured quad silver. The weather matches my mood to perfection. Ever since Monday, I've been feeling down, and nothing and no one has been able to bring me back up. I should've just phoned Lynn and nipped whatever happened back at her house in the bud, but pride kept my lips sealed shut.

Rae's out sick, so at lunchtime I grab a turkey wrap, walk past the wall of yellow lockers, and push through the school doors. It's probably not the best day to eat outside, but I crave fresh air and space to think. I round the brick walls toward the track where students are running in spite of the ceaseless drizzle.

I unroll my denim jacket from my bag and poke my arms inside the sleeves, then untangle my pink earbuds and press PLAY on my father's last album. The Derelicts made one more album after he died, but it wasn't successful. Not that their other albums were all that successful. They never went platinum or anything, even though I think they deserved more attention than they got.

The air's warm and sticky, alive with a million mosquitoes. I climb up the bleachers to the highest row and watch the bodies looping around the field, kicking up globs of red dirt. It's strangely calming, almost hypnotic. The rain pricks my bare thighs like falling needles. I stuff my hands inside my pockets and close my eyes.

The strum of my father's guitar rumbles through me, smoothing out my anxiety. Earthen tones detonate behind my closed lids—amber, khaki, garnet. Like a balm, his playing soothes me.

If only he were still alive.

If only the roads hadn't been icy.

If only the fourteen-wheeler hadn't skidded and rammed into him.

I sigh just as something grazes my elbow. I imagine it's an insect and swipe it off.

It's not an insect, though; it's a hand.

I push my stringy hair off my forehead and pivot toward the body attached to it.

Ten's mouth moves, but I can't hear what he's saying.

I pluck one earbud out. "What?"

"Do you have a bicycle license?"

My head jerks back a little.

"You're a menace on that thing."

"Um, okay." *Criticism.* Just what I need. "If you're done doling out gratuitous advice, I'd like to get back to my music."

He rests his forearms on his thighs, laces his fingers together, and lets them hang between his knees. I pop the earbud back in, hoping he gets the message I want him to leave, but he doesn't move. Well, actually, he *does* move. He extends his arm, seizes one of my earbuds, and sticks it into his ear. He wraps his palms around the edge of the metal bench and stretches his long legs out.

His head bobs.

"I thought you hated music," I say.

"Garage bands are okay."

"The Derelicts aren't a garage band."

His gym shirt with the school crest—a stylized tree of knowledge—sticks to his chest. "The Derelicts, huh? Your father's band?"

"Yeah. He was their guitar player."

"Do you play the guitar?" he asks.

"No."

"Do you play an instrument?"

"Who's the nosy one now?"

"I never called you nosy." He takes the earbud out and hands it back to me. "I said you asked a lot of questions."

"Same difference."

"Why are you sitting up here by yourself?"

"Because . . ." I loop the pink plastic cord around my index finger. "Why do you even care?"

His golden eyes darken. "You've been sitting with your back to me in class all week."

I didn't think he'd noticed.

He sticks his hand out.

I frown at it.

"I'm Tennessee Dylan, but I go by Ten. What's your name?"

I look down at his suspended hand, then look around in case this is a prank one of his track buddies is filming. No one's holding up any phones. No one's even around. How long have I been out here?

I check my watch. When I see the time, I spring up. Ten winces, mistaking my rush to head back inside for a dismissal. He stands, rubs his palms against his gym shorts, then starts down the bleachers.

"Hey, new kid," I call out.

He turns around.

"My name's Angela Conrad, but everyone calls me Angie."

His lips twitch.

I catch up to him. "I plan on being a legendary musician. What about you, Ten? What do you dream of being when you grow up?" I'm standing on the step above him, yet he's still taller than I am.

His smile turns brash. "What do you think I dream of being when I grow up?"

I tilt my head to the side. "I'm thinking it's a toss-up between talk show host and astronaut. Am I close?"

He laughs, a deep laugh that slaloms past the raindrops and sneaks into my chest.

I draw a look of mock surprise over my face. "What? Am I not even close?"

"Not even."

I skip off the step and go down a couple more. Ten follows me. I hop off the bleachers onto the squishy, sodden grass and wait for him.

"So what *do* you want to do, Ten?"

"I don't actually know."

"You don't?"

He shakes his head. "No clue."

"How can you not have a clue? Don't you have a passion?"

"Not really."

"How can you live without passion?"

"Most people don't have passions; most people enjoy certain things more than others, but that's it."

"What do you enjoy, then?" I ask as we head toward the doors that lead to the locker rooms.

"I like driving around. Running clears my mind. And I love to cook."

I stop walking so suddenly that he stops too. "So basically, you're a stay-at-home mom locked inside the body of a teenage boy?"

He kicks a stone with his mud-soaked sneakers. "That's what playing substitute for an absentee mother will do to you."

I've gone too far with my teasing. I touch his forearm. "I'm sorry, Ten. I didn't mean to . . . to make you think of *her*."

He looks at my hand. I snatch it back, return it to the strap of my tote bag.

"Try not to tell your friends about my very masculine ambitions, or I'll be turned down when I ask one of them to homecoming."

It feels as though he's just flicked my heart. Which is stupid because

I don't even like Ten. I mean, I like him more than I liked him this morning, but I don't *like him* like him.

He stuffs his hands into his pockets. "Want to go to homecoming with me?"

"Me?"

"My first choice was Mrs. Dabbs, but she was taken." He delivers his comment so seriously I blink. "That was a joke." A blush stains his jaw. "Not a funny one," he mumbles.

I'm way too shocked . . . thrilled . . . dazed to give him an answer.

He rubs the back of his neck. "You're probably already going with someone."

"Actually, I am."

He flinches.

"I'm going with Rae, Mel, and Laney. We decided to go dateless."

"Is that a thing here? Going as a group instead of as a couple?"

"Not usually." I bite my lip. "We're going to be so late for class," I say, although what I really want to say is, *Will you ask someone else?* I don't want him to go with someone else, which is all shades of selfish and strange since I have no claim on him.

Finally, he shrugs. "I didn't really want to go anyway."

"I'll save you a dance if you come." Could I sound any lamer?

"I don't dance."

"What? I assumed all good stay-at-home moms were avid ballroom dancers."

He chuckles.

I heave a theatrical sigh. "If you're really against dancing, then I'll save you a"—I push more wet hair off my face—"long, boring conversation *off* the dance floor. We can discuss sauce-making."

A soft grin settles over his face.

And that smile undoes me way more than it should.

12

Bwirling Hearts

By the end of the day, I'm still reeling that Ten asked me to homecoming. I mean, the fact that he talked to me in the first place is shocking enough, but asking me to be his date to the school dance . . . that's got my heart spinning. Or like Steffi would say—she loves naming her choreographies—*bwirling*.

By the time I reach my coaches' house, I resemble a sewer rat from all the puddles I biked through, but I don't even care. I leave my shoes by the door and go change into leggings, a workout bra, and a T-shirt with a Buddhist quote that would make Mrs. Larue proud, then go straight to the piano parlor.

"I'm sorry about Monday," Lynn says, ushering me inside.

The shy girl with the smoky voice supplants Ten's image inside my mind and squashes my high.

"I didn't mean to be so . . . nosy." Confessing this out loud makes me realize that Ten wasn't totally wrong about me. "I was so mesmerized by the girl's voice that I wanted to put a face to it." I study a patch of discolored velvet on the chaise where the sun bleached the deep teal. "And maybe I *was* a little jealous."

"You have *nothing* to be jealous about, Angie."

I'm sure she says that to reassure me.

"And I'm not saying this to stoke your ego."

Okay, so maybe she isn't.

Instead of the chaise, I look at the bun that puffs up from the top of her head like an atomic mushroom cloud.

"Someone once said that comparison was the thief of joy, and it truly is," Lynn says, stroking the varnished wood of her piano. "Never compare yourself to anyone else in this life."

Easier said than done.

"So, you wrote the lyrics to your song?"

"Yeah."

She sits on the bench and begins playing a melody. "Let's warm up first."

We start the usual way: I hum a sound that sounds like *mniam* to soften my palate. The second exercise is a smooth, soft legato *oo-o* sound, then a louder *ee*, then staccato. The series of short, sharp notes pumps my diaphragm and heats my already flushed skin. At the end of the warm-up, energy crackles through me.

I chug down half a bottle of water, then pull the sheet music I wrote on from my bag and set it in front of Lynn. The soft but frenetic tempo kicks up my pulse. I ball my fingers into fists, then stretch my jaw wide and fit the verses to the notes, adding a deep hum to the bridge. My palate vibrates with the song, and blood rushes and gushes against my eardrums, drowning out my own voice. When I'm finished, sweat beads on my upper lip. I swipe it away with my tongue.

As Lynn's fingers slide off the keys, I massage my corded neck and yawn to loosen my cramping jaw. I feel drained, like I've just finished a triathlon. I stretch my arms over my head, roll my shoulders, crack my fingers. I bet the dance studio's ceiling is vibrating from my frenzied pulse.

"So?"

My voice coach shakes her head, and the colors around me smear together in a dark, gloppy mess.

She hates it.

I pick up my bottle of water with shaky fingers and lift it to my mouth again.

"The chorus sounds *great*."

I assume the other pieces of the song must not sound all that great if she's singled out the chorus. "But the rest isn't as strong?"

"The rest is good. But do I think we can make it better? Yeah. I think we could even give Lady Antebellum a run for their money. Want to work on it?"

"Hell yeah, I want to work on it!"

Lynn laughs. We spend the next half hour piecing the verses in a different order, and then I sing everything from the top. When the last note peters out into a gentle, exhausted hum, clapping sounds from the doorway. Steffi's eyes gleam with admiration. She steps into the room and lays her hands on her wife's shoulders.

I feel like a mouse intruding on a private moment. But then Steffi puts her hand on my shoulder and connects me to them. "Angie," she murmurs. "Angie. Angie. Angie. Lynn said you were working on something, but she failed to mention how incredible it was."

I beam, because Steffi knew Mona, and Lynn is a seasoned musician, so their approval means *everything* to me. I don't even care that Mom thinks it's crap.

13

Operation Inanimate Object

"What about this one?" Rae steps out of the changing room and twirls. The burgundy dress billows around her legs.

"Um . . . why didn't I see that one?" Mel smooths out the pearl-gray fabric of the dress she's modeling in front of the full-length mirror.

"I. Love. Yours. The color really makes your eyes pop." Rae walks over to me to see the selection of dresses I plucked off the racks. "Ooh, leopard print. Nice."

I grimace. The off-the-shoulder neckline drew me in, but I'm not sure about the print.

"Try it on." She shoves me into a changing room just as Laney comes out of hers in a glittery sapphire number.

The same model hangs from my finger. No way am I even trying it on now. Attending school dances dressed identically is social suicide. A couple of years ago, a popular senior demanded that another girl go home to change.

I close the curtain and try option one first—a white dress with feathers sewn into the short hem.

Rae scrunches up her nose. "You look like you fought with a swan, and it won."

Mel smirks. "I think it's great."

Like I'd ever take *her* word.

I return to the changing room, yank off the dress, and pull on the leopard print.

Rae whistles when I exit. "Sexy."

"You don't think the print's a little loud?"

"I love the split skirt," Laney says. "You have such great legs."

Rae checks out my legs as though she hasn't seen them a million times before. "It's from all her dancing."

"I used to dance," Laney says. "Ballet. What sort of dancing do you do?"

"Mostly modern. I have an amazing teacher," I offer.

As I tell Laney about Steffi, Rae scrutinizes my dress. "It's missin' something."

Barefoot in her burgundy gown, she traipses through the aisles of clothes, stopping at a display of accessories. She returns holding a wide black belt and a hot-pink glass necklace. As I fasten the belt around my waist, she hooks the necklace around my neck, the burst of color taming the print.

"You'd make such a great stylist," Mel says, admiring Rae's work.

"She'll make an even better cardiologist," I volley back.

"Cardiologist?" Mel's nasal voice sounds uncharacteristically high-pitched.

Laney cocks one of her black eyebrows up. "Is that what you want to do, Rae?"

I'm secretly pleased neither of them knew this.

"That's the dream. But I need the grades."

"You already have them," I say.

"Actually, I'm sliding in math. I was thinking of askin' Ten to tutor me."

As though bees were poking me with their stingers, my skin begins to burn. "Why would you ask him?"

Rae gathers her blonde hair in her fist and rolls it up, holding it atop her head, then lets it unravel. "Mrs. Larue commended his math skills and thought it could help him fit in if he tutored one of his peers. Her words, obviously. Not mine. And then she told me that the Buddha once said, *Helping one person might not change the world, but it could change the world for one person.*"

I toy with the belt that feels as though it girdles my lungs instead of my waist. "The year just started. How can she even know if Ten's all that good in calculus?"

A smile curves Melody's berry-lip-balmed mouth. "Is someone jealous?"

"I don't care about being the best student," I shoot back.

"I don't think she was talking about grades," Laney says softly.

I can feel Rae watching me but don't meet her gaze. Instead I look around the store. By a mannequin stands a girl in oversized sweats and a baseball cap.

What draws me in is the cap. It's bubble gum pink.

Without realizing it, I'm fording the store straight toward her. I circle the mannequin, feigning great interest in the crop top. I think I'm being subtle, but the girl's body goes as rigid as the shiny white dummy. Scared she'll run before I can get a look at her, I speed-walk around the display, but trip over the square base. I latch on to the dummy that isn't attached to the base. I squeeze my eyes shut as I crash, dummy-first, to the floor.

On the upside, from this vantage point, I can now see the girl's face.

And yep, it's the same one I glimpsed at Lynn's house. It's even sporting the exact same expression—undiluted shock with a side of horror.

"Hi?" I venture. Not my most impressive overture.

Eyes shiny like shaken snow globes, the girl backs away but bumps into a broad body. Hands settle on her shoulders. Long fingers crease her heather-gray sweatshirt, steadying her.

My gaze scales the length of the body. When it reaches the person's face, my jaw slackens. Like rubber bands, my eyes snap back to the girl's face. I expect her to spring away from the person touching her, but she doesn't.

I wonder what my odds are of passing for a plastic dummy. Maybe if I lie perfectly still—

"Angie, are you okay?" Rae asks.

There goes operation inanimate object.

14

Ovaries Can Apparently Melt

"Hiya, Ten." Rae flips her hair.

Sucking in a sigh, I peel myself off the mannequin. I don't bother righting it. Two salesgirls have already flocked over to do just that, exceedingly concerned for the fiberglass figure and not the least bit for me.

If only I could blink out of existence—

Rae winds one arm through mine. "You okay, Angie?"

Nope. I'm not okay. I probably will never be okay. I just face-planted at Ten's feet while clutching a mannequin.

I'm animated by a very real desire to race into a changing room and hide until Tennessee leaves the store with this girl, whom I assume is the owner of the princess Band-Aids, but Mom is their decorator. I don't want them to fire her because I behaved like a lunatic stalker, so I level my gaze on the girl who's still nestled against Ten's chest and swallow my pride. "You have a real awesome voice. That's what I came over to say."

She doesn't respond. Just gapes at me.

"Nev"—Ten sighs roughly—"meet Angie."

Nev's eyebrows are as dark as Ten's, and her nose is a smaller version of his, complete with the slight bump.

"And I'm Rae," my friend says brightly, giving Nev a small wave.

"Hi." Nev's voice is adagio soft.

"So that's how you ended up at Lynn's? My mother . . ." It's not a question as much as a realization.

Nev glances up at her brother, who explains that I'm Jade's daughter.

"You sing too, Nev?" Rae asks.

Even though Nev appears spooked, she nods.

Suddenly, I realize why Ten told me I was a danger on my bike. I almost ran into a car when I was fleeing Lynn's . . . *his* car. He must've been on his way to pick up his sister. "How can you hate music when your sister has such an incredible voice?" I ask him.

Even though Nev's face is shaded by her cap, it seems to darken. She cranes her neck to look up at her brother. Her brother who still hasn't released her. Whose fingers are crimping his sister's sweatshirt.

"Ten doesn't hate music," she says.

Ten's fingers appear to dig even harder into the gray fabric. "Nev . . ."

"What? You don't," she says in a chirruping voice that clashes completely with the deep, raspy sound of her singing voice.

Why did Ten lie to me?

He lowers his gaze to the bill of his sister's cap. "We should go. We still have to pick up Dad's shirts."

Mel trots up to us. "Why were you groping a dummy, Angie?"

Wow. I shoot her the stink eye, while Rae grins.

"Sorry"—Rae tries to iron out her smile—"but it was sort of funny."

"Hi, Ten." Mel's eyes stray to Nev. "This must be your little sister. You guys look *exactly* alike. Like, exactly."

I can't imagine that being compared to your brother—however handsome he may be—is all that flattering.

"You're not in Jenny's class, are you?" Mel asks. Jenny is Mel's little sister, even though there's nothing little about the twelve-year-old.

Their father, Mr. Barnett, a former Memphis Grizzly, is one heck of a tall man. I met him at the school fair last year, and no joke, he's twice my height.

"I am," Nev says almost hesitantly. I take it Jenny isn't her friend. If Jenny's anything like her sister, I understand why.

Rae elbows me. "You should go change."

I'd forgotten all about the dress. "It was nice to meet you, Nev. Sorry if I freaked you out. I was just . . . well"—I raise a smile—"starstruck."

Her eyes go wide again, and then she whirls, pushes up on her tip-toes, and whispers something into Ten's ear. I'm guessing that whatever she's saying is about me from the way Ten's gaze strays to me.

"I don't know," he says in a low voice.

"See you around," I mumble, adding a "maybe" when I behold Ten's suspicious gaze. My smile, which had already started to fall, flattens. I'm not sure what in my character merits such suspicion.

Without so much as a goodbye, Ten drapes an arm over Nev's shoulders and tows her away. Soon they vanish in the steady stream of mall shoppers.

"How protective is he of his little sister?" Rae lets out a little sigh. "I think my ovaries just melted a little."

He *is* protective, but it felt as though he was protecting Nev from me.

Laney hoists a shopping bag onto her shoulder. "Are you all right, Angie?"

"I'm probably riddled in bruises." Especially on the inside. "But yeah, I'm all right."

Laney shoots me this strange look, which I don't even try to decipher. I finally turn back toward the changing rooms, enter mine, and yank off the accessories and then the dress. I thought that once I removed the belt, I would breathe a little easier, but my torso still feels compacted. I try to hang up the dress, but it keeps slipping off the hanger.

Grumbling, I wrench my clothes back on, pick up the pile of leopard spots and the rib-crushing strip of leather, and shove them on the stool wedged in the corner.

Rae pokes her head through the curtain. "Jasper's asking if we want to go get pizza with him and Harrison."

"Harrison?"

"The new quarterback. Mel just saw them come out of the Apple Store and waved them over."

"Is our entire school at the mall today?"

Rae's lips quirk up.

"What?" I snap.

"You're in a mood."

"And that's funny?"

"A little. You did knock over a mannequin, because you were star-struck by a kid." Rae combs her hair back. "So? Pizza? Mel really wants to hang with Jasper."

As though that'll sway me . . .

"Come on, grumpy. Grab your things, and let's go."

Sighing, I walk past Rae.

"That was way too hot to leave behind." She sweeps up the dress along with the necklace and belt, and jams all three into my arms.

And that's how, after dropping my shattered cell phone off to get it repaired, I end up with a dress I don't want to ever wear again, at a lunch I don't want to be at. The only silver lining of the meal is Laney, who tells me about her courses at the Nashville Ballet and her dashed hopes of becoming a prima ballerina (skiing accident).

"But you're healed now," I tell her, over Harrison's loud chewing, which seems to bother only me.

"My knee never healed properly." She blots her mouth, then scrutinizes the transparent patch left by the grease from her mushroom slice. "It's okay, though. I have other dreams. I want to become a kindergarten teacher. Do you have a backup plan if singing doesn't pan out?"

Backup plans are like safety nets—if you feel like you need one, then you don't have much faith in yourself.

"There's nothing I'd rather do." I slurp some soda from my giant foam cup. "For now," I add, because I sense Laney wants to give me advice, and I don't want advice. Advice is nothing but nicely packaged doubts. "So kindergarten teacher, huh?"

15

Red, White, and Super Bluesy

Homecoming week used to be my favorite week. Five days uniform-free. One big football game. One epic dance.

Today is 'Merica Monday, which means everyone will be dressed in red, white, and blue. I wear jeans, a white tank top, and red canvas lace-up shoes, but my heart isn't in it like previous years.

Glumly, I scoop up cereal and eat it.

I'm still wondering why Ten acted so weird the other day. All of Sunday, I toyed with the idea of sending him a message but never ended up clicking SEND. Our run-in did a number on my nerves, though—my balance was so screwy throughout yoga that I toppled over during tree pose, then fell flat on my face during crow.

I spent the rest of the class curled up in child's pose to avoid Mom's questioning gaze and then faked a stomachache so we could go straight home. Mom's concern was palpable, but she didn't push me to tell her what was going on.

The same way she's not pushing me this morning, even though her forehead is furrowed.

"I don't feel good, Mom. Can I stay home?"

She presses her palm against my forehead. "Is it Rae, or is it a boy?"

"Huh?"

"Obviously something's bothering you. I'm assuming it's either trouble with a friend or with a member of the opposite sex." She scoots her chair closer to me, and her long, beaded turquoise earrings swing. "Want to talk about it?"

I slurp down some more cereal. "Nope."

She sighs. "You're as stubborn as your daddy."

This isn't meant as a compliment, yet I soak it right up. I like it when Mom compares me to him. Makes Dad a little less of a stranger.

She grips the hand I've curled into my lap and gives it a slight squeeze. "Baby, you can't hide out when something's bothering you."

"Did Dad used to do that? Hide?"

Her fingers go slack, and then she releases my hand and stands. "He had other methods of getting rid of stress."

She walks over to the sink, opens the faucet, and lets the water run. I'm not sure why she turned the tap on, because she doesn't rinse her bowl of cereal or the juicer she used to press oranges. She just stands there, gripping the edge of the sink.

"Like what?"

"You're going to be late," she says way too long after I asked. She finally pulls the juicer apart with jerky movements, then sponges each piece of black plastic vigorously.

Not much ruffles Mom.

Just Dad and music. *Why?*

Pulse skittering with perplexity, I plop my bowl into the sink, then give my mother a quick hug, because I sense she needs one.

On my way to school, I listen to my peppiest playlist, but it does little to lighten my sullenness. My mood worsens when I spot a black Range Rover driving parallel to me.

As I peer through the window, my bike swerves a little. It's not Tennessee at the wheel, though, just some mom with two kids strapped into the backseat. Relieved, I straighten my trajectory, concentrating on not getting myself run over, even though I wouldn't have to go to school if I did.

As I turn into Reedwood's parking lot, I scan the rows of cars for Ten's. I don't see it. Maybe he asked to transfer to another school. Or maybe he begged his dad to stay home too, and his father—unlike my mother—showed some compassion.

I snatch my notebook from my locker just as the second bell rings, and Mrs. Larue's plucky voice crackles from the PA system. "*When you judge another, you do not define them, you define yourself.*"

Ha! Take that, Ten.

My suspicions about Mrs. Larue being a spy strengthen as I enter the classroom. The table I share with Ten is empty. I sink into my cold, hard chair, then dig through my tote for my homework sheet. Legs appear in front of me. Long legs. Clad in jeans. I follow the legs up to a white T-shirt with red lettering that reads I SPEAK FRENCH, then to the sharp Adam's apple and the jaw coated by dark scruff.

I don't look any higher. Instead, I shift on my chair, then pull my elastic off my ponytail and let my hair settle around my face like a privacy screen. I try to focus on the lecture, but it's like trying to focus on a conversation during a concert.

I tap my foot, jiggle my knee.

This is torture. Just torture.

I'm about to stick my hand up to be excused to go to the infirmary when a large hand claps my knee. Stills it.

I jerk my face toward Tennessee.

"Please stop," he murmurs, pulling his hand away.

Without doing it on purpose, I go back to bouncing my knee. I can feel him glaring at it throughout class, probably tempted to pin it down.

A scrap of paper lands on my sheet of homework. *What's wrong?*

Is he serious? Has he forgotten how weird he acted toward me at the mall? I avert my gaze from the note and feign great interest in the equation written on the whiteboard.

He filches his note back and scribbles: *Is it because I lied about hating music?*

I shake my head.

Then what? he writes.

You looked at me as though I was a nutcase in that shop.

You're mad at me because of the way I looked at you?

Now that I see it in writing, it does seem a little silly. *Forget it.*

New words appear on the piece of paper: *How much has Jade told you about my family?*

She hasn't told me anything. Just that your dad is an entertainment lawyer. Why? Frowning, I finally glance up at him.

Ten's cheek dimples. He must be biting it, because he doesn't have dimples.

It hits me then that Jeff Dylan must be a huge country star or something, that his name and job are just covers. Unless he's not into music at all. Maybe he's part of the Mafia or a runaway dignitary from another country.

Is your dad really a lawyer? I write.

Ten's eyebrows pinch together. He reaches over and writes: *He is.*

Would he tell me the truth?

Ten goes back to listening to the lecture until the end of class. As I walk to my next class, I google Jeff Dylan. I get two hits. One is a thin-faced actor in his early twenties—obviously not Ten's father—and the other is a man who survived a faulty parachute even though most of his bones didn't. Neither man is a lawyer. I add *lawyer* after Jeff Dylan's name, but find nothing about a lawyer named Jeff Dylan.

Is he such a private person that he isn't even listed on the internet, or did Ten *and* my mother lie to me?

16

The Chicken with the Bad Timing

Because I can't leave well enough alone, I drop my tray down on Ten's table at lunch. "He's not a lawyer, is he?"

"Excuse me?"

"Your dad. I looked him up. I didn't get a single hit for a lawyer named Jeff Dylan."

His features shift, composing and recomposing into several different expressions. Finally, he shakes his head. "You googled my dad?" His tone is all at once aggressive and defensive. "He *is* a lawyer, Angie."

Why is he still lying to me?

"You'd find him if I gave you our real last name."

I freeze.

"But we don't give it out because it's brought a lot of creeps into our lives. So there, satisfied?"

His confession both fans and douses the fire burning within me. It explains a hell of a lot but also fills me with questions.

Who are the Dylans?

I swallow, but my throat feels as tight as the straw poking from my apple juice.

Ten's gaze slides around the cafeteria. "If you could keep this conversation between us, I'd really appreciate it."

I nod, then leave, but double back for my tray. I set it down at my usual table, which is empty today, because Rae and Laney are helping out with homecoming decorations and Mel's sitting with the jocks.

I pick at my food but don't eat. Out of the corner of my eye, I notice Ten gather up his tray and shove it onto one of the racks. And then he leaves the cafeteria. I'm tempted to leave too, but I don't want people to think I'm following him, so I stay seated. Sticking my earbuds in, I listen to music and do a bunch of homework.

The day slides by so slowly it feels like it's going backward. When I get home, I sit at the piano and play until my fingers ache and the sun has set.

"A new song you wrote?" Mom asks, startling me.

I was so concentrated on the music I didn't even hear the front door.

I lift my fingers off the keys and curl them in my lap. "It's one of Dad's. I've just slowed the tempo." I swivel on the bench. "I know you're not allowed to talk about the Dylans, but are they good or bad people?"

She jerks her head, and the sunglasses resting on top of her hair topple onto the rug. "What?"

"Ten told me his family changed their last name."

She crouches to pick up her glasses. "Baby, I can't talk about them."

"I'm not asking you to tell me *who* they are. All I'm asking is, are they criminals or not?"

She stares at me and then at the propped lid of the piano. "They're not."

A lump grows inside my throat, invades it. The Dylans, or whoever they are, are good people. Even though a part of me still wonders who they could be, another part is telling me to stop meddling.

When Mom leaves to get dinner ready, I plod upstairs to my bedroom, take my cell phone out of my pocket, and tap on Ten's contact. I write a thousand different things. I erase nine hundred ninety-nine of them. In the end, I send: *I'm sorry.*

A short while later, hair damp from the shower, I return downstairs and set the table as Mom closes the oven door on something that already smells divine.

"The chicken'll be ready in a minute. Just crisping up the skin." She takes a seat at the table, then pats the chair next to her. "Baby, come sit. I want us to talk."

About the Dylans? Is she finally going to confide in me?

"I don't feel like I see enough of you these days," Mom says, nursing a glass of white wine between her palms. "And I'm sorry, because it's entirely my fault. I'm always runnin' from one construction site to the next." She sighs. "I've become *that* mother. The one who spends more time with people who shouldn't matter, instead of with the only person who truly matters."

I'm about to tell her that working doesn't make her any less of a mother, that if anything I'm proud of her. I think I can even use this as the perfect segue into the contest.

Before I can open my mouth, she asks, "So what's happening in your life? Have you started on your college applications? Have you written an essay yet? If you have, I'd love to read it."

I trail one finger down my glass of water, creating a path through the condensation. Water beads on the glass tabletop. "I've started looking into schools"—I haven't, but considering how every senior in Reedwood is chattering on about college, I've picked up some details I can use to substantiate my lie—"and everything else is fine."

Tell her about the Mona Stone contest. Tell her, Angie. Before playing Dad's song, I was practicing mine. It sounds better now, more polished. Maybe she'll like it.

Before I locate my backbone to fess up, she says, "When you were small, and I would ask you how your day went, you used to give me a play-by-play. Didn't leave out a single detail. But now, all I get is an *everything's fine*? That's not us, baby. At least, that's not who I want us to be." She sets her wineglass down. "Are you and Ten friends? How's Rae? Who are you going to homecoming with?"

I slide my lower lip between my teeth. "Ten and I, we're . . . I wouldn't say friends, but sort of friendly? And I'm going with the girls to homecoming. And Rae's Rae. Sunny, happy, busy Rae. She's totally into our school's new quarterback, even though she swore she wouldn't date another jock."

I think of my friend's senior bucket list and the item she will most definitely not be checking off considering Harrison's become a constant in our conversations. And then I think of my own bucket list, of the only item on it.

I inhale a lungful of courage. "Mom—"

Our fire alarm blares, and she jerks up. Batting away the pale smoke, she grabs an oven mitt, yanks open the oven door, and pulls the chicken out while I crack open the windows.

It takes a couple of minutes for the smoke to clear and the strident beeping to stop. And then Mom's on the phone with the fire department, explaining that they needn't pay us a visit, and then she's scouring the fridge for something else to make us.

I glare at the charred bird, thinking that its timing really sucked. If it could only have waited an extra minute before burning up . . .

I drop it into the trash can under the sink as though it had intentionally wronged me, but my cowardice is in no way the chicken's fault.

I'm the chicken in the story.

I scrunch up my nose, a bit appalled that I'm comparing myself to a bird.

After dinner, I check my phone. Ten hasn't answered, but he's read my apology—there's a little check mark next to the chat bubble. I take it he's still mad. At least I had enough courage to reach out to him.

If only I'd had enough courage to reach out to Mom . . .

17

The Invisible Stone and the Inflatable

Sword

On Tuesday, I only see Ten during lunch period. I watch him from across the cafeteria, but don't speak to him. Not even the colorful grass skirts and the Hawaiian-print shirts brighten Tropical Tuesday.

On Wednesday, I ready myself to face him during afternoon art class. Not that we usually sit together. Usually we sit on opposite sides of the classroom. Today, Miss Bank has us work on projects in twosomes, which screws up the seating arrangement. I try to pair up with Laney, but Brad swoops in and asks her. I'm not sure who's more startled by his proposition: me or her.

She accepts Brad's invitation, then apologizes to me. They move across the room, heads bent together in conversation.

"Did everyone find a partner?" Miss Bank asks.

I turn to ask Ron, a quiet overachiever, but someone beats me to him. I swivel around and come nose-to-chest with someone. Readjusting the Minnie Mouse headband I wore for Walt Disney Wednesday, I tip my face up.

Ten's clean, soapy scent, overlaid by notes of . . . *sweet dough*—did he spend his morning whipping up pancakes?—tickles my nostrils. "Seems like we're the last ones left."

I'm pretty sure two girls asked him to be their partner.

"Portraits!" Miss Bank announces, clapping. "You're going to be drawing your partner, costume and all. It can be as abstract as you want. And you are welcome to use whichever medium you'd like."

"I have to warn you," I tell Ten, once I've recovered from the realization that we're partners, "I'm real bad at drawing people."

"Good thing Miss Bank said it could be abstract."

"Yeah. I even botch abstract art."

He drags an easel toward a chair, and I do the same. "I won't take offense if I end up with a Picasso face."

"You'll be lucky if you end up with a Picasso face." We walk to the supply closet and grab paintbrushes and tubes of acrylic paint. As we return to our chairs, I ask, "You are aware Walt Disney didn't come up with Harry Potter, right?"

His mouth rounds in surprise. "No way!"

I'm about to say *yeah*, when his golden eyes spark with . . . amusement? "You're not a Harry Potter character, are you?"

"Nope."

I study his red graduation gown and the yellow silk scarf knotted around his neck while he starts painting me. "Are you a wizard?"

"No."

My gaze drops to the inflatable sword hooked into a rope tied around his waist. "The prince in *Cinderella*?"

"You think I look like a prince?" he asks without glancing away from his paper.

My cheeks smolder. "I said *the* prince—never mind." I direct my attention to my still-blank paper. I dab red paint on it and swirl the color around until it sort of takes on the shape of a poufy gown.

"Are you giving up? I didn't peg you for the type of girl who gave up," Ten says.

Our gazes collide. Although several conversations buzz around us, all I can hear is what Ten just said. "About your costume?"

He returns his attention to his canvas and lifts his paintbrush. "Isn't that what we were talking about?"

My heart skitters to a halt inside my rib cage. Is he kidding? Did I just totally misread him? He wants me to guess his alter ego's identity, but not his actual one? "I didn't think you wanted me to keep guessing."

He looks back at me. The gold flecks in his irises seem to have dimmed. "So you're giving up?"

"Honestly, I think it's better if I do."

I jab my paintbrush against the canvas and red paint splatters over my cleavage, which is wedged too tightly into my costume's sweetheart neckline. I should probably have bought a new dress instead of recycling the one I wore two Halloweens ago.

I try to wipe the paint away with the heel of my hand but end up smudging it and making it look like I walked off a horror movie set. I head to the sink, where I ball up scratchy paper towel and wet it to clean myself up before I give Miss Bank a heart attack.

"Arthur from *The Sword in the Stone*," Ten says after I return to my easel.

"I would never have guessed that."

For a moment, we look at each other. A long moment. And then I avert my gaze because there's too much to see in Ten's face. What's the point in seeing anything if there's no way of understanding what I'm looking at?

18

Never Have I Ever Felt This Bad

Fueled by the momentous elation of Reedwood winning the homecoming game, Rae throws a little impromptu party at her parents' pool house. There are seven of us. Four girls, three boys—me, Jasper, Laney, Brad, Rae, Melody, and Harrison, who was instrumental in demolishing our opponents.

Jasper kneads Melody's hand. "We crushed them so bad."

I don't think they've hooked up yet, but I think it's a matter of minutes before it happens.

While Harrison fiddles with a vintage iPod plugged into an equally vintage stereo, Rae opens a cupboard and whips out a bottle of vodka. A rhythmic beat vibrates against the glass walls. The singer's voice sounds hoarse, and her words don't make much sense, but it's better than the sound of Brad and Laney sucking each other's faces like leeches.

I still don't get what she sees in Brad, but hey, who am I to judge?

"Who wants to play 'Never Have I Ever'?" Rae asks.

Jasper whoops. The others alternate between nervous chuckling and excited head-bobbing.

"What's 'Never Have I Ever'?" I ask.

Brad pulls away long enough from Laney to guffaw at me. "Who wants to explain the rules to Conrad?"

The decorative green stripes Melody smeared over her cheeks for team spirit are smudged, giving the impression she's wearing an avocado mud mask. I don't think she cares, considering Jasper is still rubbing her hand. "One person says, 'Never have I ever gone swimming.' If you *have* gone swimming, you drink. If you haven't, you pass."

"I found the vodka and suggested the game. I get to start," Rae says as Harrison sits next to her.

He sets multicolored plastic cups on the glass coffee table, then pushes his longish black hair off his forehead. I eye him and then I eye Rae. Like humidity thickening the air before a storm, something's brewing between them.

Talk about being a fifth wheel. Or seventh in this case.

Rae pours a finger of alcohol in all the glasses. "So this one's for Jasper." She winks at him. "Never have I ever read an entire book."

Jasper sucks air through his teeth. "That's harsh, RaeRae."

She grins, then shoots down the contents of her glass. Everyone drinks, except for Jasper and me.

"Angie, you've read tons of books. Bottoms up, hon," Rae says, already pouring a second round.

Right . . . I drink if I've done it.

I shoot it down, and it leaves a trail of fire on my tongue and throat. I cough and my eyes water. I wipe them on the sleeve of my green hoodie.

"You've seriously never read an entire book, man?" Brad asks Jasper.

"Nope."

"My turn," Laney says. "Never have I ever kissed a girl."

The boys and Melody drink. We all stare at Melody, who raises a brazen smile. "What?"

"Any chance we can get a repeat performance?" he asks her.

She leans over and pecks Laney's lips. Jasper whistles.

"You have to drink now," Brad tells Laney.

She laughs. "Fine." She shoots her vodka down, after which he kisses her with wet, slurpy noises.

"Never have I ever had a crush on someone younger," Melody says.

The boys and Laney drink. As Brad asks who, Rae says, "Never have I ever gotten a C."

Everyone but Rae drinks. The vodka goes down like hot lava.

"Your turn, Angie," she says, filling up all the empty glasses.

I bite my lower lip. "Never have I ever gone a day without listening to music."

Only Harrison drinks. After he slams his glass down, he says, "Never have I ever gone skinny-dipping."

All the cups are drained except his. I can't help but begin to relax as heat threads through my veins and into my arms, legs, and head.

"There's a pool right there, dude." Brad points to the shimmery turquoise water beyond the glass.

Harrison glances at Rae, who grins and says, "Be my guest."

"Not alone," he replies sultrily into her ear but loud enough for me to pick up.

Never have I ever felt like more of a fifth wheel, I think but don't say out loud, because one, it's not my turn, and two, I always feel like a fifth wheel.

I wish Ten were here. *Ugh.* Why am I so hung up on him?

"Never have I ever had sex," Mel says.

Everyone drinks except her and me.

Jasper raises an eyebrow at Mel. "Never?"

She blushes but laughs it off.

Has Ten ever had sex? The thought dampens the lilt in my mood. Why must my brain conjure him up? Why can't I just stop thinking about him altogether?

"Never have I ever driven a car," I say, even though it's not my turn.

Everyone drinks except me.

"Never have I ever lied to Principal Larue," Rae says.

We all drink except her and Laney.

"Never have I ever played volleyball," Laney says.

We all drink but her.

"Never have I ever enjoyed volleyball," Harrison ventures.

I drink. I don't like volleyball. It hurts my wrists. Wait, was I supposed to drink? The rules are blurry.

"Never have I ever painted my nails," Jasper says.

The girls drink.

I've had six, seven, maybe ten shots.

Ten.

Ugh.

I tap on my phone and bring up my last conversation with him and type, *Are you a virgin?* and click SEND. Then I stare at the words, the horror of what I've just done registering. I want to erase my message but since I can't, I add, *Rae asked,* and send it. I silently apologize to my friend but doubt she'll care considering how little physical space remains between Harrison and her. They're definitely well on their way to hooking up. Come to think of it, she didn't mention Ten once this week. Not that we've spent an extensive amount of time together what with her spearheading the homecoming committee.

I drink the next shot without listening to the question. Three little dots light up on my screen.

Ten is writing back.

I'm not sure whether to feel glad or nervous, so I feel both. I gnaw on my fingernail, chipping the green polish Laney brushed on before the game.

BEAST: Why does she want to know?

His text makes throbbing erupt in the pit of my stomach.

ME: Playing a drinking game at Rae's. It was 1 of the questions.

BEAST: And the question was about me?

Kill me now . . .

"Conrad, your turn!" Jasper's voice makes me drop my phone. I whisk it up before anyone can read my texts. Then I put it screen-side down in my lap. It vibrates as I say, "Never have I ever texted drunk."

Everyone drinks, and it comforts me.

I flip my phone back over and read Ten's message. *Did you bike to her house?*

ME: Maybe.

I'm expecting him to tell me not to cycle drunk, but he doesn't message me again. I reread our chat. Why, oh why, did I ask Tennessee if he was a virgin? What's wrong with me? I toss my phone into my bag before I stupid-text anyone else.

After another five rounds, I stand up to go to the bathroom. My head spins. I place a hand on the couch behind me, then stagger to the toilet. After peeing, I wash my hands and splash freezing water on my face. My mirror reflection comes in and out of focus.

I'm very drunk. Very, very drunk. *Crap.* Mom is going to flip.

I totter back out, scoop my bag off the floor, and hook it on my shoulder. "I should get home. Curfew," I mumble. Way better than admitting I can't see straight.

"Aw." Rae pouts. "Call me tomorrow, hon."

I give her a thumbs-up—I should probably have done something cooler, like wave. Is waving cool? I stumble through Rae's twinkling backyard until I reach the light pole around which I secured my bike. I dig through my bag for the keys. I come up with a tube of lip gloss, a pair of sunglasses, and some quarters.

Frustrated, I squat and dump my entire bag on the sidewalk. My plastic doughnut key chain lands on top of an almost empty pack of chewing gum. As I shovel everything back inside, I grab a piece of gum and stick it in my mouth. I drop my bag into the basket, put my helmet on—backward at first, but then I get it right. After several attempts, I manage to insert my key in the lock. I think it's a good thing I don't drive, because I'm in no state to operate a big vehicle. I'm not sure I'm in any state to operate a small one for that matter. But I do need to get home, and walking will take way too long.

Plopping my U-lock on top of my bag, I think of my friends who are still at it. I hope none of them drive tonight.

I steer my bike onto the deserted street and hop on. A car honks, and my feet skid off the pedals, and then my bike tips.

At the same time that my heart plunges all the way down to my stomach, I swan dive into the asphalt. My gum gets jammed in my throat, and I cough until it stops obstructing my airway.

I tremble so hard I can't tell if anything hurts after I stand. Blood trickles down my calf, but I quickly forget about it as a dusky figure, backlit by the beams of the car that honked at me, looms larger. The person looks like an angel.

I squint into the brightness. The headlights are like twin suns in a pitch-black universe. I turn away before they permanently damage my retinas. Thighs shaking like tambourines, I crouch to pick up the cap-sized contents of my bag.

"Are you insane?"

I recognize that voice. I tip my head up, and my helmet slides back, giving me a clear view of Ten's scowling face.

"Seriously, Angie!"

My pulse flattens with embarrassment.

"Were you seriously going to bike all the way back to your house?"

"What are you doing here?" My voice is as wobbly as my legs feel.

"You can't bike drunk!"

As I toss my stuff back into my bag, I moisten my lips. "I'm not drunk."

"You're right. You're *wasted*."

My throat feels as dry as a rice cake. "I'm fine."

"You're anything but fine. Your leg is bleeding."

"It's just a scratch."

"Scratches don't bleed that much." Ten's voice echoes around me and inside of me.

"How did you even know where I was?" I mumble.

He's silent for a moment. "Rae texted me earlier. Invited me to stop by."

Rae? Why? She has Harrison . . . If Ten had showed up, would she have made a move on him instead?

On the brink of tears, I right my bike and start rolling it away when Ten grips the handlebar.

"Angie—"

"I need to get home."

"I'll get you home."

"I can't leave my bike here."

"We'll put it in the car."

"I'll walk home," I whisper, my voice breaking.

He mutters something under his breath, then: "Just let me give you a ride home. That's the least you can do after . . . after you sprang *that* question on me."

Yep. I wasn't embarrassed enough. "I don't know why I sent that."

"Because you're drunk." He wrestles the bike out of my clammy hands, then rolls it to the back of his SUV while I climb into the passenger seat.

I'm too ashamed to look at him, but not too ashamed to accept a ride. He lowers the back seats, then hoists my bike up. He attempts to close the trunk, but it doesn't close. He pushes against my bike's back wheel, but the door still doesn't close.

"I guess we're driving with the trunk open," he says.

I unhook my helmet and place it on my lap. Cold air gushes in through the wide-open trunk. I shiver. Ten turns the heater up full blast, then begins driving. I grab ahold of the handlebar to keep my bike from falling out. The car beeps to indicate a door is open.

"What drinking game were you playing?" he asks.

Keeping my eyes on everything but his face, I say, "'Never Have I Ever.'"

"That's a lethal one."

I nod.

"In what state are the others?"

"Drunk."

"Maybe I should offer to drive them home after I drop you off."

"I doubt they're ready to leave." They're probably all making out by now.

Ten takes a right.

"That's not where I live."

He doesn't answer, just drives until we come to a twenty-four-hour gas station. He orders me to stay put. Which I do. It's not as though I want to get out. I let go of the handlebar and concentrate on a sticker glued to the inside of my helmet. I manage the extraordinary feat of peeling it off just as my door opens.

"Show me your leg, Angie."

I gape at Ten.

He agitates a bottle of disinfectant in front of my face. "Your knee." He nods toward my leg.

Slowly, I slide my injured leg out of the car. He pours rubbing alcohol over my wound, and I grind my teeth. He keeps pouring until the cold antiseptic trickles clear down my leg.

He gives me the bottle, then rips open a pack of Band-Aids and sticks one against my skin, the pressure and heat of his fingertips making me forget all about the vicious sting.

"Were they out of princess Band-Aids?"

He snorts but flashes me a lopsided grin. Plucking the bottle of rubbing alcohol from my fingers, he wets a handful of cotton balls and lifts it to my face.

Horrified, I feel for blood on my cheeks and forehead. "Did I cut up my face?"

"Just your chin."

I touch it, then hold my fingers in front of my eyes. I have too many fingers, and most of them are coated in blood.

Ten presses my hands down and dabs the cotton against the underside of my chin.

I gasp from the burn. He blows against it, and the sting is replaced with another burn, a slower burn not located anywhere near my injury.

Ten peels the back off a smaller Band-Aid. As he pastes it against my chin, I stare at his long lashes. I'm afraid to speak with his face this close to mine.

Afraid he'll smell my rancid breath.

Afraid I'll say something stupid.

I wait until he packs everything back into the bag and gets in the driver's seat before whispering, "Thank you for . . . taking care of me." I grip my bike's handlebar again.

He shrugs, as though he's done nothing to deserve my gratitude, then takes out a granola bar and a bottle of Tylenol, and shakes out two pills into my palm. I swallow them without water. He gives me the granola bar, but I lay it inside my helmet, since I'm pretty sure anything I put in my stomach will find its way out.

As he backs out of the parking spot, he says, "You should eat that."

"I really can't."

He turns the radio on. It's one of those late-night club beats that all sound the same. The pounding from the speakers travels down to my navel. A wave of queasiness slams into me. I rip my hand off my bike's handlebar, and even though the car is moving, I fling the passenger door wide just in time to retch outside.

Ten hits the brakes so hard I flail. Another surge of vomit sprays out of my mouth. My pulse intensifies like the music, drumming so wildly spots swim before my eyes. I close them.

Ten's hand wraps around my loose hair. Tears of humiliation drip out of my clenched lids. A third acid wave swells up my throat and shoots out of my mouth. I clamp my lips shut, hoping that will be enough to calm the spasms, but it doesn't. My stomach contracts, then eases. Nothing comes out this time. It contracts again. And again it eases.

I'm empty.

Empty of vodka but full of shame.

Sweat beads on my throbbing forehead.

Ten releases my hair. I can't bear turning back toward him, so I close the door and stare at the power window switch. It comes in and out of focus. I swipe my hand discreetly over my eyes, and even though I'm cold, I power the window down.

"I'm never drinking again," I whisper.

"That's what we all say."

"It's happened to you?"

"Too many times."

I concentrate on breathing. "I'm sorry I asked if you were a virgin."

He doesn't respond.

I yawn as the car glides down one road and then another. He drives slowly. The wind gently buffets my face as the silence grows denser, all-enveloping, like the darkness outside the vehicle.

"I'm not."

I blink at him.

He shrugs. "A virgin."

Even though I presumably lost a large quantity of blood after falling off my bike, apparently I didn't lose enough. It rushes up to my cheeks until they blaze, and since the lights are on in the car because the trunk is still open, it's not as though I can hide my blush.

I turn back toward the window. When my street sign appears, I blow out a soft breath. "I'm not either."

I'm not sure why I lie . . . Maybe so he doesn't think I'm lame. But that's a stupid way of thinking. Virginity isn't lame.

I'm lame for thinking it's lame.

I should probably stop thinking altogether.

Ten arrows the car up the driveway. The redbrick house with its white columns looms over us like a menacing, judgmental giant.

"I'll get your bike out," he says.

"Thanks." I look up toward Mom's bedroom window expecting to meet her disappointed glare, but no one stares back. Praying she's asleep,

I get out of the car. When my feet hit the white gravel, I wince and almost collapse, but catch myself on the car.

Ten jogs back toward me.

My head spins, but it's my leg that's killing me. It feels as though someone's hacking at it with a knife.

"Maybe we should go to the ER. Have you checked out for a concussion," Ten says.

"No, it's my knee." It feels like liquid is swishing in my stomach, but that's probably my imagination. I doubt anything's left inside.

"You're sure?"

I nod slowly, careful not to aggravate the throbbing.

"Here. Take my arm."

Even though that's pretty much the last thing I want to do right now, I grip his arm for support. "My bag!" I exclaim.

"I've got it."

I take it from him and hike it up my shoulder, then limp down the path, careful not to put too much weight on my bad leg. "How the heck am I going to dance tomorrow?"

"I think my grandpa has a spare walker."

"Funny," I say, even though I'm wondering if Ten really has a grandpa. I know so little about him. Besides the fact that he's no longer a virgin. I wish I'd asked him to tell me what his real last name was instead.

"Or you could skip it, and we could hang out."

I freeze. "You'd want to hang out with me after tonight?"

He shrugs as we climb the porch steps. Once we reach the front door, he releases me.

"I shouldn't complain." I dig through my bag for my keys. "Mona Stone once performed crazy acrobatics eight months pregnant during one of her shows. A battered knee shouldn't stop me."

He doesn't say anything for a long second. Then: "She was probably hoping to lose the baby."

My fingers freeze on the plastic doughnut key chain. "That's a horrible thing to say."

His face shutters as quickly as falling dominoes. Without another word, he walks down the steps and strides back to the car. I shake my head as he drives away, then let myself in quietly and tiptoe up to my room. I should take a shower, drink a gallon of water, and brush my teeth, but those three tasks require energy. Energy I don't have. As though I've been clocked, I fall into a deep, dreamless sleep.

19

A License to Drive People Insane

I wake up feeling like Mona Stone's band is performing a live concert inside my body. Her drummer is pounding my skull with his sticks, while her guitar player is strumming my intestines with his plastic pick, and her backup dancers are stomping against each one of my bones. To make everything worse, the sun pours through my window like the megawatt spotlights at the Grand Ole Opry.

The evening returns in vivid detail. I cringe and then cringe some more. Who asks a boy they barely know if he's a virgin?

I swipe my phone off my nightstand and click on our chat. After rereading our volley of texts, I delete the whole conversation. It won't erase it from his phone, but at least it'll no longer be on mine. Out of sight, out of mind.

While I wait for my brain to stop wobbling, I scroll through my Instagram feed and find a picture that has me sitting up in bed so fast my eyesight short-circuits. I wait until the room swims back into focus before calling Rae.

After the third ring, she picks up with a groggy, "Yeah?"

"You hooked up with Harrison?" My voice reverberates between my left and right temples. Is that normal? I've never had a hangover before.

I squeeze my forehead between my thumb and middle finger, then swing my legs off the bed and slowly stand. A small ache throbs in the knee Ten patched up, but it's not debilitating enough to keep me in bed. Holding on to the wall, I plod to the bathroom, then turn on the shower.

"Morning to you too, hon."

"You hooked up with the quarterback?"

"I did." There's a lilt to her voice.

"What about Ten?"

Her sheets rustle as though she's flipping over in bed. "What about Ten?"

I grimace at the sight of my haggard reflection in the beveled mirror over my sink. "I thought"—I touch the Band-Aid on my chin before slowly peeling it off—"I thought you were into him."

Isn't that why you invited him over? I don't say this out loud, afraid of how petty it'll make me sound.

"Angie, you do realize Ten's got it bad for *you*, don't you?"

I want to say no. That it isn't remotely true. That what happened on the school bleachers was a total fluke . . . It hits me that I never even told Rae about the bleachers.

"It took Laney knocking some sense into me after the mall," Rae says. "The second she pointed it out, though, I wondered how I'd missed it. I'm real sorry."

"About what?"

"That I didn't see it sooner."

Steam rises to the mirror and cloaks the glass, blurring my reflection. "Rae, first off, you have nothing to be sorry for. Secondly, nothing's ever gonna happen between Ten and me."

I shudder just thinking about my text. I'm tempted to send Ten an apology along with a thank-you, but I'm forbidding myself from further indelible forms of communication.

"Why not?" Rae asks.

Because I'm a lunatic, and he's secretive. Because when I get into a relationship, I want complete honesty. How can anyone build a future on top of concealed foundations?

"Mom's working for his dad. She told me not to get involved." It's a lie, but sadly, it's probably not too far from the truth.

"Seriously? That sucks."

"It's okay. Anyway, I need to focus on my music what with the contest coming up. Boys are too much of a distraction."

"But what a fab distraction they are." Rae yawns.

"I thought you were done with jocks."

"I was, but the heart wants what it wants. You should write a song about that."

"Selena Gomez already did."

"Ah, damn." There's some more rustling on her end. And then: "Crap. I promised the parents I'd brunch with them. Crap," she repeats, as drawers creak and slam. "I'll pick you up on my way home. Around three?"

"I'll be ready."

After we disconnect, I step under the shower's spray and loofah my skin until I feel more human punching bag than roadkill. I change into my comfiest leggings and my all-time favorite T-shirt that reads NOT ANOTHER ROLLING STONE.

I bought it at the Mona Stone concert Rae invited me to. Most people in Nashville get the double meaning, but not Mom. It took me spelling it out for her to understand the slogan had nothing to do with the rock band.

Even though my stomach feels like a piece of trampled gum, it lets out a pathetic grumble, so I head down to the kitchen, where Mom's frying some eggs. I walk over to the percolator, and although I'm not usually a coffee fan, I pour myself a cup. It's bitter and hot, and scorches the lining of my throat. Lynn's always on my case about drinking lukewarm beverages to preserve my vocal cords, but I can't do tepid. Water has to be cold and tea has to be hot.

Mom side-eyes me. "How was the football game? Heard the home team won."

"It was fun."

"What'd you do after?"

I shrug, and the tiny movement makes my head ache anew. I should've swallowed some painkillers before coming down. "Hung out at Rae's."

"What happened to your chin?"

I touch the spot I left bandage-free so the puckered, reddened skin could scab over. Thankfully, it's on the underside of my jaw, so not too visible. "I fell off my bike." I point to my leg, which she can't see through my leggings. "My knee got the brunt of it."

Mom slides the crispy eggs onto a plate. "Baby, I'd really like you to consider getting your driver's license. Bicycles aren't safe—"

"Dad was driving a car."

Mom's fingers tighten around the spatula. "And what? You think he would've survived had he been on a *bicycle*?"

I jerk from the intensity of her voice, and coffee sloshes out of my cup and trickles down my wrist. "No. That's not what—"

"Angie, I know you have it in your mind that cars aren't safe because of what happened to your father, but they're a hell of a lot safer than a scrap of metal with two wheels and a handlebar. I'm signing you up for driver's ed. Once you get your license, it'll be your choice whether to drive or not, but at least you'll have the tools to make an informed decision."

This isn't the first time we've fought about my preferred method of transportation, but it's the first time Mom has put her foot down so hard. I half expect the tiles to crack from the impact of her ultimatum.

I'm about to tell her that she can sign me up but I won't go, when I realize I can milk this. "I'll do it if you agree to let me enter the Mona Stone songwriting contest."

Her summer tan leaks right off her face. "What?"

"I want to submit the song I wrote. The one I played you."

"Is that"—her voice falters—"why you wrote it?"

My migraine feels like it's migrated to my chest. "Yes." I wait with bated breath for my mother to say something. Preferably *okay*.

She eyes the congealing eggs as though waiting for them to advise her.

"You didn't even like my song, so I probably won't win. That should reassure you."

She squeezes her eyes shut for a millisecond, but then reopens them and sets them on me. Before her lips even move, I predict what she's going to say.

She says it anyway. "No."

My heart twists and twists. "Please?" I whisper.

"No."

I set my mug down so brutally coffee splashes over the rim. "That's not fair. *You're* not fair. I do everything you ask me to. I even go to yoga with you every week, and you won't even let me do one thing for myself!"

"Because you have so much more to lose than to gain!"

"Wow . . ." Tears sting my eyes. "You don't even think I have a chance to win."

"I didn't say that, Angie."

"But you're thinking it." I start up the stairs, my bad knee smarting from the rapid movements. "Dad would understand. I wish he were alive! I wish you'd been the one in that car instead of him!"

Something clatters in the kitchen.

I went too far, but I'm too proud and angry and shocked to head back down, so I fling my bedroom door shut, jump into bed, and curl up to mourn my crushed dream.

I wait for Mom to come upstairs. I'm certain she will. She's one of those people who have to fight until there's no more fight to be had. Until the anger has defused, and the parties have reconciled. She would've made a good lawyer.

I sob, and it angers the pounding in my head.

Soon, it's been an hour, and she still hasn't come upstairs.

I haven't heard the front door so I know she hasn't left the house. I pad over to the window just to make sure her car's still in the driveway. It is.

She's waiting me out.

Or maybe she's so appalled by what I shouted at her that she never wants to talk to me again.

My mother's all the family I have . . . all the family I need.

I can't lose her.

I open my door. It creaks, and then the floorboards groan under my footsteps.

Mom's lying on the couch, reading a book with a smashed pink flower on the cover. It pretty much sums up how I feel—crushed. I approach her slowly.

She doesn't lower the book.

Doesn't even glance at me.

Lips trembling, I whisper, "I didn't mean it, Mom. I didn't mean it."

She sets the novel down beside her on the couch, and then she sighs and opens her arms, and I tumble into them.

Tears drip down my cheeks and soak into the ruffles of her camisole. I didn't earn the right to sob—*I'm* the insensitive one—and yet I just can't seem to contain my emotions.

Mom smooths my hair back.

"You didn't come upstairs. Why didn't you come upstairs?" I croak, resting my cheek against her chest.

Her labored heartbeats drum against my ear. "I thought it was about time you learn to put out the fires you light, baby. Most people aren't bulls. They won't charge into you. They'll hold grudges, and it'll fester. And that's the absolute worst. Your daddy used to do that." Her voice has dropped to a whisper. "He held so many grudges it killed him before he even died."

I wipe my eyes and sniff, then push myself off Mom. "Like what?"

Mom presses her lips together so snugly they vanish. "I don't want to talk about him right now. Not when I'm feeling so emotional. I'm afraid I might say something I'll regret."

It takes everything in me not to beg her to toss me one more scrap about the man I don't remember.

"About that contest . . . I understand you've got your sights set on it, but I don't want you entering it."

My lips start to wobble anew. "Why not?"

"Because, baby, I don't like that woman."

I untangle myself from her hug. "You don't even know her!"

"But you do?"

"No." I pause. "It's so unfair."

"Life's not always fair. Something else you gotta learn."

I mutter something about needing to get ready for the dance.

"Don't be mad at me, baby."

"Yeah. Sure. Whatever."

I'm going to have to do it behind her back.

If I don't win, she'll never find out. If I do win, she'll have to live with it.

20

Crash Into Me, Why Don't You?

The gym sparkles with gold streamers, green balloons, and dangling cutouts of our school's football players—to which Rae and her decorating crew added comical facial hair, painted-on crowns, and superhero capes. A giant green tablecloth covers a long row of desks topped with drinks, bowls of allergen-free snacks, and clear vases filled with green apples.

The second we enter the gym, Rae, Laney, and Mel are reeled into the beefy arms of their respective boyfriends. I toy with the hot-pink glass necklace girdling my neck, jealousy niggling at me. But then I think of Mona Stone. Superstars don't need anyone to hold them up.

Alone, I move closer to the stage, where a hired band is playing a medley of the latest hits. Careful not to put too much weight on my sore knee, I sway to the beat. I feared I would have to wear flats, but in the end, I managed to walk just fine in the black heels I borrowed from Mom.

I lift my arms and let the music travel through me. The singer, dressed in black jeans and a black T-shirt, paces the stage, mic in hand. The only hints of color are his piercing blue eyes, enhanced by black eyeliner, and his horseshoe belt buckle inlaid with turquoise. Even his hair is black and falls in waves across his forehead. He winks at me.

Or at least I think he does. He probably can't even see me what with the stage lights. I bob my head to the twang of the guitar, musing about what it would feel like to be up on that stage, to play in front of people, to have my voice carry over a crowd. Just imagining it makes my palms clammy. I rub them on my leopard-print dress.

The song ends. I clap along with everyone else. The singer strides across the makeshift stage in my direction and lifts his mic to his mouth. Right before launching into a new number, he winks at me. This time, I'm sure I'm not imagining it.

Maybe the wink was meant for someone else, though. I check over my shoulder. People have stopped clapping and have started bobbing their heads and hands to the new song. It's unfamiliar, probably an original. It's not bad. The pitch could use some tweaking and some high notes would work better as low notes, but the rhythm is catchy. As I sway to it, locks of hair escape my waterfall braid and fall in tendrils around my face.

At some point, I close my eyes and let the music guide my motions. It's not like I can step on anyone's toes. I'm not even lifting my feet. Besides, I love to feel music, and when you suspend one sense, the others heighten.

But I feel much more than music.

I feel a hand on my waist.

My lids snap up.

My gaze lands on a set of hooded eyes.

Tennessee leans over until his mouth is level with my ear. The pounding of blood inside my veins increases so suddenly that if he moves any closer, my pulse will nip his mouth.

"I see the leg still works."

Because my heart has usurped all of my brain's capacities, I don't speak. I simply stare up at him. When that gets awkward, I whiz my gaze back to the band.

The blue-eyed boy has returned to my side of the stage. As he hops to the beat of a dizzying tune, he shoots me another wink. Or maybe he didn't wink. Maybe he just has a seriously twitchy eye. Magnesium deficiency will do that to you . . .

"A friend of yours?" Ten has pulled back up to his full height, features tensed.

"What? Who?"

"The singer."

"Never seen him before." I shout-speak over the instrumental din. "I didn't think you were coming!"

"I wasn't planning on it."

"What changed your mind?"

"I heard the food was good."

I smile. "Ha! The infamous gourmet offerings of Reedwood High homecoming."

Ten smiles back.

Since I'm guessing he didn't turn up for the buffet, I ask, "Did your dad make you come?"

"He *strongly* suggested I should attend. Besides, it was either home-coming or another viewing of Nev's favorite movie."

"What's her favorite movie?"

"*Grease.*"

"Ooh. I love *Grease!*"

Ten grins. "Of course you do."

I flick his chest, then stare at the black fabric of his button-down. What got into me to touch Ten? I ball my fingers and drag them down to my sides, locking them there. "You must really hate it if you picked homecoming."

A soft chuckle reverberates through the thin space between our bodies. The sound is as surprising as it is beautiful.

"What?" he asks.

"You have a nice laugh."

"I think that is the first time someone's complimented my laugh."

"Maybe because it's the first time you've laughed?"

"That must be it." He shoots me a crooked grin. He must practice them in front of the mirror because he nails them every time. His gaze lingers on my face and then moves to a spot behind me. "I thought you and your friends were all coming dateless?"

I turn my head and sure enough, Laney's dancing with Brad alongside Rae and Harrison. "The golden boys of football become irresistible after a win."

"Should've picked football instead of track." He tips his head to the side. "No football player for you?"

"I'm not into jocks."

"What sort of boys are you into?" His gaze darts back to the stage. "Musicians?"

"I don't think I could ever go out with a musician. It would be too explosive, what with all the rivalry and passion." I touch the little arrow speared through the top of my ear.

His eyes move to my ear.

"What about yourself, Tennessee Dylan? What sort of girls do it for you?"

"Hmm . . ." He lifts his hand, then runs the pad of his thumb over my chin, over the scab I camouflaged with foundation.

I think the band has stopped playing, but I could be wrong. The feel of his thumb, the smell of spice and soap lifting from his neck, is confusing the heck out of my senses.

"Spirited ones," he finally answers, voice so raspy my skin bursts into goose bumps.

"You'll be happy to know I didn't bike here," I blurt out before I can ask if I fall into that category.

"How wise." He frees my chin, but the heat of his fingers lingers. "Should we get some punch?"

"Punch?"

The dance floor has become a mosh pit of excited shrieking. Not surprising, considering the band's playing Taylor Swift's new song.

"Don't they have punch at American school gatherings?" he asks.

I frown. "Didn't you attend an American school before?"

"No. Only French lycées for *moi*."

"Really? Why?"

"Because my dad thought it would be neat that I spoke French," he says.

"And here I thought you enjoyed T-shirts with random slogans." When his eyebrows slant, I say, "On Monday, your shirt said you spoke French."

"It was the only item of clothing I owned that was red."

"Your cape-slash-gown was red."

His lips hike up into another lopsided smile. "That look is harder to pull off than you'd think."

"If anyone can do it, it's you. The guy who doesn't care what people think."

His smile fades. "Is that the impression I give? That I don't care?"

"I didn't mean it in a bad way. I wish I didn't care what people thought of me." Because I haven't dug a deep enough trench, I add, "Then again, Ten, I don't know much about you. Besides the facts that your last name is made up, that this state gives you hives, and that you enjoy running, cooking, and driving."

"That's more than most people know about me."

Suddenly a hand closes over mine, and it isn't Ten's. I'm whisked backward and then twirled.

Rae shouts into my ear, "Just checking if you need me to stage an intervention!"

I frown.

She jogs my memory. "Momma Jade's instructions about the boss's son?"

Right. I glance over my shoulder at Ten, who's watching me right back.

"Should I spin you back into his arms?"

Even though I'm nervous, I nod.

An eloquent smile starts on her lips and then takes over her entire face. Rae is positively radiant.

Earlier, I dusted her cheekbones with gold bronzer—I did all the girls' makeup because I need training if I want to become as talented as Mona—but that's not what's making Rae sparkle. She's just one of these people who glow no matter the lighting, no matter the makeup.

Harrison steps toward Rae in a suit as black as his hair, nods to me, then grabs her hand and reels her into him. Rae throws her head back and laughs. If I'm to be completely honest, I'm glad she's set her sights on a boy other than Ten. Although I've always fought for what I wanted, I could never have fought with my best friend over a boy.

I return to Ten's side. Thanks to Mom's vertiginous pumps, I'm only a few inches shorter than he is. "Sorry Rae interrupted our long and boring conversation."

His lips curve. "Want to pursue it somewhere more quiet?"

Even though my pulse thumps in time with the heady beat of the drums, my body becomes as quiet as the Bluebird after closing time. "I don't think we could get off this dance floor even if we tried right now."

Just as I say that, a body slams into my back, sending me flying into Ten. There wasn't much space separating us, but now there's absolutely none.

Ten catches my waist, steadies me. Instead of releasing me, though, he keeps me close. And then he starts moving to a rhythm that's much slower than the one erupting from the stage, but right on beat. I place my hands on the nape of his warm neck, keeping my touch light so he won't feel how clammy my palms have become.

I haven't slow-danced since drama camp two summers ago. If what we'd done then could even be deemed dancing. Killian had two left feet and thirty-three zits—I'd spent the entire song counting them while he'd crushed my toes.

Ten hasn't stepped on my feet once, and his skin is absolutely flawless. I'm dying to run my fingers over his jaw, to learn if his stubble is soft, or spiky like his hair.

"How's your knee?" His mouth is so close to mine that I can't feel my knee anymore.

I can hardly feel my face.

"Why can't you feel your face?"

I snap out of my trance. "What?"

"You just said you can't feel your face." His eyes are wide with genuine alarm.

"I—um . . . I meant I can hardly feel my knee."

When I get nervous, I voice my thoughts. One of my many quirks. Obviously this isn't something I feel like explaining to Ten. He said he liked girls who were spirited, not crazy.

The concern leaves his face, but the tiny groove between his eyebrows remains. "Angie?" He dips his face toward mine.

"Yes?" I breathe.

He dips his head lower but stops again, as though asking for permission to move any closer.

I part my lips and wait for him to bridge the distance between us, but instead of coming closer, his head jerks back violently. I'm not sure what happened. At first, I think someone's yanked him backward, but no one's touching him. Gradually, the fog of Ten's proximity lifts, and I hear the song the band has decided to play. One of Mona Stone's most epic love songs.

I always dreamed of being kissed to this song, but Ten looks likelier to punch than to kiss. His grip hardens, becomes almost bruising. Carefully, I pry his fingers off my waist, but I don't let him go.

He tries to remove his hands from mine, but I clasp them tighter.

"I'm sorry. I need to get out of here," he says.

"Ten . . ."

He looks down at our joined hands.

"What just happened?" I ask.

His gaze swings back up to my face. As though my idol's voice is causing him physical pain, the skin around his mouth puckers.

"Why do you have this reaction to Mona Stone's music?"

He studies every millimeter of my face, as though trying to decide whether I'm trustworthy. In the end, he must decide I'm not, because he says, "I can't tell you. I'm sorry . . ."

"Don't shut me out."

His hands slide out of mine, and then he strides through the mesh of swaying bodies.

21

Spite and Stones Can Hurt Your Bones

I'm hurt but mostly mad.

Before I even realize that I'm walking, I'm halfway across the gym. The doors swing shut. I pick up my pace, knee burning from my mad dash in sky-high heels.

When I push through the doors, I find Ten trudging down the yellow-lockered hallway.

My heels click on the linoleum. If he hears them, he doesn't turn. "Ten!"

He pauses but keeps his back to me. "Angie, please. Don't push me."

I finally manage to catch up. "You just went Jekyll and Hyde on me. The least you can do is tell me why." I circle him until we're face-to-face. "What is it about Mona Stone's music that sets you off?"

He palms his hair. "Just leave it alone. I'll be transferring schools soon, and—"

It feels like he's just slapped me. "You're leaving?"

"I'm applying to a boarding school outside of Boston. Hopefully I'll be out of here before the end of the term."

I can still taste his breath on my lips. "Because of Mona Stone?" My voice has never sounded flatter. Emotions create melody, and right now, I feel numb inside.

"Angie—"

"No. Don't *Angie* me." My pink glass necklace casts jeweled pin-pricks of light over his wary face. "The least you can do is explain why Mona Stone triggers so much anger in you."

He eyes the door next to us that leads into a deserted classroom. Is he planning on hiding inside and waiting me out? He clasps one of my wrists and tows me into the moonlit room. My heart erupts with heart-beats. Once the door snicks shut, Ten releases me and paces the narrow space between the whiteboard and the teacher's desk, hands stuffed in the pockets of his black suit trousers.

After what feels like an eternity, he stops his frenzied prowling. "Why do you think we changed our name?"

"I'm not sure . . . witness protection? Oh my God." My eyes go very wide. "Did Mona Stone threaten your family or something?"

He barks a laugh as dark as the sky beyond the windows.

I cross my arms. "I'm guessing that's not it."

"Nope. Not even close."

As though the leopard spots have penetrated my skin and altered my nature, I growl at him. "Can you just tell me already? I've never seen someone get so angry at a singer." I sense I'm close to the truth. A couple more swings, and it'll pour out of Ten like candy from a piñata. "At first, I thought it was music in general, but you don't hate all music, you just hate *her* music."

Shadows tarnish the gilded brightness of Ten's eyes.

"Did your sister ask Mona to be her mentor, and Mona turned her down? Is that—" I stop talking.

Mona Stone has children.

A boy and a girl.

I sweep my gaze up and down Ten's face. At first, he keeps his eyes leveled on mine, but then, slowly, he lowers them to his patent loafers. I'm not sure whether to take a step toward him or away.

I feel like I've just trespassed into a room I have no right or desire to be in.

Mona went through a terrible divorce. Her husband, a big-shot lawyer, proved to the court she was unfit to be a parent, and then, to add insult to injury, he had her stripped of visitation rights.

"Your last name . . . it was Stone." It's not a question. I just need to hear myself say it.

He raises his gaze back to my face.

The oxygen in the room seems to have thinned. I place a palm on my belt, but don't fiddle with the buckle. I just need something to hold me up, and somehow a hand against my abdomen does the trick.

"My father gave up his own family name in the divorce settlement. To protect us, he gave up his own name."

Ten behaves as though Mona deserted them, but the choice wasn't hers. It was her husband's. He took everything from Mona, and then excluded her completely by altering his last name along with their children's. And then worse, he set his son and daughter against their mother.

Heart cancer . . . "You told me she was dead," I whisper.

"She is. To me, she is."

The rows of desks seem to undulate like the streamers sparkling in the gym. I need to get out, get away from Ten. I back up until I hit the door and then I swing around, pull it open, and escape the airless classroom.

22

Back Rolls and Spring Rolls

Last night has toppled my entire world.

I danced with Mona Stone's son.

I'd been about to let him kiss me.

I'm still reeling from how betrayed I feel. Not by Ten, but by my mother. Considering how evasive she's been about them, I have no doubt she's aware of their connection to Mona. How could she not tell me? Don't I deserve to know who I'm sitting next to in school?

Maybe she was hoping I would never find out since Ten is transferring schools soon. Or maybe she was hoping I'd like Ten so much that I'd change my opinion of my idol.

Unless Mom doesn't know who the Dylans really are . . .

I stare at her upside-down head. She's so concentrated on her yoga flow that she doesn't feel my eyes on her.

"Warrior three," our yoga teacher says.

Mom puts her right foot between her hands, then lifts her back leg. I follow suit. She lifts her palms and stretches her arms in front of her. I attempt to do the same, but lose my balance. I topple, whacking my hip bone so hard against the vinyl-wood flooring that a breath rushes though my parted lips.

Mom mouths, *You okay?*

No. I'm not okay. I don't shake or nod my head, don't answer her vocally. Instead, I go back to attempting mediocre poses while watching the wall clock.

As we pick up our mats, Mom says, "Is everything okay, baby?"

I have never rolled up my mat so tight. "Yeah." I lead the way out of the glassed-in yoga studio.

She beeps the car open, and I toss my mat in the back alongside hers, then sink into the passenger seat.

"Did something happen at homecoming?" she asks, settling behind the wheel.

I eye Mom. Debate whether to tell her about my discovery. She'll probably just take the Dylans' side. "Nope. Nothing."

She combs her fingers through her hair, then starts the car and drives out of the lot. "You know you can talk to me."

Why would I when you don't talk to me?

I fiddle with my phone the rest of the way to Golden Dragon. I hate that Ten gave it to me. Hate it so much that I decide to erase the content and give it back to him tomorrow. As though the tech gods heard my thoughts, I find a text from the Apple Store informing me that my old phone is fixed.

We park across from the restaurant, then get out.

"Hey, Mom, can you pick up my phone tomorrow at the mall?"

Her forehead grooves. "Your phone?"

"I dropped it off to have it fixed." When she glances at the one Ten gave me, I say, "This was just a loaner."

"Okay . . ."

"Jade. Hey!" A man with dark eyes and a closely trimmed beard is smiling at my mother.

I tuck my phone into my hoodie pocket.

Mom's cheeks have dimpled with a wide smile. Whoever this man is, she likes him. As though remembering I'm standing there, she drapes her arm over my shoulder and pulls me to her.

"This must be Angela," the man says, sticking out his hand toward me.

"Just Angie." I shake his hand. "Angela's when I'm in trouble."

The man laughs. He has a nice, deep laugh. "Pleasure to meet you, Angie. I'm Jeff."

He releases my hand, but instead of arcing downward, my fingers stay suspended in midair.

Jeff . . . Did I just shake Jeff Dylan's hand or is this some other Jeff?

Two people come up behind him—one tall, one short. My limp hand finally drops. Wiping my palm on my camo-print leggings, I duck out from underneath my mother's arm.

"Hey, honey." My mom steps forward and gives Nev a quick hug.

I hear my name. Jeff must've asked me a question. I snap my attention to him, but my ears are ringing too loudly for me to grasp anything he's saying. Mom's hand lands on my forearm. She squeezes, and the ringing begins to lessen.

"Baby?" One of her eyebrows tips up.

"What?"

"Jeff just asked if we want to join them."

"Join them?"

"Share a meal with them?" She gestures toward Golden Dragon.

I suck in a breath. I don't want to share a meal with them, much less the same air.

Nev and her father are watching me, waiting. Ten's concentrated on his cell phone.

I force my lids up real high. "I completely forgot about an assignment that's due tomorrow!"

Mom's brow furrows in surprise or in disappointment—probably both. "Can it wait until after dinner?"

"It's a diorama. It's going to take me all night."

Jeff glances at his son. "Did you also have a diorama to make, Ten?"

Ten looks at his dad. They're the same height and have the same lean, solid build. But Ten has his mother's eyes, and her hair color, and her mouth . . .

"Angie and I aren't in all the same classes, Dad."

"Well, that's a shame."

That we aren't in the same classes? It's a godsend.

Maybe he was referring to us not being able to have dinner with them.

Jeff tucks Nev against him. "Is it still okay for next weekend, Jade?"

Nev's not wearing her pink baseball cap, but her hair's combed forward, obscuring most of her face. She peeks at me, and although her eyes are gray brown like her father's and her pale face is splashed with freckles, I see a lot of Mona in her.

"Of course," Mom says, all smiley.

"What's going on next weekend?" I ask, my voice a little shrill.

"Nev will be staying with us, because Jeff and Ten are going out of town."

Was she planning on telling me about our surprise houseguest?

Ten lowers his phone. "Or you can just come with us, Nev."

"Don't be silly, Ten," Mom says. "I've got a girls' weekend all planned out."

Nev's lips quirk into a smile, but then her gaze snags on me, and the smile slips away. She interprets my surprise as reticence and flattens herself against her father's side.

Well, crap. Now I feel bad. "Mom plans the most fun stuff," I say, even though I have no clue what Mom intends to do.

A sliver of space appears between Jeff's and Nev's bodies.

I add a smile. Nev might be a Dylan, but she enjoys singing. If she enjoys singing, she can't possibly hate her mother, can she?

"Oh, Jade, I had time to look over those rug samples," Jeff says. "I have them in the car. Let me give them to you now, because I have an early meeting tomorrow and I don't think I'll have time to discuss anything before I leave." He lets go of Nev, then tips his head toward a gleaming navy sports car parked down the street. It's a little evil of me, but I can't help wondering if it was paid for out of Mona's alimony.

According to *People* magazine, she has to pay him spousal support since she's the more successful of the two.

Mom follows Jeff to his car, leaving me alone with the siblings.

"A diorama, huh?" Ten says, the second our parents are out of earshot.

Nev frowns at him, then at me. "What's a diorama?"

"A three-dimensional model," I answer.

"Oh, that's cool," she says. "I've never made one."

"Maybe Angie'll have another one to make next weekend," Ten mutters.

"We'll be doing way more fun stuff than that," I lob back.

Ten's expression becomes as stiff as the geometric wolf face on his mustard-yellow T-shirt.

"Jade told us this is the best Chinese food in town," Nev says.

"It's our favorite, but I don't know if it's the best." Mom and Jeff are standing by his trunk, heads bent over a thick binder. "You guys are probably used to better ones in New York."

Nev toes an old cigarette butt with her gray Converse. "You really don't have time to stay and eat?"

She seems so frail and delicate, but maybe it's because she's dressed in wide cargo pants and an oversized Henley. Her choice of clothes makes me wonder if she's not allowed to wear anything but Ten's hand-me-downs. Then again, I did cross paths with her at the mall. Maybe she has lots of girlie stuff but is forbidden to wear it out of the house or something.

"I really need to get home," I say.

The door of the restaurant opens as diners exit trailing the scent of vinegary shrimp dumplings and deep-fried spring rolls. My stomach emits a ravenous growl.

Nev pushes some hair out of her eyes. "Was that your stomach?"

I rest my palm on my abdomen, which is still gurgling with hunger. "Yeah. I'm always hungry. Plus we just went to yoga."

"I've never done yoga."

"Maybe you'll get to do that too on your *superfun* girls' weekend." Ten's voice drips with sarcasm.

Nev's lips pucker. "Forgive Ten. He's been grumpy all day."

Ten doesn't blush, but a nerve twitches in his jaw. He turns his face ever so slightly toward our approaching parents. Mom is laughing. Friends exchange jokes, not business colleagues . . . or whatever redoing a house makes her and Jeff. Their camaraderie twists the knife she planted in my back the day she accepted work from this family.

I lock my knees to tamp down the desire to bolt toward the Volvo. "Are you also going away to boarding school, Nev?"

"Nope. I'm super excited to be in Nashville."

Jeff slings an arm around his daughter's shoulder, making her lose her balance.

"Dad," she admonishes him.

He tickles her side. "What?"

She giggles. "Stop."

"Stop what?"

"Tickling me," she says between bursts of laughter.

"Oh, that." Jeff grins down at her. "Fine. I'll stop." And he does stop.

As I stare at them, I see a loving father, but then I remember how vicious he was to Mona, and my sympathy fades like the closing bars of a song.

"Have a pleasant night, ladies," he tells us before guiding his kids into my favorite restaurant.

I hate that Mom shared it with him. It was our place.

The knife twists some more.

When we're back in the car, Mom asks, "You and Ten had a fight?"

I whip my face toward her.

"Come on, baby. I wasn't born yesterday."

"I don't want to talk about it."

As she backs out of the parking spot, Mom makes a small clucking sound with her tongue, because she imagines my chilliness stems from a romantic quarrel.

Halfway home, I decide to come right out with it. If I keep it in any longer, it will fester. "Were you ever going to tell me Ten and Nev are Mona Stone's kids?"

Mom hits the brakes so hard my seat belt digs into my chest. All her earlier amusement drains from her face. There are no more dimples. No more smiles. No more glittery eyes. Just a hard jaw and an even harder stare.

23

The Destruction of Idols

We end up at the Dairy Fairy. At this hour, the place is real quiet, but Mom still picks a table in the farthest corner. I don't feel like frozen yogurt, but I eat it anyway. It goes down like cold, goopy cement.

"Jeff didn't want me talking about his private life."

"But I'm your daughter. I go to school with Ten." I stab the swirly cream. "I just feel so blindsided."

"How did you find out?"

My cheeks warm. I'm so not giving Mom a play-by-play of homecoming, but I do tell her how, when Mona's song came on at the dance, Ten flipped out. "I ended up guessing."

Mom sighs and sets down her plastic spoon, then reaches over to take my hand. "Mona walked out on him. It's normal that he feels angry."

I snatch my hand out of hers. "Stop saying she abandoned them! It's Jeff who shoved her out of their lives."

Mom's expression tightens. "Were you *there*, Angela?"

I flinch.

"Were you present when they decided to split?"

"No." I lift my chin a fraction. "But you weren't either."

"True. But I've lived many more years than you, and let me tell you, a divorce is never black and white. There are a lot of gray areas. A lot of them."

"How would you know? It's not like you ever got divorced."

Mom stares at her mountain of chocolate frozen yogurt. "I filed for divorce a couple of hours before your daddy died."

Goose bumps crawl all over my bare arms. "What?"

"We didn't have a happy marriage."

"I thought you loved him."

Mom looks up. "I did love him. Until he started drinking." Her eyes begin to glitter. "He wasn't very nice when he drank. I told him that if he didn't clean up his act, I would take you and we would leave. And he said . . ." She blots the inner corners of her eyes with her napkin. "He said . . . *fine*."

All the tender images I conjured of my father and mother go up in smoke.

"He didn't even fight to keep us, so I called him and informed him that I'd filed for divorce, and he told me he'd sign the papers, and then I didn't hear back from him." Mom's voice has become so low I can barely hear her. "That night, a cop called. Said your daddy had gotten into a car accident." She lets out a ragged breath. "Ran a red light." She releases another breath. "Collided with a truck." Another breath. "Died on impact." Her chest stills, as though she's all out of exhales.

How did we go from speaking about Mona and Jeff to Mom and Dad?

"I thought . . . I thought—" But everything I've ever thought is wrong wrong wrong.

My life frays and unravels heartbeat by heartbeat.

"The accident was Dad's fault?" I croak. That part seems so inconsequential compared to all the other things Mom has told me.

Mom nods as she rolls the tip of her paper napkin between her fingers. "He had so much alcohol in his system that the insurance company refused to pay out his life insurance policy."

Silence stretches between us.

"I idolized him," I finally whisper.

Mom gives me a sad smile.

I hug my arms around me. "I feel so stupid right now."

"No." Mom scoots her chair closer to mine and laces her arms around my hunched back, and then she sets her chin in the crook of my neck. "Don't feel this way."

"Why—" *Why did you keep it from me? Why are you telling me now?* I don't speak my questions, yet Mom understands. She always understands. I feel even more stupid because I've never understood her.

"Your father loved you, baby. He just didn't love *me* enough."

"He left us . . ."

"I know, but before he did . . . before he started drinking . . . he was a good father."

"You mean for the three years he stuck around?"

She bites her lower lip, which makes me wonder if he was a good father for all three years or just a couple of weeks here and there?

"When you were born, he would sit by your crib and play you lullabies on his guitar to put you to sleep." Mom smooths back my hair. "And then, while I was completing my decoratin' certificate course, he'd take you with him to band practice. He even got you a tiny pair of pink headphones. I still have them somewhere."

"I don't want them."

Her hand rhythmically sweeps my hair back. "This is why I didn't want to tell you. Because I don't want you to hate him. He loved you. And he was talented. Besides, hating him will only hurt you."

I stare past her.

"He's gone, baby."

I keep my gaze on the Dairy Fairy's cheery turquoise wall.

Mom sighs deeply, then picks up her plastic spoon and rotates it slowly in the swirled cream. "I don't know what happened between Jeff and Mona. What I believe happened, though, because I've seen it with

121

friends of mine, is that her success made them drift apart. When you stop lookin' in the same direction, you start going in different directions. And it takes a lot for people to stop and turn around, to check where their partners are at. And it takes a heck of a lot more for people to concede and retrace their steps. Hop over all those little cracks in the road. Sometimes, those cracks are so wide, hoppin' over them becomes impossible." She keeps churning her frozen yogurt. "But maybe I'm wrong. Maybe that's not what happened between Mona and Jeff. Maybe they just fell out of love. Whatever it is, though, you shouldn't judge people without getting the entire story."

"You judged Mona. You've always judged her and you don't know her personally. Unless you do . . ." I narrow my eyes. "You're good at keeping secrets."

Mom draws away from me. "I was trying to protect you. That's what mothers *should* do. And that's probably why I'm so harsh in my judgment of Mona. Because she's a mother. But you're right . . . it's unfair of me." She palms her shiny cheeks.

"Can I enter her contest, then?"

"Angela Conrad!"

"What?"

"Just because I'm admitting to judgin' her unfairly does not change my opinion."

I grit my teeth. "Are you worried it'll get you fired?"

"Of course not. I just want more for you than—"

"Doesn't what I want matter?"

"It's a phase."

"It's not a phase!" My ambition is the *only* thing that hasn't changed—the chorus that forever repeats and never varies when all the verses around it shift. "Stop thinking I'll outgrow it, because I won't."

Mom's disappointment is as pungent as the sweet vanilla scent of the Dairy Fairy. She lowers her gaze to her shoes—an übertrendy pair of white sneakers with sparkly smiley faces on the back.

I want to spring out of my chair and storm away, but a tear rolls down her cheek, and it drains the rage right out of me.

For now.

For today.

I clasp her hand. Her skin is cold. Mine isn't much warmer.

I think back on our fortunes that day at Golden Dragon. "Should've worn your booties."

She finally looks up from her sneakers. "What?" she croaks.

"Those made you happy, remember?"

Mom's blotched forehead furrows, but then it must come back to her, because a laugh bursts out of her mouth.

"I love you, Mom." Secrets and opinions and all, I love her, because I understand she's trying to protect me from a passion she thinks turns people mean and miserable. It reinforces my desire to participate in the contest, if only to disprove her theory.

Her chair legs scrape, and then she stamps a long kiss on my temple. "You are my world." Her hands flutter over my brow, my nose, my chin as though marking me as hers.

After a beat, I ask, "Mom, why didn't you get involved with another man?"

She exhales a protracted breath. "I was frightened of getting attached . . . of you getting attached . . . and it not working out. And then I got used to the rhythm of the two of us."

"What happens next year when I'm gone?" *If I end up going away to college . . .*

Both corners of her lips turn up. "I'll visit you a lot."

"You know what I mean . . ."

"I'm open to meeting someone."

As Mom smooths a lock of hair behind my ear, something occurs to me. "Why is Nev staying over at our house by the way? Doesn't she have friends?"

"Apparently, she's been having trouble fitting in. Jeff was going to hire a nanny to watch her, but I suggested she could stay with us." She stands, then picks up her cup of frozen yogurt. "You should give the Dylans another chance. They're good people."

Uh-huh . . . "Fine."

Mom smiles. "Now we should probably get home so you have time to make that diorama of yours."

"I don't have a diorama to make."

"What?" She claps a hand over her chest. "You lied to me?"

I roll my eyes as I rise from my chair and swipe my own paper cup from the little table.

"You're a terrible liar," she says with a grin.

"Must've gotten that from Daddy, since you're a terribly good one."

For a second, Mom's features crinkle and smooth, crinkle and smooth, as though she can't decide whether to smile or frown.

I grab her hand and squeeze it. "You're also a terribly good mother."

Her eyes get misty again, and then waterworks. It's strange to see your mother weep, because parents should be strong . . . solid. But then I think of how strong and solid she's been over the years during which she raised me on her own on ample amounts of love and on measly salaries—not supplemented by my father's life insurance like I assumed—and I think that if anyone deserves a break from being so strong, it's her.

24

The Drawer of Abandoned Gifts

On Monday morning, as I walk toward my first class, Mrs. Larue's voice booms from the PA system: *"If you create a storm, don't get upset when it rains."*

I mull her words over as I head down the aisle toward my seat. Mrs. Dabbs hasn't shown up yet, so the classroom is lively. I like the noise and movement. I like the way both screen off the nervous hush that settled over me after I got home from the Dairy Fairy.

I spent the darkest hours of the night thinking about my father and the palest hours of the morning thinking about Ten's mother. Head spinning, I went downstairs and sat in front of the piano. Mom was already gone—she had an early meeting with a restaurateur out in Nashville—so I played long and hard. Pieces ranging from Ravel's "Boléro" to Journey's "Don't Stop Believin'" to Kelly Clarkson's "Stronger." The only songs I didn't play were my father's. I was afraid his music would make my heart cramp all over again.

After jotting down Mrs. Larue's quote in my notebook, I ask Ten, "How did you like Golden Dragon?"

Ten doesn't answer for so long that I think my question got lost in the din surrounding us. "It was good."

Probably not up to his standards. I bet he goes to way fancier places with his dad. I draw a squiggly frame around the quote.

"How did your diorama turn out?" he asks.

I add a second squiggly frame, and it feels like I'm drawing the rhythm strip of my heart. "It didn't turn out as expected."

He snorts softly.

Five minutes go by and still no Mrs. Dabbs.

I dig through my tote for the phone, then slide the sleek apparatus over to him.

He sits up straighter. "You took pictures of your diorama?"

I smile. "I know you don't need the phone, but I really can't take it. Not after . . . Anyway, I've rebooted it."

"My mother sent it to me as a welcome-home present." His jaw is smooth today. No stubble in sight. It makes him look a little younger, a little softer. "If you don't want it, I'll leave it in the lost-and-found box. I want nothing to do with it."

Just like he wants nothing to do with his mother. And yet she sent him a housewarming gift. I don't get it, but I promised Mom I'd try to.

"Don't give me that look," he says.

My lids pull up. "What look?"

"The one like I'm this evil, ungrateful kid."

I bite my lower lip and lower my eyes. I don't think that's the way I'm looking at him, but I doubt he'll see anything else after our conversation at homecoming.

Mrs. Larue's assistant walks into the classroom and announces that Mrs. Dabbs is out sick, then urges us to get some homework done, that she's trying to find us a supervisor for the hour.

The second she walks back out into the hallway, the noise level grows. I doubt anyone's going to be doing any homework, but I'm wrong. Ten pulls out his history notebook and starts making annotations in the margins.

"Are you visiting the boarding school this weekend?" I ask.

"No. Colleges."

"Which ones?"

"Brown. Cornell. Princeton."

"You really like New England."

"I really like any place that isn't geographically close to Tennessee. Or Nevada."

"Why Nevada?"

"Mona got her start here, but blew up with her Vegas show."

Right . . .

He underlines a sentence in his notebook, then adds, "Our names were her idea."

I frown. His sister's name is Nev—*oh* . . . "Nev is short for Nevada?"

"You didn't know?"

I must've read about it but filed it in the dusky recesses of my brain. "I like your names."

He grunts. "Of course you do. *She* came up with them. You like everything about her."

I flinch but don't lash out. I allow him to be angry. "Will you look at colleges on the West Coast? Or maybe in Europe?"

Ten's eyebrows pull together. "Maybe." He leans back in his chair and crosses his arms. "Did Jade tell you to be nice to me or something?"

My pen jerks across my paper, slashing through the quote.

"She did, didn't she?" He shakes his head, and his hair, which seems spikier than usual, doesn't even budge. "You don't have to act interested in my life."

I'm too tongue-tied to tell him that I'm genuinely intrigued by his choice of colleges. I haven't given college any thought because I'm planning on taking a sabbatical next year to work on my music. I'll probably have to send some applications out, but I'm choosing easy schools in the area. Hopefully, Mom won't make me go to any of them.

We don't talk the rest of study period even though every single other person around us is chatting. Ten's silence is louder than all their voices put together. As soon as the bell shrills, he puts his stuff away and barrels out of the classroom. I'm about to leave when I notice the cell phone he's left behind.

I'm tempted to leave it behind too, but don't. I take it. He might not need it—functionally speaking—but it's a gift from his mother. If my father had left me a gift, I'd keep it. In a drawer, but I'd keep it.

As though the universe has conspired to make me prove it, I return home to a tiny set of pink, noise-canceling headphones nestled on my comforter beside my refurbished cell phone.

Last night's Angie would've shoved the headphones into the InSinkErator, but today's Angie picks them up reverently, studies them for a heartbeat, and then places them in a drawer, alongside Ten's phone.

25

Some Ashtrays Have Warts

I don't cross paths with Ten on Tuesday. I see him from afar even though he doesn't see me. He's not looking for me.

On Wednesday, though, we have art together. Miss Bank has set out pottery wheels and globs of wet clay, which we're supposed to fashion into vases. I haven't done any pottery since middle school, and that was a major fail as my mug turned into a saucer after it accidentally slipped from my fingers and got trampled by two students who gave me grief for getting clay on their shoes.

Laney pats the empty chair next to hers.

As I sit, I ask, "Where's Brad?"

"He's sick. Stomach flu. Apparently it's going around."

I wrinkle my nose and stroke my wet clay, then start shaping it. Well, Laney starts shaping hers; I'm still trying to figure out how to use the wheel. I copy what she's doing, adjusting my pressure and my fingertip placement. Just when I'm getting the hang of it, my concentration breaks. A couple of desks down from Laney's, Ten is helping Samantha, one of the blonde cheerleading twins, with her vase. He has his hands over hers, guiding them.

My clay whizzes off my wheel and slaps the back of Overachieving Ron's chair.

He spins around and shoots me a disgruntled look, then makes sure no clay sprayed his shirt and backpack. Thankfully both were spared.

"Angie." Laney elbows me when I still haven't moved to pick up the clay. "Your clay."

I stare down at the wheel, trying to sort through the tsunami of emotions.

"Angie," she says again.

This time I look up at her. And then I look beyond her. Ten's fingers are back on his own vase, and yet I can still picture them covering the cheerleader's hands. On wooden legs, I rise, circle my desk, and retrieve the gray lump from the floor.

I stick it on my wheel, but don't press the pedal. I just coax the clay into something resembling a receptacle the same way I used to shape the play dough Mom would make on our stovetop out of flour, baking soda, and water. For the first time, I wonder if she made it at home because it was cheaper than buying it.

"What's going on?" Laney whispers.

I pinch my clay and end up tearing off a piece. God, I suck at this. "I didn't sleep well."

"Uh-huh."

I glance at her, trying my hardest not to let my gaze drift beyond her shoulder.

She leans close to me and whispers, "What happened at homecoming?"

"Nothing."

"I got that nothing happened. I guess I'm wondering *why* nothing happened, because it looked like a lot was happening on the dance floor."

I stiffen. Her voice is low, but is it low enough not to carry to Ten?

"FYI, Ten keeps looking at you."

My face goes real hot, which makes Laney smirk.

"That's what I thought," she says.

"What did you think?"

"That whatever's eating you has to do with him." She lengthens her vase, then manages to give it a curvy lip. "I know Rae's been wrapped up in Harrison, so if you need someone to talk to, you can try me. My track record's a little skewed, what with all the Brad drama, but I'm a good listener."

"Thanks, Laney."

She shoots me a smile that disperses some of my glum mood.

I go back to trying to mold my clay into something . . . anything at this point. Unlike Samantha, no nimble fingers guide my own. By miserable attempt number forty-seven, I give up and carry my lumpy creation to the drying rack. Of course someone has to set their perfectly symmetrical vase next to mine.

"You're better at singing, right?"

I turn to find Ten looking down at me, one corner of his mouth kicked up.

I gesture to the gray thing. "I was going for ashtray with warts. I think I nailed it."

The other corner of his mouth rises. "I think you did."

Samantha sets her vase down on the other side of Ten's. "Thanks for all your help, Ten. You have real awesome hands."

As though he's embarrassed by the attention called to his hands, he slips them into the pockets of his khakis.

"Happy to help," he says.

I stare at the bulge in his pockets, but then lift my gaze as I realize how staring at that general area could be misconstrued.

Without another word, I return to my table and swipe my tote off the floor. It feels like it weighs a ton.

"Want to sit out on the bleachers for lunch?" Laney asks.

"That sounds nice."

"By the way, I called your dance coach."

"Really?"

"Yeah. I'm going for my first lesson tomorrow after class."

"You're going to love her."

I tell Laney about Steffi's quirks, and then I tell her not to be alarmed by the brightness of her wife's hair. Rae meets us halfway through lunch—Harrison-free. I'm not jealous, but I'm glad to have my friend to myself. When she's with him, I fade into the background, become one with the yellow lockers. It's not her fault, though; it's all me. I step back to make room for him. I did the same thing when she was dating Jasper's older brother.

"So one of Harrison's old teammates is coming into town next weekend," Rae says.

I chew on my tuna fish sandwich, watching the track team run laps—the entire team . . . not just one runner. Sure, Ten stands out more than the others, but that's because he's so tall. It wasn't even my idea to come out here.

"And I was thinking we could double-date," Rae says. "Or triple-date if you and Brad are free, Laney."

Ten tilts his face up in my direction, or maybe he's looking at the sky. Probably the sky. I'm too far up to see what his eyes are focused on.

Rae flicks my knee. "Earth to Angie."

"What?"

"The triple date. You in?"

"What triple date?"

Rae and Laney exchange a look.

"I just asked you if you want to go out with me, Harrison, and his friend next Friday. Laney and Brad might join us too."

"Um." I ball up my sandwich wrapper.

"Rae, I don't think Angie wants—" Laney starts.

"Sure, I'll go."

Laney raises one of her black eyebrows. "Why?"

"Because it's never gonna happen with him." I tip my head toward the track so I don't have to utter his name.

"Why not?" Laney asks.

"Because . . ." I squeeze my water bottle, and the plastic crinkles. "It's complicated."

"I don't get it," she says.

I bite my lower lip. "Like I said, it's complicated."

Laney narrows her blue eyes. "You like him; he likes you. Seems pretty simple to me."

"But it's not, okay? It's not simple." I say this too harshly, but I can't discuss Ten with them. It's not like I can tell Laney and Rae whose son he is.

Laney presses her lips together and stands, balling up her napkin and sandwich wrapper.

"Laney—" Rae starts.

"I promised Brad I'd call him." She heads down the metal stairs, heeled boots clunking.

For a while, Rae doesn't say anything. She lets me wallow.

"I should apologize," I say.

Rae still doesn't say anything. Just studies her shoelaces, which are plain and white—really nothing to look at.

I drink some water, then cap the bottle.

Rae finally lifts her gaze from her laces. "You'll tell me at some point, right?"

"Yeah." Once Ten leaves Reedwood, I'll tell her. I probably shouldn't, but it's Rae. Rae can keep secrets. "I really wish I could tell you now."

She pats my hand. "I know, hon. I know." And then she drowns out my inside voice with talk of Harrison's friend.

I'm not real excited for this date, but if it can help get my mind off the boy who's leaving soon, I'm game.

B-Side
Nev

26

Nevada in Nashville

The following day, I try to find Laney to apologize, but she's out sick with a stomach flu, so my apology has to wait until Friday. But she's still not in school on Friday, and Ten isn't either, but I don't think it's because of any bug. I assume he left early for his college visits.

After school I bike to Lynn and Steffi's. I don't practice my song today. I don't want to think of Mona Stone, because she inevitably makes me think of Ten, and spending the weekend with his little sister will be reminder enough. I almost ask Lynn if she knows who Nev's mother is, if that's the reason she flipped out the day I spied on their lesson.

Lungs aching from my singing exercises, I head down to the dance studio and attempt to sweat out my stress, but stress, sadly, is thicker than perspiration.

When I get home, the house smells like melted cheese and cilantro, which automatically makes my stomach grumble. I walk into the kitchen and freeze when I spot Mom and Nev rolling up soft tortillas.

"Hey, baby. I'm teaching Nev how to make my famous tacos." Mom has a smear of guacamole on her chin.

Nev, whose face is mostly hidden behind her hippie hair, blushes. I give her a tentative smile. She flashes me the tiniest smile in the history of smiles.

"Is she a better disciple than me?" I ask.

Mom grins. "Well, she understands the difference between a cup and a tablespoon."

I hook my tote on the back of a chair, then take a seat on a cowhide barstool. "Ha ha."

Because Nev's eyebrows pop up, I tell her about the glazed carrot incident. She's full-on smiling by the end of my account.

I plop my elbows on the island. "And that's the reason I stick to singing."

"Why don't you go take your shower, baby? Food will be ready in ten," Mom says.

"Are you saying I smell?"

Mom rolls her eyes. "Unless you want to set the table . . ."

I bounce off the stool. "Shower it is." I rush up the stairs and take a long, warm shower, and then slip into a loose-fitting dress and head back to the kitchen.

Dinner is nice, even though Mom insists on talking college. To deflect the attention, I pummel Nev with questions about middle school. Her answers are mostly monosyllabic, but that doesn't deter me. By the end of the meal, I've learned three crucial things about Ten's sister.

She doesn't like her name—surprise, surprise.

She started singing two years ago.

She's made one friend in school, but he's unpopular, which seems to bother her.

"Being popular is overrated. Not that I would know," I tell her after Mom goes to change into comfier clothes before our Friday-night movie showing.

"Ten said you were very popular."

"Um. No. My best friend is, but not me. I'm the weird one who loves singing."

Nev rinses the plates while I slot them into the dishwasher.

"You're just saying that to make me feel better," she says in a low voice, handing me the water glasses.

"Nope. I'm being totally honest." I close the dishwasher and turn it on, then grab the dish towel and wipe my hands. I hold it out, but Nev doesn't take it; she's too concentrated on the empty sink. I touch one of her hands. "Being different is cool."

She peeks up at me. "I don't want to be different."

For a moment, I feel like I'm looking at a younger version of myself. Like Nev, I was riddled with insecurities. Unlike Nev, I had a friend who helped me through them.

"Is that boy you hang out with a good friend?"

She grimaces. "He's quiet. And he makes a lot of noise when he eats. And he always has stains everywhere."

"But can you talk to him about . . . *things*?"

"We don't really talk. He's always studying."

"So why are you friends?"

"Because he sits with me at lunch. And he doesn't tell me I should wash my hair or eat more."

"Who tells you that?"

Her nose crinkles. "Some girls."

She's wearing baggy sweatpants, so I don't see how those girls can even see the shape of her body, but then I remember her middle school has a uniform like ours.

"And your friend doesn't stand up for you?"

She finally takes the dishrag from my hand and dries her fingers before burrowing them in the too-long sleeves of her hoodie. "I never asked him to."

"You shouldn't have to ask a friend to stand up for you." Sensing this conversation is making her uneasy, I change the topic.

"How do you like Skittles?"

"Skittles?"

"I mean Lynn." I never call her Skittles out loud, so it's weird that it popped out. "That's what Steffi calls her."

"Because she likes the candy?" Nev asks.

"No, because of her hair color. You'll see. She changes it once a year to something insane. Last winter, it was Granny Smith green."

"No way." Nev's openmouthed stare turns into a full-on grin.

"Look at that. The kitchen is immaculate," Mom says, reappearing in slinky gray pajamas that look more like a pantsuit than PJs. "How about we watch—"

"Please not *When Harry Met Sally*," I say, walking toward the couch. Nev takes the armchair.

"What's wrong with *When Harry Met Sally*?" Mom asks.

"It's old. And we've seen it, like, a trillion times."

"Maybe Nev hasn't seen it."

"I've seen it," she says. "It's one of Dad's favorites."

"See . . . someone with good taste," Mom says.

"Then spare us and watch it with him." I snap my mouth shut. I can't believe I just suggested that.

Mom's cheeks turn a little pink. "That wasn't even the movie I was going to suggest."

We bicker about which movie to watch for the next fifteen minutes. Finally we all agree on *Dumplin'*. It strangely mirrors what Mom and I are going through, except the roles are reversed. Does Mom see the parallel?

After the end credits roll to one of Dolly Parton's tunes, I don't feel very tired, but I set a good example for Nev and head to my room. I text with Rae for a little while and then shoot off an apologetic message to Laney.

Just as I click off my bedside light, I hear snuffling. I assume it's not Mom considering her bedroom's on the other side of the house. I stare at my dark ceiling. Maybe Nev has a cold . . .

I hear it again, and this time it's louder.

I cross the narrow hallway to the guest bedroom and knuckle the door. "Nev?"

An almost inaudible *yes* reaches me.

I push open the door. "Are you okay?" I ask, which is stupid, because people who snuffle are obviously not okay. They're either sick or sad.

Nev digs the heels of her hands into her eyes. "Yes," she murmurs, eyes and cheeks shiny with tears. *Sad.*

I walk over to her and sit on the edge of the bed. "Did you have a nightmare?"

"No."

"Then why are you crying?"

She shuts her eyes, squeezing them so tight it makes her entire face pucker. "I've never slept away from home."

Oh. I chew on my bottom lip, trying to think of something to say that will reassure her. "I cried on my first sleepover, too." *I didn't.* "I was staying over at my best friend Rae's house." *True.* I was eight and incredibly excited. "I cried so much that her mother let us have ice cream in the middle of the night." *True and not true*—we'd snuck down to the kitchen to eat it once her parents were asleep. It was probably nine o'clock but felt like midnight. "Want some ice cream?"

Nev's eyes widen, as though I suggested we go run a mile in our underwear while singing the national anthem at the top of our lungs. "Your mom won't be mad?"

"If she hears us, she'll probably join us."

Nev gets out of bed, and we pad through the dark house toward the kitchen. Even though I'm not particularly hungry, I eat rocky road straight from the tub. You don't have to be hungry to eat ice cream.

Nev is quiet for a while, and then she says, "I wish Ten wasn't going away to boarding school."

I pour us two glasses of milk.

"He's leaving because this state reminds him of Mom, but she never visits us, so I don't get why he needs to go."

I peer at her over the rim of my glass.

"You know who our mom is, right?" Nev asks.

"Yeah."

"He really hates her."

"And you?" I ask carefully.

"I try to hate her."

I frown.

"But I can't. You can't hate someone you don't know."

Exactly!

"Don't tell Ten or my dad," she says.

I feign zipping up my lips. "I'll keep it between us. Promise."

After our high-calorie feast, we head back upstairs. I'm about to go into my bedroom when Nev tenses up. She looks positively frightened to be going back into her room alone.

"Want to sleep in my room?" I ask her. "I promise I don't snore."

She nods, then all but runs into my bedroom as though worried I might rescind the invitation.

After we get into bed, and I turn off the light, she says, "Ten snores, but I don't mind."

I smile.

I think she's fallen asleep, because her breathing has slowed, but then she adds, "He always lets me sleep with him."

"He sounds like a good brother."

Again, it gets very quiet.

"I don't want him to leave, Angie."

"Maybe he'll change his mind," I say.

"Ten never changes his mind. Dad says he's as stubborn as a mule."

I smirk. I'm about to ask her if she wants me to talk to him, but why would anything I tell him change his mind? Besides, I'd prefer it if he left. It would make everything easier.

I turn to look at Nev. Her eyelashes palpitate against her cheeks, and her nostrils pulse with measured breaths. Her hair's swept off her face, and for a moment, she looks so much like Mona that it disconcerts me. It's almost like I'm sleeping beside my idol, which is real odd. As much as I want to spend time with Mona, I definitely never envisioned us sharing a bed.

Not that I'd ever envisioned myself sharing a bed with her daughter. Or wanting to kiss her son.

27

The Shade of Water

Nev wakes up early. Since I'm a light sleeper, the slight rustling pulls me from my dream. I was starring in a talent show in a place that was supposed to be my school but looked a lot like an aviary, and all these bluebirds were flocking around me, creating the melody of a song I desperately try to recall but can't.

I yawn, then turn toward Nev. "I just had the weirdest—" I sit up so fast my autographed poster of Mona Stone swims in and out of focus. "*Whoa.* Maybe it's a sign."

"What is?" Nev is studying my framed poster. Her upper lip isn't hiked up in disgust, but her eyes, which peek through her tangled hair, glitter quietly.

I tell her about my dream, that the birds were bluebirds. She's still frowning, so I say, "As in the Bluebird Café."

"The place where Mom got her start?"

It hits me that she doesn't refer to her as Mona.

She scoots up in bed, then smooths out a wrinkle in the duvet cover. "Have you ever sung there?"

"Me? No way. But Lynn's a regular."

Last month, Steffi, Mom, and I went to hear Lynn play. She tried to get me to sing with her, but I froze. I'm well aware that someday, if I want to be a real vocal artist, I'll have to actually sing in front of an audience. I'm hoping the new song I wrote will be the mallet that shatters my stage fright.

I swing my feet off the bed and head to the bathroom, while Nev picks at a piece of goose down sticking out of the comforter. The pale sunlight filtering through the drawn curtains limns the white feather.

I pause next to her. "Speaking of singing, I meant what I said at the mall . . . you have an incredible voice."

She twists up her lips. "Thank you."

"Is that what you want to do? Sing professionally like your mom?"

Her gaze settles on Mona's poster again. "Dad would never let me. And Ten would never talk to me again."

"Mom hates my choice of career, but it's my dream," I say, before going into the bathroom, leaving Nev to contemplate her mother in peace.

When I come back out, Nev's gone. I pull on a pair of ripped denim shorts and a white tank top, then head down to the kitchen. In spite of our late-night snack, I'm ravenous and dig up an energy bar in the pantry. After guzzling a tall glass of water, I plod toward the living room and sit at the piano. The keys are cool and stiff like my fingers, which I stretch before trying—unsuccessfully—to re-create the song from my dream. I end up playing the one I'm submitting to Mona's contest. I don't sing, though, just work on the melody. I add a little bridge right before the chorus, then hum my lyrics to see if the bridge adds anything.

"That's really pretty."

My fingers stumble, then disengage from the keys. I turn around and find Nev sitting on the couch, hands folded in her lap. She's wearing gray leggings and a black T-shirt, which tents over her bony upper body.

"Thanks. Do you play the piano?"

She shakes her head.

"The guitar?"

"No."

"The harmonica?"

She smiles a little, then shakes her head again. Her hair seems more tangled than yesterday, which does have me wondering if she has an aversion to brushes and combs.

"Want to sing something?"

Her face turns as red as Mrs. Dabbs's hair.

I pat the bench. "Come."

Her knees seem to wobble as she approaches. I half think she won't make it all the way to me, but she does.

After she sits, I ask her, "What do you want to sing?"

"Um. I like Amy Winehouse."

I smile, not surprised by her choice. From what I remember, Nev's timbre is real close to Amy's. "'Valerie'?"

She nods enthusiastically.

I was so obsessed with that song when I first heard it that I spent hours at the piano mastering the tune. At first, Nev doesn't sing. Only I sing and I butcher the song, because my voice isn't deep, but I keep singing anyway, hoping Nev will jump in. I glance sideways at her, find her nibbling on her bottom lip.

Just as I'm thinking I've pushed Nev too hard too fast, she lets out a breathy sound that surges across the room like a gush of steam. She snaps her mouth closed, her cheeks two flaming dots.

Afraid she'll clam back up, I let out a wrong note, then mouth, *Help!* She swallows, and then her lips part. This time the sound that comes out of her mouth is perfection. It ripples and sways through the air. As her singing gains power, goose bumps scatter over my arms, lend vigor to my frolicking fingers. The air becomes electric and jaunty, a jungle of violets, oranges, and blues. The colors tinge the piano keys and edge the pale furniture, highlighting every angle and curve around us.

Little by little, I lower my voice to a mere hum and listen as Nev gives a performance worthy of a *great* . . . worthy of her mother. Possibly greater because there's *nothing* commercial about Nev's sound. The second the song ends, I segue into a new song—a recent hit by Kelly

Clarkson. I'm afraid that if I stop playing, Nev will stop singing, and I don't want her to stop. I could listen to her for hours.

I sing with her this time. Although an octave separates our voices, we somehow manage to braid them into something thick and dazzling. When I play the last chords, a low whistle sounds from the doorway. Mom's leaning against the doorframe, hair slicked back and shiny like the gold hoops speared through her lobes.

"What a voice, Nev." She slow-claps.

Nev smiles sheepishly at me, then at Mom, freckles ablaze.

Mom pushes away from the doorframe. "Your range is startling."

The bright colors in the room darken. Mom's right—Nev's voice is startling, but what about mine?

It's silly.

So silly.

But couldn't she have said my voice was nice too, even if she didn't mean it?

Nev wrings her hands. "Thanks, Jade." Her voice is wispy and unremarkable again.

I lower the cover over the piano keys, trying to slug away my stupid jealousy. "Are we going to brunch?"

We usually brunch on Saturdays before I go off with friends. This weekend is a rare exception where I have no plans for the rest of the day. Rae is busy with Harrison, and Laney hasn't answered my message, so I'm not sure where we stand.

Not that Laney and I ever made plans before . . .

"I booked a table at the country club," Mom says. "I thought we could go swimming afterward since it's so nice out. Nev, did you bring your bathing suit, sweetie? I told your daddy you might need one."

At least she didn't call her *baby.*

I stand and stick my hands in the back pockets of my cutoffs. Seconds ago, I was surfing on waves of psychedelic colors and now I'm drowning in murky waters.

"It's upstairs," Nev says.

"Well, go grab it. You too, Angie."

Nev trots up the stairs. There's a spring in her step that wasn't there last night. I follow her slowly, having left my spring somewhere underneath the fallboard.

Nev pauses at the top of the staircase, fingers gripping the steel railing. "Are you okay?"

I give her a tight nod.

"Did I . . . did I *do* something?"

"What?" I paste on a frown. "Of course not."

She draws her hand off the banister and murmurs, "Okay." She doesn't sound convinced.

I grab my bathing suit and stuff it inside a bag along with a pair of sunglasses, my earbuds, and a book. Knowing Mom, she'll run into some friends at the club, and we'll be sitting by the pool a *long* time. Not that I mind if I'm listening to music. I just hope she's not expecting me to babysit Nev.

28

Back in Sync

After scarfing down an entire hamburger, I don my bathing suit. Thank God it's stretchy, because I feel like a snake who's just ingested an egg. I come out of the changing room at the same time as Nev. Her beach towel is wound so tightly around her diminutive frame she resembles a burrito.

We didn't talk much during lunch. Well, I didn't. Mom and Nev discussed the Dylans' mansion decoration at great length. Even though Nev asked me for input on a color scheme and furniture for her bedroom, I was vague with my answers, afraid residual jealousy might tint my feedback. I don't want to be the reason she ends up with green shag carpeting on her ceiling.

Mom's already outside when we emerge from the locker room. She's managed to secure three lounge chairs in the sun. I drop my bag on the glass side table, then lay my towel out. Nev climbs onto her lounge chair, still shrink-wrapped in her towel. Maybe she's chilly?

I stick my earbuds in and close my eyes. After the third song, I lift my lids and stare at the blazing sun until my eyes water. When did I become the girl who needs her mommy to pat her back? *Ugh* . . . Mom doesn't even like the type of music I like, so her praise wouldn't mean all that much.

The only person's recognition I need is Mona Stone's. Thinking about her has me glancing over at Nev. It's not fair that I've taken my insecurities out on a twelve-year-old. I pull out my earbuds and sit up, a drop of sweat slinking down my spine.

Mom's on the other side of the pool, chatting with an elderly couple. If I'm not mistaken, she redid their ranch house last year.

"Want to go for a swim?" I ask Nev.

She looks at me, anguish lacquering her gray eyes silver.

"Do you not know how to swim?"

She keeps her gaze on the bracelet glinting on her wrist. Like Ten's, it reads I ROCK. Unlike Ten's, hers is yellow gold instead of silver.

Even though I'm dying to hear the story behind the matching bracelets, I stay on topic. "Nev?"

I think of the image of the swing suspended over the pool that Mom showed me a couple of weeks back. Nev must know how to swim. If she didn't, a swing would be incredibly unsafe.

Her lips finally pull apart. "What did I do?" she whispers.

"What?"

She's staring down at her knees, which peek out from her towel, round and knobby like a newborn foal's. "You haven't talked to me once since we got here."

I tip my head to the side, seeking out her downturned eyes. "Okay . . . I'm not proud of what I'm about to tell you."

Am I really about to admit to a twelve-year-old that she made me feel insecure? I glance at her stringy hair and skinny form, and they remind me that she, too, is full of insecurities.

"*Iwasjealousofyou.*" I say this the same way I rip off Band-Aids—fast, because speed makes things less painful. In this case . . . less shameful.

She jerks her shiny gaze up. "What?"

It also makes things less intelligible. "I was jealous of you," I repeat slowly, cheeks hot, but that's partly due to the sun beating down on me. I pick at a cuticle, stripping off a tiny piece of skin, flinching from the quick burn. "Mom's never complimented my voice."

Nev is silent for a beat, then: "Angie, your voice is *so* pretty."

I heave a sigh, then roll my taut neck, finding relief in the whisper-soft series of cracks.

"No one's ever been jealous of me," she adds.

I straighten my neck. "I doubt that's true."

"I mean, back in New York, my friends were jealous we had a pool in our house, but no one's ever been jealous of me *for me*."

"You had your own pool?"

"Yeah." She hoists one shoulder as though having a pool inside a house in Manhattan is a completely normal thing. Maybe it is?

"So you really love swimming, huh?" I say.

"Not especially. Ten and Dad do. Especially Dad."

"Was it his idea to put a swing over your pool?"

Her eyes flash. "All mine."

"Can I come over and try it once it's set up?"

"Yes!"

I smile. She smiles.

Even though we're not singing, Nev and I are in sync again.

"I think you could fry an egg on my thigh right now." I toss my sunglasses on the lounge chair and stand, gesturing toward the pool. "Come with me?"

Nev fiddles with the hem of her purple towel, but finally peels it off her legs. Together, we race to the edge of the pool and leap in, making a great big splash.

Once we come up for air, I ask, "Why do you and Ten have matching bracelets? And what's with the inscription?"

"Oh." She blushes. "Ten had them made two years ago." She strokes the etched gold plaque. "He said that if I ever feel lonely or down, it'll remind me that I'm not alone, and that I *am* cool."

I grip the rough edge of the pool.

Nev makes a face. "I should probably take it off."

"Why?"

"Because it's silly."

"No, it's not."

The red on her cheeks deepens. "His ex thought it was weird."

I push my wet hair out of my eyes. "Well, his ex is stupid, because it's not weird. It's supersweet."

Nev seems to float a little higher in the glittery water. "She *was* stupid. I don't even know why he went out with her for so long."

My pulse jackhammers in my chest. I don't want to talk about Ten's ex, and yet I want to learn every sordid detail about her. But I don't ask. Instead, I challenge Nev to a race, which she happily agrees to. I desperately try to get rid of thoughts of Ten as I swim, but in the steady, liquid swoosh, he's all I can think about.

I race harder, giving it my all. Unfortunately, the only thing it saps is my energy. It doesn't even put a dent in my infatuation with Nev's brother. Why did I have to develop feelings for someone who hates everything I love?

29

The Short Stranger from My Cookie

On our way home, Mom tunes in to her favorite classical station and explains to Nev how she designs each house while listening to a specific composer.

"Which one's inspiring our house?" Nev asks.

"Debussy."

Nev sits on the edge of the backseat. "I don't know him."

Mom slaps a palm against her chest. "What?"

"I . . . uh, don't listen to classical music, Jade."

"Hang out with us a few more weekends, and you'll be well-versed in everything instrumental," I tell her.

"Do you like classical music, Angie?" Nev asks.

"She hates it." Mom says this with a smile. "I drive her crazy with it."

Which is true. The *driving-me-crazy* part. I don't *actually* hate classical music. If I did, I wouldn't play it for fun on our baby grand. "I'd rather listen to music with words. I think voices are the most special instruments."

Even if you don't agree with me, Mom.

Even if you don't think my voice is all that special.

My heart sways with the insecurities that tarnished most of my morning. Stupid, stupid insecurities.

"I agree with Angie. I mean"—Nev points to the radio—"it's pretty, but it's not as pretty as a song," she adds, as the purple notes slink around us like yards of chiffon.

Can she, too, perceive the thick dark-violet spool of Rachmaninoff's Piano Concerto no. 3? Lots of people on forums claim music shows itself to them in color.

Mom's smile stretches, dimpling her cheeks. Sometimes I wish I'd inherited her cheek dimples instead of my father's chin one. "Gang up on me, why don't you?"

Nev flushes.

"Maybe when we're old, we'll get your fascination," I say.

"Old? Old! Oh, you're going to pay for that." She reaches over the center console and tickles me until I'm bent double.

I bat her hand away, trying to catch my breath. She used to tickle me all the time when I was a kid. Did Dad ever tickle me? I don't dare ask, because talking about him will sour her mood, and I like to see Mom happy. It reassures me that all is right in the universe.

Once we're home, Mom heads down to start on dinner. She's making lasagna from scratch. I tug Nev into the living room and turn on the TV. As we watch a series about witchy sisters, she tucks her long hair behind her ears and pulls her knees against her. Unlike Ten and Mona, and Jeff for that matter, Nev's face is heart-shaped.

"You should wear your hair up," I say.

Her entire body turns as rigid as the marble console in the foyer. "Uh. I . . . Uh. My cheeks are so round."

I frown. "No, they're not."

"Carrie says my head looks like a bowling ball," she adds.

"Who's Carrie?"

"The daughter of Dad's best friend. She's a year older than me, but everyone thinks she's sixteen."

"Well, Carrie's an idiot. Your head does *not* look like a bowling ball."

Her forehead pleats as though she's unsure whether to take my word or Carrie's.

"Nev, you're, like, the prettiest twelve-year-old I've ever met."

Her freckles turn as pink as the modern painting on our wall.

"And I'm not saying that to pump up your ego or anything. Although I think your ego definitely needs some serious pumping."

A smile forms on her lips, as blinding as the beams on her brother's car.

"*Whoa!*" I sit up ramrod straight.

Nev's expression warps with concern. "What?"

"The fortune cookie!"

"Fortune cookie?"

"Before school started, I got a fortune cookie that told me a short stranger would come into my life this year. It's you!"

For some reason, her level of confusion escalates. Unless she's perplexed that I inadvertently called her short. Or maybe she thinks I'm mental. Probably the latter.

"Look, I don't really believe in fate or fortune cookies—well, I didn't used to—but isn't it sort of weird—*funny-weird*—that a scroll wedged into a piece of cooked dough forewarned me that you'd pop into my life?"

Finally, her lips ease back into a smile.

"For a while there, I was worried I was going to have a short boyfriend," I say.

Nev laughs, and the sound is wispy, as though she's trying to catch her breath but can't.

I crack up too, until she says, "Good thing for Ten that fortune cookie was about me."

I sober up so quickly I let out a very unladylike snort.

Her laughter teeters. "Um. He likes you." She twirls the end of a still-tucked lock around her finger. "You know that, right?"

She might've felt like a sister for a second, but Nevada's not *my* sister—she's Ten's.

Ten who's leaving.

I stand up suddenly. "Want some water? I'm real thirsty." I should say something else but can't think of anything that would make the moment less awkward.

When I return clutching two glasses of ice-cold water, Nev whispers, "Don't tell Ten I told you, okay?" Her hair's curtaining off her face again. "He'll kill me."

I nod. Never in a million years would I ever entertain having that sort of conversation with her brother. I swallow back the wad of nerves clogging my throat and paste on a smile that distills some of the tension floating around the living room.

Before sitting down, my eyes run over her boxy clothes. "Why do you always wear sweats and hoodies?"

She wrinkles her nose. "Because."

"Because what?"

"I'm so . . . *bony*."

I frown. "So?"

"So it's ugly."

I sigh. "Come with me."

She hesitates, but stands and follows me up the stairs to my bedroom. I walk to my closet and pull out a pair of shorts I haven't worn since freshman year but haven't been able to part with because I emblazoned the denim with funky patches one long, hot summer afternoon. Rae has a matching pair. We wore them all the time, so proud of our handiwork. I still find them cool, which is a lot more than I can say about the rest of my wardrobe at that age.

I toss Nev the shorts. "These used to be my favorites, but I can't fit into them anymore."

She gapes at the shorts. For a moment, I'm not sure if she'll don them, but then she takes them back to her bedroom. A minute later, she's back. Although a little loose, the shorts look a heck of a lot better than the gray sweatpants. Her gaze moves over the full-length mirror, before landing on her mother's poster next to it.

I really should take the poster down.

"Thank you." Her arms go around my neck so suddenly that I emit a little choking sound.

I smile into the chlorine scent of her hair and pat her back.

"Thank you for being nice to me, Angie."

I press her away. "Don't ever thank someone for being nice to you!"

She gnaws on her bottom lip. "Not many people are."

"Because you hide from them. You should let people see the real you."

Her eyes silver as they return to her mother's poster. "Maybe."

30

Crushing My Crush

Since a thunderstorm has been buffeting Nashville since dawn, Nev and I have become one with the living room couch. While we watch Netflix, alternately tossing popcorn into our mouths and at each other, Mom reads a book, drinking chai tea and rolling her eyes at our antics. The house smells delicious, like cloves and melted butter—the scent of lazy days.

As a new bag of popcorn bloats in the microwave, the kernels snapping like the rain against the window, I spy a big black car turning into our driveway.

I draw the front door open before Ten even has time to ring.

He stands on the doormat, rain trickling down the sides of his face. His hair's all mussed, as though he's just rolled out of bed, but if he's rolled out of anywhere, it's probably an airplane.

"How was your trip?" I ask.

"Good. How was your . . . *girls'* weekend?"

"Nev survived, so there's that."

He doesn't smile, but his stiff jaw softens. He didn't shave over the weekend.

"Is she ready to go?"

"Who is it, baby?" The floorboards squeak as my mother walks over to us. "Oh, hi, Ten. How did all your visits go? Did you find the school of your dreams?"

"I did."

"Which one?"

"Cornell."

"Ooh. That's such a great school," Mom gushes, then peeks beyond him. "Where's your dad?"

"He ended up prolonging his trip. He had some meetings in the city. He said he'd call you later."

"Where are our manners? Come right on in." Mom steps aside. "Nev, your brother's here!" she calls out louder than necessary. Unlike the Dylans' mansion, our house is normal-sized. "Can I get you anything to drink?"

Ten strides over the threshold. "Just some water, please."

As the door snicks shut behind him, he gazes around, takes in the kitchen, the staircase, and finally the living room. Our home is stylish but must seem dwarf-sized to him. I cross my arms and scrutinize his expression, but can't figure out what he's thinking.

"Here you go." Mom places a tall glass on the kitchen island, then empties the popcorn into the glass bowl and glides it toward Ten, grabbing a handful on the way.

"Ten!" Nev launches herself at him and strangles his waist.

When they break apart, she looks around the kitchen. "Where's Dad?"

"Still in New York." He gives her a once-over, and his eyebrows pull in, forming an almost uninterrupted line. "Where are your pants?"

"My sweatpants? In my bag."

Just then, Mom's cell phone rings in the living room. "I'll be right back," she says.

"It's raining," Ten says. "Go put them on."

Nev's smile flickers like a faulty light bulb. "But it's hot."

"You can't walk around without pants."

She blinks, but then her surprise is replaced by giggles, and she lifts the hem of her hoodie. "I have shorts."

His expression is devoid of amusement. "Well, they're too short."

"Oh." She peeps at me through her curtain of hair.

Before I can remind Ten how shorts got their name, Nev bows her head and climbs the stairs.

After the bedroom door shuts, I hiss, "You shouldn't do that, Ten."

"Do what?"

"Make her feel self-conscious about her body."

"I didn't say anything about her body. Just about her clothing choice. Which I'm guessing is yours, not hers . . ."

"It's what girls today wear."

His eyes flash. "What you choose to do, Angie, doesn't concern me. What my kid sister chooses to do, that concerns me."

"She's twelve. Twelve-year-old girls wear cutoffs and crop tops."

"Dad and I would rather she doesn't walk around half-naked."

I want to shake my head, but shock has hardened the tendons in my neck. "You're protective, I get it, but she's old enough to pick her own clothes."

I can tell he doesn't agree. His lips are as tight as my tank top.

"I'm ready," Nev says softly.

Slowly, I turn toward her. How much has she heard? I move toward her and give her a one-armed hug.

"Come back whenever you want," I tell her.

She answers me with a silent nod. Then she pulls away, and, ducking her head, she trails Ten to his car.

Upstairs, on my bed, lie the shorts I gave her. That isn't the only thing she's left behind, though—a tiny spot of wetness darkens my tank top.

Tears.

Stupid Ten managed to make his sister cry.

He's also managed to crush my crush on him.

31

Twelve Isn't Ten

The following morning, Rae is waiting for me next to the bike track. "Okay, you and me . . . we need some serious catch-up time. I'm scheduling a mandatory sleepover Saturday night after our double date."

I bend over to fasten my U-lock. "Double date?"

"Don't tell me you forgot! We're having dinner with Harrison and his friend."

"Right."

She smirks. "Don't sound *sooo* enthusiastic."

"Sorry."

"Did I mention he's super hot?"

I smile. "You might've. I just hope he's *super* interesting."

"That, I cannot guarantee." She hooks one arm through mine, then pulls me up the flagstone path toward school. "But I'll be there. If he's a total snooze, we'll just snub the boys and talk to each other."

The glass doors slide open and let us into the loud, sunny hallway. Several people wave to Rae or call out *hey* as she walks by. I'm convinced my friend exerts a gravitational pull over people, just like Mona Stone.

"Is Laney coming to dinner?" I ask when I spot her.

Brad has her flattened against his locker, and he's either whispering into her ear or licking her eardrum. Whatever he's doing has got her smiling.

"She and Brad already had a thing," Rae says.

I take it Laney's still mad at me. At least she was kind enough to pretend to be otherwise engaged. Or maybe that's Rae's way of softening up Laney's refusal.

As we pass by them, Rae flicks Brad's shoulder. "Keep it PG, guys."

He crooks his head and smiles at her.

Laney ducks out from the cage of his arms, cheeks aglow. "Hey, Rae, Angie. Wait up."

I freeze, surprised she said hi to me. "You got my text?"

"Yeah. You're forgiven." She shoots me a smile that zaps away the dumbbells of guilt I've been toting around since last Thursday.

"See you later, babe." Brad pinches Laney's waist before sauntering into his classroom.

"How about we go to Party Central on Sunday to buy our Halloween costumes?" Rae suggests, excitement edging her tone.

The mention of Halloween makes my spine snap ramrod straight. It's the deadline for Mona Stone's contest. More than ever, I want to enter it . . . if simply to spite Tennessee.

He's standing by his locker. Our gazes lock, loaded like two guns about to go off.

"Sounds good," I say.

"Can I join?" Laney asks, tearing my attention from Ten.

"No, hon, you can't."

Laney's pasty cheeks pinken.

Rae rolls her eyes. "I'm kidding. Of course you can come! I'll ask Mel, too." She tosses her shimmering blonde hair over her shoulder. "Catch you two at lunch."

Neither Laney nor I rush off into our respective classrooms. I hoist the straps of my bag higher on my shoulder.

"Still can't tell me why you snapped at me?" she asks.

I shake my head.

"*So* . . . you're going on the double date?"

Ten vanishes into our classroom just as the first bell sounds.

"Yeah. What are you and Brad doing?"

She tightens the ribbon tied around her sleek black ponytail. "He surprised me with tickets to the ballet."

"Really?"

She laughs softly. "Don't look so shocked."

"Sorry. I just can't picture Brad attending a ballet."

"He's going for me."

Which is something else I can't picture Brad doing: something for someone other than himself.

I gesture to her leg. "It doesn't break your heart to sit in the audience?"

"I get a little nostalgic, sure, but I still really enjoy watching it." She pulls a hefty science textbook to her chest. "Would you stop listening to music if you lost your voice?"

Or lost Mona Stone's contest . . .

The thought takes me by surprise. My odds of winning are so slight that I shouldn't even be considering it. Besides, I'm going to forge Mom's signature on my application form, so if I *did* win, I'd probably be stripped of the prize.

"I couldn't live without music," I end up saying.

The second bell rings, and Laney squeezes my arm. "Gotta get down to the lab before Mr. Olson notices I'm not in my seat."

I don't think he would. He's one of those teachers who's so passionate about his subject matter that the apocalypse could hit and he'd keep prattling on about subatomic particles. Mrs. Dabbs, on the other hand, would notice. *Nothing* escapes her.

When I enter the classroom, Mrs. Dabbs is jotting a formula on the whiteboard, her felt-tip pen squeaking on the slick surface. Without looking up, she says, "Did you not hear the second bell, Miss Conrad?"

Like I said, nothing escapes her.

I trudge to my seat without glancing at Ten. Even though I don't angle my chair away, I don't look at him once during the entire class. I'm actually quite proud of myself, as I sense him looking over at me several times. As soon as the bell rings, I spring out of my seat.

"Thought you'd like to know Nev's not talking to me," he says.

I study the contents of my tote, then flick through my notebooks to make it seem like I'm busy looking for something, like I'm not avoiding his gaze, which is searing the top of my head. "Why would I like to know that?"

"Because you're not talking to me either."

"I'm not talking to you because I have nothing to say to you." That's not true. I have a mountain of things to say to him.

"I didn't mean to insult you."

"I don't care," I lie.

"Yeah, you do."

"I don't." I stop fake-scoping out the contents of my bag and look up. "Nev was so excited to wear something other than your hand-me-downs, and you ruined that for her. You made her cry."

Ten stiffens. I shake my head and turn, but stop in the doorway and wheel around. Ten halts inches from me. He's so close I can feel the heat coming off his body.

I step back and crane my neck to better glare at him. "Do you even know how miserable she is in school? Apparently people make fun of her."

His brow juts forward, casting shadows over his eyes. "What are you talking about?"

"If she hasn't told you, I'm certainly not going to, but understand that what she needs right now is to feel good in her skin, and you telling her she looks like a skank—"

"I didn't say that."

"—you *implying* she looks like a skank is exactly what she *doesn't* need. She adulates you, hangs on to your every word, so be supportive, remind her that she rocks." I flick my gaze to his bracelet.

He looks at it too, then crosses his arms. "I *am* supportive. But like you said, I'm also protective. I don't want her wearing shorts that display her underwear."

"Oh. My. God. They don't! They're not *that* short."

"She's twelve."

"I know!"

No one's in the classroom anymore, but our heated conversation has attracted the attention of students lingering in the hallway.

"I *know* she's twelve," I continue, my voice a dozen decibels lower, "but I don't think *you* realize that. If you did, you wouldn't still be buying her Disney princess Band-Aids."

He jerks back as though I've slapped him.

I might've gone a tad too far, but there's no way I'm taking it back, because it's true. At twelve, I would rather have bled out than plastered my skin with the Little Mermaid.

Suddenly, I want to tell him that she slept in my bed all weekend, that she's miserable that he's leaving, but I don't say anything. Maybe because I sense I've inflicted enough pain on Tennessee.

32

A Knight in Moisture-Wicking Armor

I spend the rest of the morning thinking about my dad, Nev, and Ten. But mostly about Nev. At lunchtime, instead of eating with Rae, I decide to head over to the middle school to check up on her. The campus isn't huge, but walking would take me at least ten minutes, so I cycle over. Granted, I could run, but then I'd be sweaty, and I don't feel like having my shirt plastered to my skin. It's humid enough out—a remnant of yesterday's never-ending storm. The grass is slick, and the ground sticky with mud. Although the grayness has dispersed, the sky is scratched up like the DVDs Mom refuses to part with even though we no longer own the equipment to play them.

Unlike our yellow lockers, the ones in the middle school are powder blue and coated in stickers—skulls and bones, hearts, unicorns, monsters. I run my fingertips over the crisp edges of a glittery rainbow. My last year of junior high, I had a matching one on my locker. I also had a bunch of musical notes arranged to match the lyrics of Mona Stone's "Rainbow Road."

I lower my hand and wade down the vibrant ocean of lockers. I wonder which one is Nev's. What sort of stickers would she paste? One locker is bare, and I think it might be hers, but I could be wrong. Hers could be the one next to it that's covered in glow-in-the-dark stars.

Fording the school hallway is like a trip down memory lane. I see the tiny dent in the white-plastered wall where Brad shoved a boy who called Brad's mom a MILF. I see the water fountain we used as a sprinkler when the weather hit the nineties. I see the girls' bathroom sign, which Rae and I switched with the boys' to confuse the new sixth graders. Somehow Jasper got in trouble for it and never told on us. I was never sure why he took the blame, but I suspected it was either because he was a stand-up guy or because his popularity skyrocketed after the incident.

The cafeteria hasn't changed an iota. The white rectangular tables are arranged in neat rows that reach the cement wall inlaid with three horizontal windows that look out onto a huge sports field hedged by a tight fence of flamboyant myrtles and tall poplars. And no, I'm not some tree-hugging devotee. Tennessean flora and fauna made up a huge chunk of our seventh-grade syllabus.

I scan the loud space for a skinny girl sitting next to an antisocial boy. I locate them during my first sweep—their table is the only one occupied by just two people. As I make my way toward it, I pass a gaggle of eighth-grade girls sporting pink lip gloss, elaborate hairdos, neon nail polish, and uniforms altered to display more skin than allowed.

The popular table.

The one Rae spent all junior high ogling while I worked extra hard to keep her entertained. I'd been so afraid she'd grow out of our friendship, but more loyal than Rae doesn't exist.

When I reach Nev's table, I slide onto the bench across from her. "Hey."

Her face tilts from her tray of food, and her lips part a little, then a lot.

The chubby boy a couple of spaces down from her looks up from a thick textbook that seems way above his grade level. His face swivels between Nev and me, but he loses interest fast and returns to his studying, popping a paprika chip into his mouth. He scrubs his fingers against his white button-down, leaving orange smears.

"What are you doing here?" Nev's soft voice tiptoes into my ears.

I shift my attention back to her. "They ran out of food in the high school cafeteria."

She blinks. "They did?"

I smile. "No."

"So why did you come?" she asks a tad louder. Which isn't saying much. The sound of her friend crunching on his chips largely overpowers her voice.

"I wanted to see how you were doing."

"You came here to see *me*?"

"That's what friends do. They check up on each other."

Emotion ripples across her features.

"Also, I might've heard you were giving Ten the cold shoulder."

She knots her skinny arms in front of her, bones jutting against her shirtsleeves. "He doesn't deserve to be talked to."

"Boys are clueless."

Muncher looks up from his textbook, then licks his fingers before dipping them back into his extra-large bag.

Even though I'm still angry at Ten, I don't want a rift to form between sister and brother. "I was thinking we could go shopping on Saturday. *With* Ten." I wasn't thinking this at all. "That way, you'll get to pick your own clothes, but both he and I have to approve of your choices. Does that sound fair?"

Nev's eyes light up like the QB-sized blow-up ghost my neighbors always stick by their front door on Halloween. "Yes!"

I don't want to talk to Ten, but here I am suggesting shopping with him? "Great."

She nibbles on her lower lip. "He probably won't approve of anything I choose . . ."

"He can't be *that* pigheaded."

She lets out a little giggle. "Yeah. He can." Her cheeks have become all rosy.

I lean over the table. "So, which ones made fun of you?"

The color in her cheeks spreads to the rest of her face. "Uh . . ." She picks at the label on her juice bottle. "It doesn't matter. I'm over it."

"Well, I'm not."

"Angie, it's okay. I promise."

"I'm not going to make a scene." I might, though.

She tears off a piece of the plasticky paper and rolls it between her fingers, flicking it onto her tray.

Her "friend," whose nose is still wedged in his book, surprisingly denounces them—or perhaps unsurprisingly . . . he doesn't seem to care about school politics at all. "Jenny and Crystal," he says, jutting his chin toward the table of glammed-up girls.

"Mark," Nev hisses.

"What? It's not a secret. Even I saw that snap of you in the locker room, and I don't even have Snapchat."

Nev has gone so pale that she matches the laminated tabletop.

"I didn't like it or anything," he reassures her.

Nev knocks over her juice bottle, and a translucent yellow stream trickles onto my lap in time with the anger coursing through my veins.

"They snapped a picture of you in the locker room?" I grab a paper napkin from her plate to stanch the flow of juice.

"All you could see was her back and legs," Mark the Muncher supplies, sucking the orange powder off his fingers.

"Angie. It's no big deal," Nev murmurs.

But it is. My thighs harden against the bench. All of my muscles harden. "Does Ten know?"

She shakes her head. "And you can't tell him. Or Dad. I don't want to be homeschooled again."

Homeschooled? Nev was homeschooled? "I won't tell them. I promise." Tossing the wet napkin back onto her tray, I spring off the bench, and then my black combat boots devour the floor.

I think I hear Nev calling my name, but I could be wrong. Too much anger is swooshing against my eardrums. I stop next to a blonde whose lips are so shiny they reflect my face.

"Jenny Barnett," I grumble.

She blows a large pink bubble that snaps against her lips. "And you are?"

Does she really not recognize me? *Whatever* . . . "I'm someone who has something to say to Jenny. And to Crystal, too." My fingers ball into fists at my sides. I relax them, because it isn't like I'm going to clock anyone, even though the desire isn't lacking.

A girl with almond-shaped green eyes and hair as black as Laney's lowers a blinged-out smartphone to peer at me. "I'm Crystal."

Her voice doesn't waver, her expression doesn't flinch. She's not scared of me. None of them are. Why would they be? Because I'm a high school senior? I suddenly wish Rae were here. She would've inspired fear in them and would've known what to say.

"It's not okay to bully people." Jeez, I sound like my mom. Worse than my mom . . . I sound like Mrs. Larue. I wedge my lips shut before I quote the Buddha.

Crystal smiles, but it isn't kind. And then her eyes rove over the cafeteria, finally settling on someone beyond me. Probably Nev. "Whatever are you talking about?"

That elicits snickers from the girls around her.

She knows exactly what I'm talking about.

Whom I'm talking about.

Anger simmers in my veins.

Vicious. They are so vicious. Some go back to scrolling through their feeds, some keep eyeing me.

Come on, Angie, think of something that will make them shrink . . .
But not a single solid comeback slots into my mind. If they knew whose daughter Nev was, they would all be sidling up to her, but obviously

I can't tell them who Nev's mom is. Besides, people shouldn't be kind because of who you are or who you know.

I curl my fingers back into balls. "If you ever hurt her again, I'll hurt you even more."

Jenny grins so wide I can see her tonsils, but then her smile wilts as her eyes settle on a spot higher than my head. I turn, expecting to see a figure of authority, but it's not a supervisor.

All of the girls stop smirking at me to stare at Ten, who stands behind me in his track attire. He glowers down at them, sweat glossing his forehead and neck.

"What are you doing here?" I choke out.

His eyes surf over the stunned, pinkening faces. He hasn't said a word, yet he's somehow chastened them. "My sister is off-limits. If I fucking find out any of you bully her, I will involve the principal *and* your parents."

Cheeks turn scarlet, and eyes go wide. Ten's no-shit demeanor and crisp tone has their gazes bouncing off one another nervously. Had I said the same words, would their ears have gone flat too?

Probably not.

They probably would've kept simpering.

I look for Nev, find her spot empty. I step around Ten to get a clearer view of the incredibly quiet cafeteria. Everyone's staring, but I don't care. All I care about is finding Ten's little sister.

"Where is she?" Ten's voice is low and raspy.

"I—I don't know."

"You have your phone?" he asks.

I nod, rushing back over to the bench where I left my tote. I dig my phone out and, fingers shaking from the confrontation, dial Nev's number. Ten stalks over to me. Like magnets, people's eyes stick to the knight in moisture-wicking armor.

"She's not answering." The apple juice pooled on the tabletop seems to quiver, like my harried pulse.

I'm hoping she had to meet with a teacher before classes resume, but I'm pretty certain she left because I embarrassed her. I gnaw on the inside of my cheek as I text her: *Where are you?*

Ten looks behind me at Mark the Muncher. "Sam, right?"

"It's Mark."

"Mark, where did my sister go?"

"No clue."

I sling my tote over my shoulder. "What's her next class?" I ask, not expecting Mark to be familiar with her schedule, but it can't hurt to ask.

"We have history together."

"Which classroom?"

"E7. By the gy—"

I don't wait for him to finish his sentence. I remember where E7 is. I bolt down the hallway, then down a flight of stairs. My chest hurts, my lungs are on fire, and my muscles burn. Unlike Ten, who's already caught up to me, I wasn't born to run *or* to confront people.

We bypass the entrance to the gym, then burst into E7.

33

Ten Facets of Ten

Even though the lights are off in the classroom, the pink puffiness of Nev's lids and nose are unmistakable. I dig my heels into the floor, afraid to come any closer, afraid my presence will just make her cry more.

She sniffles and looks up.

"I'm sorry," I say, at the same time as she squeaks, "Ten?"

Ten looks at me. "Why would you be sorry?"

"Did you tell him to come?" Nev scrubs her shiny cheeks.

I shake my head.

Ten waits another second for an answer from me. When none comes, he strides to the back of the room and drops into the chair closest to Nev's. "Nev, why didn't you tell me people were being mean to you?"

"Because—" She lets out a sigh that's as weak as the air wafting through the vent over my head.

I shiver when the air hits my skin.

"It doesn't matter," she mutters.

"The fuck it doesn't!" Ten snaps.

I finally unglue the soles of my boots from the floor and inch toward them. "Please don't be mad at me, Nev."

She picks at her purple nail polish, which is already peeling. "I'm not mad. But it'll probably just get worse now."

Ten's gaze ping-pongs between us. I can tell the moment he finally understands the reason for my apology, because he sits up straighter. "You're mad at Angie because she went to talk with those girls?"

I lean against the table behind me. "She asked me not to make a scene, and I made a scene." *A lame one at that.*

"It's okay," Nev murmurs weakly.

Breaths pulse out of Ten's nostrils. "How long has this been going on?"

She shrugs.

"Nevada Dylan, how long—"

"I don't want to talk about it, okay?" She pulls on her hair as though she's trying to tighten the fence around her face.

"Because you think I'm going to give you a choice? If someone's bullying you, you have to tell me. I'm your brother. I'm here—"

"*For now!*" Nev's voice is so sharp that Ten shrinks back. "You might be here for the next few weeks, but then—then you'll be gone." Her voice wavers, losing its bite but not its sting. "Just like Mom."

Ten goes as still as a corpse.

A charged silence brews between the siblings and thickens the air.

Barely moving his lips, Ten says, "I'm going away to study. I'm not abandoning you. It's not even remotely the same thing."

"But it feels the same," Nev croaks.

He palms his hair. "Fine. I won't go, then!"

Her eyes fill up and leak big, fat tears that make her narrow chest heave.

Ten mutters something under his breath, then his chair legs scrape, and he leans over and envelops her in a hug.

How am I supposed to stay mad at someone who loves his little sister so damn much? I push away from the desk and start toward the door. I don't feel like things are resolved between Nev and me, but I also don't feel like I should be intruding on this moment.

"Wait for me outside, Angie," Ten calls out.

I halt, cast one last look at Nev, then nod before leaving. I stand outside the door like a vigil. I check the time on my phone, figuring the first bell should ring soon.

I sigh. It will. In this school and in ours.

Five minutes later, the door to the classroom snicks open. I'm half expecting to see both Ten and Nev, but it's only him.

"She decided to stay?" I ask, trying to glimpse her through the door, which Ten left ajar.

"Yeah."

"Is she okay?" I murmur.

"Not really, but she doesn't want me to take her home. She says it'll just give them ammunition against her." He rubs the back of his neck. "Fuck. I'm so pissed she didn't tell me what was going on."

I wonder if she told him everything. "She didn't want to worry you."

His hand stills on his taut neck. "But she told you after one weekend."

"It's easier to talk about certain things with strangers." I want to go back in the room, but it's probably best to leave Nev alone. I favor solitude when I'm processing emotional stuff. "We should head back. We're going to be massively late."

Ten glances over his shoulder, as though hesitant to leave his sister. In the end, though, he strides alongside me toward the school entrance, hands shoved deep in the pockets of his gym shorts.

When I can't stand the silence any longer, I say, "So . . . will you stay?"

He swallows, and his Adam's apple bobs. "I don't know what to do anymore. Nev said it was just her anger speaking, that she didn't mean it, that I *should* go."

"You might not want my advice, but if you're going to be miserable here, it probably won't help her."

He raises his eyes off the flagstones and sets them on the brick building in the distance.

"Anyway, I'll see you in class," I say.

When he frowns, I nod toward my bike.

"You biked here?" he asks.

"It was quicker."

"You're one strange girl, Angela Conrad."

"No, I'm a practical one." I undo the U-lock, then walk my bike back up the path toward him since it's easier to cycle on stone than mud. I don't climb on right away. "Are you free on Saturday?" Before he assumes I'm asking him out, I add, "Because I told Nev we'd take her clothes shopping."

His face goes through a myriad of emotions before settling on cautious amusement. "Clothes shopping?"

His nonanswer makes the whole situation all the more awkward, so I start down the path, rolling my bike along. Ten's footfalls are quiet but steady next to mine.

"Am I going along to pay or do I get a say in what she buys?"

"I told her she was only allowed to buy what we both okayed." I glance over at him. "So you're not allowed to veto *everything*."

A crooked smile lights up his whole, darn gorgeous face. The air suddenly feels a hundred degrees warmer, and yet the sun is playing hide-and-seek behind the clouds.

I train my eyes on my handlebar in an attempt to cool off.

"A shopping trip with two headstrong girls . . . what's there not to look forward to?"

My heart feels like it's made of a trillion guitar strings. Each smile and glance from Ten plucks at them. I think of my double date . . . pray it will quiet my body's reaction to this boy, because nothing else seems to work.

"By the way—" he starts.

I can feel his eyes call to mine but don't meet his gaze.

"Thanks for having her back."

"I think I made it worse. I suck at confrontations."

"Could've fooled me."

I peek at him. "About having made it worse?"

"No. About the last part. You're incredibly good at making a person feel like crap."

"Are you kidding? I was totally pathetic back there."

"I wasn't talking about *back there*. I was talking about earlier." He juts his chin toward our building, which is looming larger even though we still have a ways to walk.

"Oh. Well, you were a jerk yesterday."

He fixes his gaze on the sinuous path. He's no longer smiling. He's contemplative and serious. So serious. "Sometimes I forget she's growing up, because she's still so small." The weight of his confession presses down on the usual taut line of his shoulders, making him stoop.

This shows me yet another facet of Tennessee Dylan, and like most of the others that constitute him, it's shiny and beautiful.

"I really wish you could make it easier for me to dislike you."

He stops walking and pulls his shoulders back, pulls his head up. "Why?"

Oh . . .

No . . .

I said that out loud.

"Um. Because—" I rack my brain for something. Anything. "Because you don't like music, and I don't want to be friends with someone who doesn't like music."

A smirk tugs at his lips. "I thought we established that I *do* like music."

"Your mom's music, I mean," I add quickly.

His expression shutters up so fast I flinch. I almost apologize for bringing her up, but realize that perhaps it isn't such a rotten argument. However much he wishes his mother were dead, she's not.

She's alive, and I'm entering her contest.

How deeply will he hate me once he finds out?

"I'll see you later," I say as I hop onto my bike and pedal away before he becomes a roadblock on the path to my success.

34

A Fleck of Light

Since Monday, Ten has acted extraordinarily cold toward me, and I can't fault him for it. It's what I want.

No . . . Not what I want. What I need.

Thankfully, Nev's thawed out completely toward me. All week, we've texted. We mostly sent each other song recommendations and screenshots of cute outfits that she hopes to find at the mall this weekend. I sense Saturday's going to be painfully awkward with Ten, but I also sense it's going to be incredibly important for Nev, which is the whole point of the expedition.

It's funny how quickly I connected to Ten's sister. Perhaps it's because of our shared passion for singing. Or maybe it's because Rae's been sort of absent from my life, so I suddenly have room for other people. Or maybe it's because I see a little of myself in Nev. A little of myself and a lot of Mona.

My fingers freeze on the U-lock of my bike.

Is that it? Is this why I've gotten close to Nev so fast? Because getting close to her somehow feels as though I'm getting closer to her mother?

I snap the lock in place around the railing of Lynn's house before ringing the doorbell.

That can't be it.

This can't be the sort of person I've become.

Piano music resounds from inside, and then a voice joins the instrument and harmonizes. As the scales escalate to high tones, the voice breaks. Nev mentioned she was taking a class today. Even though she didn't tell me what time she'd be here, I'm almost certain she's the one practicing. Every voice has a specific signature, and the gritty growl of this one tells me it's Nev's.

Steffi opens the door wide, wiping her sweat-slicked forehead on a hand towel. "Hey, Angie. Lynn's just finishing up."

"I know. I'm early."

"You want to come see my new choreography?"

"Sure."

Another voice exercise begins behind the closed parlor door. This time Lynn's tapping the lower octaves on the piano. And this time, the voice doesn't even rattle.

Steffi worries the towel in her hands. "Come," she says. When I don't move, she utters my name forcefully.

Realizing her new routine is a ploy to lure me away from the ground floor, I blurt out, "I know Nev."

"You do?"

"Yeah. We're friends."

I'm not using her.

I listen to another remarkable chromatic succession. The haunting depth of Nev's voice chills me. "She has so much talent."

"She *is* incredibly gifted, but so are you, Angie."

"I wasn't fishing for a compliment."

Steffi runs the towel over her buzzed hair. "Just stating a fact."

"So, did you really have a routine to show me, or was it a ruse to get me downstairs?"

"I actually do have something new in the works."

I trail her downstairs and sit on the bench propped against the wall.

Steffi blasts a Sia song, then positions herself in the center of the room and lets the music flow through her body, possess her. She presses her fingers together as if in prayer, shoots her arms up, locks her elbows, dips backward, then sucks in her stomach and plunges her upper body forward, curving her neck, her shoulders, her spine. She executes this flow rapidly, successively, to the right, to the left, forward again. Her body moves like a ribbon, seemingly devoid of bones.

When the music fades, I clap. "That was awesome!"

Her flushed skin glistens with sweat. "Want to try it?"

"Sure!" I skip to the middle of the dance floor.

Steffi grins, then runs me through each move without the music. Once I've gotten the steps down, she makes me repeat the series, clapping her hands to give me a tempo. When she deems me ready, she hits PLAY. Keeping my gaze locked on her body, I follow her footwork, shoot my arms in the air, bend, curve, slide, repeat.

The music penetrates my skin, rolls over my flesh. The lights blind me. The floor vanishes from underneath my toes. The exertion burns away my earlier worries. But then the last notes evaporate, and I'm back in my body, back in the dance studio, back to pondering my motivations.

Stupid conscience.

There's whistling at the bottom of the stairs. Lynn and Nev. Steffi shakes her head, whereas I gape at Nev, at the smile puffing her cheeks, and I think that I somehow put it there. I'm not evil and calculating. Besides, I don't need Nev to reach Mona. I need my *music* to reach Mona.

I grab a rolled hand towel from the stack Steffi replenishes obsessively. "I heard you practicing. How the heck do you hit those low notes?"

Nev's face colors with delight.

"You two have completely different ranges." Maybe it's because they've lived together for so long, but Lynn has the same knee-jerk reaction as Steffi—reassuring me that I'm good. It's sweet and appreciated, but not what I'm after. "We better get started, Angie. I have a lesson right after yours," Lynn continues.

I seize my tote and wave to Steffi.

She winks at me.

Nev climbs the basement stairs behind Lynn. She's traded her pleated blue uniform skirt for a pair of slouchy white track pants.

When we get upstairs, I ask her, "Can you stay a bit longer?"

"Let me go ask Ten."

"He's here?"

"He always picks me up." She flings the front door open, then dashes down the porch stairs, her matchstick legs pumping extra rapidly.

Barely a minute later, she bounds back toward the house. "He said he can wait."

Together we walk into the piano parlor.

"Have you been practicing your song for the—" Lynn's sentence cuts off when she spots Nev next to me.

"Yeah," I say.

Lynn drums her fingertips against the piano keys.

"I added a bridge," I say, sitting beside her. "Can I play it for you?"

Lynn's gaze bumps into Nev again. "Of course." She removes her hand from the keys and runs it through her orange hair, crushing the frizzy flyaways around her face.

Nev shuffles over to the chaise and sits with her back straight and her knees wedged together.

After a beat, I close my eyes and play the song. As I hit the chorus, I open my eyes, wrench my shoulders back, and soften my jaw. My diaphragm expands as my voice rips up my throat. It vibrates everywhere: on my forehead, in my cheeks, against my palate. It even pulses inside my nostrils and underneath my nails.

When I finish, the room is so quiet my shoulder blades pinch together. "So?"

"It's perfect," Lynn whispers. "It's honest-to-goodness perfect. If she—"

I widen my eyes, and she falters.

"It's for my mother's contest, isn't it?" Nev's quiet voice sounds as strident as acoustic feedback.

Neither Lynn nor I answer.

"If you don't win, then Mom's stupid."

Lynn, who's already not moving much, grows even stiller.

Nev flattens her hands so hard against the velour that her knuckles protrude and whiten like knobs of chalk. She stands and then walks over to the door, emotion gusting over the sliver of face that peeks out from behind her unkempt hair.

"You're angry," I say, right before she exits.

The smile she sends my way is tight. "I'm not."

"Then why are you leaving?"

"Because"—she pushes a lock of hair behind her ear, then, as though realizing what she's done, combs it right back in front of her face— "because Ten's waiting."

"You promise you aren't mad?"

She nods, but it's so choppy that it doesn't comfort me. Maybe she's just emotional.

Right before she leaves, I say, "Don't tell Ten about the contest, okay?"

"I won't. See you tomorrow, Angie."

After the door shuts, I ask Lynn, "She was angry, wasn't she?"

Lynn stares out the window at the stocky magnolia tree. "I don't think she was mad, Angie. At least not at you. I think she's struggling with her feelings for her mother, which will inherently cloud everything that involves Mona." She sighs. "Even though Nev hasn't mentioned her once to me, I think she wishes her mother would take notice of her. I think that's why she sings. To get closer to her." She fingers the piano keys. "If only she weren't so talented."

"Who?"

Without stopping the repeating melody, Lynn says, "Nev."

"Why do you say that?"

"Because . . . unless she gets as big as her mother, she'll always feel like a failure. And attaining Mona Stone's level of success, well, it's not easy."

I tilt my head to the side as I absorb this. "If she's doing it for recognition, then she's not out for success."

Unlike me. I crave Mona's success. Is it such an impossible dream? I suddenly feel downright gloomy. For the first time in my life, I wish I were more like Ten, like my mother. I wish I weren't devoured by a single, all-encompassing passion.

Maybe I shouldn't submit my song, because truth is, losing would be crushing.

I pour my qualms and hesitation into my practice session, and as I sing, my defeatist attitude strips away layer by layer before finally flaking off completely.

I might have to adjust my aim, shoot for the stars instead of the moon. Stars might not light up the world as brightly as the moon, but it doesn't make their shine any less dazzling. I'd rather be a fleck of light in the darkness than not burn at all.

35

The Boy Who Blushes

At eleven a.m. sharp, a shrill honk makes me jolt so hard my hand jerks, dragging a squiggle of ink into the margin of my home ec homework. Mom looks up from the decorating magazine she's flipping through. When she spots Ten's Range Rover through the kitchen window, she waves.

I tuck my cell phone and keys into my suede cross-body bag, then drop a kiss on her cheek before striding toward the front door.

"Have fun at the mall, baby."

I bet she didn't put much stock in me trying to spend time with her client's kids, much less enjoy spending time with them.

I pause at the door. "I'm going out with Rae tonight. You should make plans. Maybe go out on a date?"

A blush streaks across Mom's face, as pink as her quartz cuff. "I'll—I'll call Nora."

"Rae's mom isn't a man."

Mom's dimples appear. "I was going to call her so she could introduce me to one."

"Okay. Call her."

"I will."

"Now."

She flicks her hand to shoo me away.

"Not until you call her."

"Angie—"

"Come on, Mom."

"Fine." She picks up her phone and taps the screen. Then she brings it up to her ear. "Nora? Hey."

She could be faking it, but I doubt it. *Bye*, I mouth, and shut the door.

I head over to the backseat when I spot Nev gesturing to the front one. *Shoot*. I don't want to sit next to Ten, but it seems like I don't have a choice, so I draw open the passenger door and get in.

"Mornin'." I smile at Nev, then at Ten, because what am I supposed to do? Pretend he's not there?

Even though he turns my way, he's wearing sunglasses, so I can't see his eyes. From the tight press of his lips, I fathom he's not too thrilled about this trip, or about my presence.

"Did you just wake up?" Nev asks, leaning over the center console.

"No," I say at the same time as Ten says, "Nev, seat belt."

"It's on," she grouses, forearms splayed on the back of both my and Ten's headrests.

"Not just the lap part."

Grumbling, she glides back and slides the strap over her upper body. "Dad doesn't make me wear a seat belt when I'm in the backseat."

"Well, he should."

"Yes, *Mom*." She rolls her eyes.

Ten's fingers stiffen around the steering wheel.

"Angie, can you put on some music?" Nev asks.

Even though I'm a little apprehensive to touch anything in Ten's car, I spin the volume dial, and a terrible, grating song fills the closed space.

"What is this crap?" Nev says.

"Language, Nev."

"*Crap* isn't a bad word."

I scan through the satellite presets until I locate the pop station.

"*Crap* isn't a nice word," Ten says after some time.

"You say way worse words."

"Yes, but I'm not a twelve-year-old girl."

Nev huffs. "You're *sooo* lucky to be an only child, Angie. Older brothers are a pain in the—"

Ten's gaze jerks to the rearview mirror.

"—bottom," she finishes.

Ten looks back out his windshield. "*Who* takes care of you?"

"I take care of myself."

"Who drives you around?"

She sticks out her tongue. "Because you and Dad won't let me get a bike."

I spin around in my seat. "You asked for a bike?"

She nods just as Ten mutters, "I wonder where she got that idea."

I gnaw on my bottom lip, feeling guilty, even though I never suggested she get a bicycle.

"Who makes you breakfast every morning?" Ten continues.

I jerk my gaze to Ten. "You make breakfast every morning?"

"Dad doesn't know how to cook," Nev explains.

Ten stops at a traffic light and rotates in his seat to face his sister. "So what you're saying is, it won't matter if I go to boarding school?"

Nev's face becomes pinched. "I never said that."

"Still haven't decided?" I venture.

He turns back around and stares at the bumper of the car in front. "I need to send my application by Wednesday."

An entire Maroon 5 song plays before Nev says, "You know I'd miss you like crazy."

That seems to thaw Ten out. His stiff jaw softens, and his fingers loosen on the steering wheel. "Imagine all the time you'll get to spend with Angie singing and talking about singing if I'm not around."

"We can still do that." Nev leans over the console again. "Did you hear Taylor Swift's new song, Angie? It doesn't sound like her. I'm not sure I like it." Then: "Ooh. Louder."

I turn the volume dial.

"I *love* this guy's voice," Nev gushes.

I tap the rhythm out on my bare knee, listen to the distinctive, slightly nasally, falsetto voice. "It's catchy."

"He sounds like a girl," Ten says.

"No, he doesn't," Nev counters.

"Yeah, he does."

"And I sound like a boy," Nev says.

"What?" Ten's eyes flick to the rearview mirror. "No, you don't."

"When I sing, I do."

"But not when you speak," he says.

"You should hear Angie sing."

My body temperature rises so fast I check that I didn't accidentally bump the dial of the seat warmer.

"I heard her yesterday," Ten says. "While I was waiting."

I didn't think I could get any hotter, but here I am, getting hotter. A couple of degrees from evaporation.

"She wrote the song you heard." Nev's words are laced with such pride that it lessens the sting of Ten not commenting on what he thought of my singing.

Mannered people don't comment about things they don't like. Since Ten is mannered, his silence tells me he doesn't think very highly of my singing.

"All those hours of calculus finally paying off," Ten says.

"What?" I croak, while Nev frowns.

"You spend the entire period composing music," he says.

Nev sighs. "I wish I could compose music." I'm about to suggest she take music theory when she asks, "Ten, what time's your track meet this afternoon?"

"Three."

"You really like running, huh?" I say.

"It's a good stress reliever," he says. "Like singing is for you."

Singing usually relaxes me, but these days, it's been winding me up tight. Between keeping my desire to enter the contest from Mom and—

"We're here!" Nev shrieks, cutting off my musings and ridding me of a decibel of hearing. After we park, she skips all the way to the mall.

"Did you make her marshmallow pancakes this morning?" I ask Ten, who's lumbering alongside me.

His brow furrows, so I point to Nev.

"No." Ten smacks his forehead. "Crap."

I readjust the strap of my handbag that's digging into my collarbone. "What?"

"I forgot to bring a book."

Nev pirouettes around. "That'll just give you more time to speak to Angie."

I don't think Ten wants more time to speak with me.

"Lucky me," he murmurs.

Nev rolls her eyes. "You can thank me by buying me *everything* I want."

I've rarely seen Ten's skin redden, but his jaw definitely looks a little flushed. I pin it on annoyance, because what other feeling could he be harboring for the girl who's obsessed with the mother he abhors?

36

Sweet-Toothed and Weak-Kneed

"**N**o way," Ten says, glaring at the crop top that shows off his sister's midriff. It's the eighth outfit she's modeled and the eighth one he's turned down.

"But it has sleeves!" she carps. "Angie?"

I study the top, which is short but not extraordinarily so considering Nev is flat-chested.

Ten crosses his arms. "Get it in a larger size."

"It's a one size fits all!"

"That's misleading labeling."

Nev presses her palms together and folds her fingers. "Please, Ten."

He grumbles an almost inaudible, "Fine, but definitely not those shorts."

"They do seem a little small," I concede. "I'll try to find them in a size up."

Nev jumps and claps before pouncing back into the changing room.

I turn toward a rack and riffle through it. I lift a distressed black denim mini from the rack and hold it up. Even though I haven't given much thought to my date tonight, it wouldn't hurt to come up with something to wear.

"Don't even."

Still clutching the hanger, I turn toward Ten. "Don't even what?"

"Don't even think about handing her *that*."

"Oh." I smile. "I wasn't. I was thinking of getting it for myself."

He looks at it, then at me, then at my legs, and then his gaze whizzes back to the chrome rack.

"What? No *that's revoltingly short*?"

"You're not my sister. You can wear whatever you want."

I keep smiling as I hold the skirt in front of me to see if it'll fit since I don't feel like trying it on. Worse comes to worst, I'll return it when I come back to the mall with Rae tomorrow for our Halloween shopping trip.

Nev reappears in a denim romper that hits right above her knee.

"Yes," Ten says, but I shake my head.

Nev checks her reflection, then wrinkles her nose. She's so thin it hangs from her frame. She disappears back inside the fitting room.

"What was wrong with that one?" Ten asks me.

"It was shapeless."

"So?"

"So no girl wants to wear a burlap sack."

He tugs on his spiky hair, then sinks down on a bench that's propped against the wall of the changing area. "I really don't get women's fashion."

I smile down at him. "You're only realizing this now?" I take a seat next to him, laying the mini over my lap. "Basically, whatever you think is awful, you can be sure we'll find cute."

Nev prances out of the stall in a black dress scattered with tiny red hearts.

"Too short," Ten says.

"I love it," I say.

Nev spins around, then flattens her palms in prayer again. "Please, Ten. Pretty please. *Pleasepleaseplea—*"

"Fine, but promise to wear it over tights or jeans."

"Deal."

She bounds back behind the curtain.

The bench is so close to the ground that Ten's knees are almost to his shoulders. Okay, the bench isn't *that* low, but he does look like a giant on it. He spreads his legs, probably to get more comfortable, and one of his knees knocks into mine. A spot of heat blooms around the area of contact. I assume he'll notice our bodies are touching, and he'll move, but he doesn't move.

I'm about to shift away, when he says, "You have plans tonight?"

I stare at our joined knees, my pulse picking up speed. "Yeah. I'm having dinner with Rae. You?" Before he can sense my skittering pulse through my kneecap, I unglue my leg from his. I'm tempted to put more distance between us, but I can't exactly scoot discreetly away.

"I was planning on grabbing dinner with Bolt and Archie after the meet. They run track with me," he adds.

"I know who they are. Been in Reedwood my entire life, remember?" I fidget with the frayed hem of the skirt on my lap. "You should go to Guido's. Best pizza in Nashville."

Nev struts back out in a pair of black leggings and a plaid shirt that ties at the waist.

"The shirt's cute," I say. "Ten?"

He nods.

Nev's freckles grow as bright as the red squares on her new top.

Once she's back inside the changing room, Ten asks, "You and Rae want to come with us?"

"Um." My nail snags on one of the black cotton threads. "We can't tonight." I don't have to look at my reflection in the wall of mirrors opposite us to know I'm blushing. "But thanks for asking."

Ten stays silent for so long that I sense my rejection bothers him. No one likes rejection, even when they don't especially like the person rejecting them. Humans are strange like that.

"Where's the meet taking place?" I ask him.

"Down in Arrington."

"Cool."

"Have you ever been to a track meet?"

I shake my head. "Do you have lots of cheerleaders and fans?"

A smile curves his lips. "It's not that sort of sport. We have supportive parents and girlfriends. *Some* have girlfriends, I mean. Bolt's girlfriend always shows up. She bakes the best blondies."

"I *love* blondies!"

"You should come. For the blondies."

Nev pops back out, models a faux suede jacket and army-print cargos. Both get our approval, which earns us a massive grin.

"Blondies are my Achilles' heel," I say.

He leans against the wall and crosses his muscled arms. Maybe the coach has them run wheelbarrow races during practice, because his arms are spectacular. "You should never tell others about your weakness. They might use it against you."

"Good point. Only fair you tell me your weakness now."

His gaze roves over my face, then lands on my chin, my neck, before rising back to my lips. My stomach folds and bends under his quiet, careful observation.

"Um, guys, yea or nay?" Nev asks.

She twirls, displaying her low-slung black jeans and a tight boatneck T-shirt. I give her a thumbs-up.

"Ten?" she asks.

He's scrutinizing his sneakers, which are crusted with red clay. From the track, I suspect. "That outfit's fine."

Did he even see it?

Nev fires off a brilliant smile.

"Can't believe you okayed those fishnets," I tease Ten after his sister vanishes into the changing room.

He whips his head up so fast his neck cracks, then stares in panic at the settling curtain. "What—She was—"

I touch his forearm lightly. "Relax. Nev wasn't wearing any fishnets. Just jeans. Real conservative ones at that."

He glances down at my fingers.

I remove them, return my hand to my lap. "*So . . .* you were telling me about your weakness."

"I wasn't."

"One of those fancy KitchenAid mixers?"

He frowns.

"Your weakness?" I repeat.

He smirks. "Call me old-fashioned, but I enjoy whisking batter by hand."

Probably the source of all that muscle . . .

"Calculus, then?"

He lets out a soft snort. "No."

"Am I close?"

"Not even a little."

"Running shoes."

He eyes his sneakers. "I like them but not excessively."

"T-shirts with sayings?"

He tips his head this way and that. "I do have a thing for expressive T-shirts, huh?" He's wearing a royal-blue one today with a stylized white wave stenciled with the words FIND YOUR OWN WAVE. "But I could stop buying new ones and have zero regrets."

I sigh. "I'm starting to think you're one of those people who have no weaknesses," I say, just as two girls burst into the dressing room area. Both give Ten a once-over before entering a changing room together, whispering animatedly.

"How many more outfits do you have in there, Nev?" he asks.

"Two," she says, dragging the curtain open. "In this store."

"There are more stores?"

"There are always more stores."

He observes her outfit. "Why can't girls settle for one store?"

"Because they might miss out on something incredible. Thumbs-up," I tell Nev.

Ten nods his approval, then rests the back of his head against the wall and side-eyes me. "Or they might miss out on something incredible because they don't look long enough around the first store."

I rub my neck, which feels warm against my clammy palm. "That was deep."

He stares at me so hard that I stand up to put some distance between us.

The next outfit Nev models is vetoed by Ten even though I don't see anything wrong with it, but I don't argue, because her loot is already considerable.

The other two girls who came in to try clothes step out of their dressing room. Ten looks at them, and it annoys me so much that I march to the register with my skirt.

I have a date tonight, I remind myself.

And he's leaving.

And he's Mona's son.

37

A Slice of Boredom

If I were a football player, Harrison's friend, Mike, would be the best date ever, but I'm neither a linebacker nor a fan of the sport. For Rae's sake, I ask lots of questions about technique and strategy.

Mike answers me with words like *buttonhooks*, *Hail Marys*, and *blitzes*. When I ask him what those are, he shoots me looks that make me shrink into the burgundy vinyl seat.

At least I ask questions. Unlike him. Mike hasn't asked me a single question since the one at the start of dinner: "Do you like football?" to which I answered, "I'm not sure."

After the waitress removes our empty plates, I excuse myself to go to the bathroom. I don't ask Rae to come with me, although I'm sort of hoping she'll jump out of her seat and tag along. She doesn't. Unlike me, she enjoys football talk and is leaning into Harrison's shoulder, eating up all his anecdotes.

I walk to the bathroom wishing it were the front door.

I wash my hands, then wipe them against my new denim mini instead of using the high-speed dryer. Since childhood, I've been terrified one of those things will suck me up and spit me out into some rat-infested tunnel. I don't actually believe that anymore; I just really hate the violent noise they make.

"Nice skirt," someone says as I retrace my steps toward the booth.

I stop to hunt down the owner of the familiar voice, which is a feat considering how dark Guido keeps this place.

"Ten?"

I hear one of his friends—Archie—whisper, "Dude . . ."

Archie's a very blond and very soft-spoken guy, the sort who'd be shocked by such a forward comment. Bolt, on the other hand, is the exact opposite. Dark hair, dark skin, and incredibly outspoken. He was class president several years in a row.

I amble over to their table, smiling. "You don't have to pretend to like it." I spy empty plates piled high with fire-browned crusts. "What did you think of the pizza?"

"It was almost as good as the ones back in New York." I'm sure Ten's saying this to rile me. Pizza in New York can't possibly be better than the puffy yet thin dough here.

"You guys knew this place, right?" I ask his friends.

"I come here with my grandma once a week," Archie says.

I can totally picture him bringing his grandma here.

"I'm a regular, too. My girl's obsessed with their cheesy bread," Bolt says.

"Ooh. It kicks butt here," I gush.

Ten cocks his head toward my table, which he can see over the partition separating the booths. How I didn't see him is beyond me. Then again, I wasn't looking around. *And* it's dark.

"How's the double date?" he asks.

I look away from where I should be sitting. "Awesome."

He tilts his head to the side. "Really?"

I can sense his friends looking at us.

"Okay. No, it sucks." I perch on the edge of the booth next to Ten. "You think I can hide out here until the check comes?"

Ten grins as though he's so damn happy I'm having a crap time.

"How was your track meet?" I ask.

"You're looking at number one, two, and four," Bolt announces.

"Whoa! Which one of you won?"

Ten tips his glass of Coke toward Bolt. "Where do you think this guy got his name?"

I grin. "Congrats, Bolt. Who came in second?"

Archie palms his hair. "Unfortunately, not me."

I elbow Ten. "Nice. We're going to have to find you a nickname now."

Ten chuckles.

I catch Mike scanning the aisle that leads to the bathroom, and then Rae's turning around. I duck a little, but Rae and I are connected on some other plane, so I'm totally not surprised when she struts up to the divider and rests her forearms on top of it.

"Hey, Ten, Bolt, Archie."

Archie goes red, which makes his blond eyebrows resemble crescent moons.

"Hon, did you lose yourself on the way back?" She's smiling, so I know she's not mad.

"Did the check come yet?" I ask.

"We just asked for it."

Beyond her, I see Harrison and Mike looking our way.

I sigh and stand up, tugging on the hem of my miniskirt. I give Ten and his friends a little wave, then slink around the aisle of booths to reach ours. "Sorry," I say, sliding back in next to Mike.

I take in a long lungful of air that smells like roasted garlic and menthol—a scent I will forever associate with crap dates from now on. Mike spent a good portion of our meal explaining how he has to rub this cooling cream into his muscles after every game. He went as far as displaying his muscles, as though I wouldn't know what they were . . . Not only do I dance but I am a human, so I know what muscles are and where they can be found in the body. I can even name most of them, but I didn't get into that. I felt it would be a tad snarky of me.

The waitress slides our check onto the table. I reach for my purse and unzip it while Harrison calculates how much we owe.

"Fifteen bucks a head," he says.

Since I don't consider this a real date, I don't expect Mike to pay for me. However, I'm expecting Harrison to pay for Rae—which might be antiquated of me, but I don't know . . . it's just fifteen dollars. When she takes out the exact change, he doesn't tell her to put her money away.

I pull out a twenty and lay it flat on the tray.

"You sure, man?" Mike yanks the check out of Harrison's hands. "I only got a plain pie and tap water. I remember it saying twelve dollars on the menu." He reads over the bill. "Yep. Twelve bucks." He digs into his pocket and comes up with a handful of ones and a balled flyer. He smooths it out. It's a rebate for five dollars. He peels off seven ones and puts them on the tray along with his coupon. "Rae, your vegetarian pizza was eighteen bucks."

Her eyes widen a little, and she starts for her bag again, but I reach over and touch the back of her hand. "I got you, Rae. Hey, Harrison, did you factor in tip?"

He rubs the back of his neck. "I forgot."

I take another ten out and toss it on the pile of green bills.

"Angie, you don't have to do that," Rae says.

"It's okay." There's nothing I dislike more than that moment at the end of meals when everyone's tallying up what they owe. Since this dinner was already painful, I want to expedite this part, even if it means paying more than my share.

"Your daddy has a good job, huh?" Mike asks.

"My daddy's dead." Which he would know if he'd asked me a single question.

Mike flinches.

I stand up and hook my bag over my shoulder.

"So what'll it be? *Guardians of the Galaxy* or *Outbreak*?" Harrison asks, pulling Rae into his side.

I frown.

Rae tucks a blonde lock behind her ear. "I suggested a movie at my place. What would you rather see?"

I'd rather see Harrison and Mike drive off. Since I don't think that's one of my options, I say, "I think I'm going to head home. Mom texted me that her date didn't go too well."

"Oh no." If Rae senses I'm lying, she doesn't let on.

"Rain check on our sleepover?" I ask.

"Sure, hon. I'll drop you off."

"That'd be great."

As we head out, Mike falls in step next to me. "My homecoming's next weekend. Want to go with me?"

I blink at him. "Are you serious?" Did he think this date went well?

"You don't have to be a bitch about it," he huffs.

The fringes of my long, sheer vest swing against the backs of my thighs as I walk through the door Harrison is holding open.

Since Mike's still giving me the stink eye, I mutter, "Sorry. I'm trying to get over someone."

Can this night be done already?

The door of the restaurant flies open and out strides Ten. I wait for his friends to materialize, but it's only him. He stops beside us and nods at Harrison.

"Hey, Ten," Harrison says.

"You're named after a number?" Mike asks.

Ten gets that crooked, provocative grin of his that gets me *every* time. He slides his gaze off Mike and onto me. "I was on my way home. Want a ride?"

My heart *bwirls*.

"It'll save Rae a detour," he adds.

"I don't mind." She hooks her hands around Harrison's arm. "Angie?"

I choose Ten.

Rae blows me a kiss before heading toward her Beemer. Harrison gets behind the wheel. Rae loves driving, so I'm a little surprised she's relinquished control of her steering wheel to her boyfriend. Then again, I feel like she's relinquished control over a lot of things since hooking up with Harrison. I realize that dating requires concessions, but molding yourself into someone you're not seems wrong. Which is one of the reasons I can't entertain thoughts of Ten and me together. I could never shun Mona Stone to please him.

Mike walks away without so much as a goodbye and gets into his own car.

"Are you having regrets?" Ten asks.

"About not spending more time with a guy who called me a bitch? Not really."

Ten stiffens beside me. "He called you a bitch?"

"In his defense, I was rude to him."

Ten rests one hand on my shoulder, his palm making contact with a piece of skin that feels acutely sensitive. "Never make excuses for a guy who insults you."

His quick pulse nips my skin, beat-matching my own. For a second, I forget what we're talking about, but then a car revs up and I'm reminded of my sucky date.

Ten's hand slips off my shoulder, and I shiver from the sudden nippiness that replaces his fingers' warmth.

I look at the door of the restaurant, still expecting Archie and Bolt to step out. "Where are your friends?"

"They wanted dessert; I didn't."

"Oh. Okay." *Real glib, Angie.*

"Unless you want dessert? I noticed you passed on it."

I fold my arms, unsure what to think that he noticed this. Then again, Ten seems to notice a lot of things most people miss. "I'm not hungry anymore," I end up saying, not because I couldn't have dessert—I always have room for dessert—but I'm not sure what it would mean to go back inside with Ten.

"All right. Let's go, then."

We head toward his gleaming steed, which is parked at the end of the full lot. He powers his car open. For a split second, he hesitates by the front bumper, as though debating whether to open my door. I hurry to do it to make things less awkward.

A thick envelope rests on the passenger seat. I lift it and am about to chuck it into the backseat when I see the address and the row of stamps.

38

Mailing My Heart Away

I squeeze the envelope. "Is this your application?"

The beams of a car turning into the lot highlight the nerve fluttering in Ten's jaw.

"There's a mailbox right over there." I jut my chin toward the street corner. "Want me to drop it inside?"

"No."

"But you're gonna mail it, right?"

The envelope crinkles in my tense grip. I ease up before I inflict irreparable damage.

"I haven't decided."

A gust of wind dances through the fringes of my sheer vest, making my thighs pebble with goose bumps where fabric meets bare skin. "Seems like you did." I nod to the stamps.

"Angie, just toss it in the back, will you?"

For some reason, I can't unglue my fingers from the envelope. Just like I can't unstick the soles of my black cowboy boots from the pavement. I'm frozen, and so is Ten. But then he manages to move. He takes the envelope from me, his knuckles skimming my wrist.

His tongue wets his lips, making them glisten in the darkness. "You know what?"

My heart pops and sizzles like birthday sparklers.

"I've never made a good decision in my life, so here." He places the envelope back into my hands.

I frown at him as another car turns into the lot, splashing the back of his head with light. His face is suddenly dark, unreadable.

"Are you asking me to choose for you?"

He nods.

My next breath catches in my lungs. "Why me?"

"Because I can't tell if you want me to leave or to stay."

I understand what he's asking, and although I want to pitch the envelope into the gutter, I don't want to make him stay . . . I want him to *want* to stay.

I spin around, stride to the mailbox, and push the envelope through the flap.

In a few quick strides, Ten's at my side. "Angie!"

I think my heart might've slipped through the slot too, because it's become real quiet in my rib cage.

"What did you do?" Ten tries to thrust his fingers through the flap, but of course the opening isn't wide enough to accommodate his hand. "Angie, I thought—" He tugs on his thorny hair. "I guess I thought wrong."

A lone cigarette butt blights the pavement's smooth shimmer. I kick it out of the way, and it lands on the road, gets smooshed under the tires of a pickup. If only I could get rid of my feelings for Ten the same way . . . these feelings that have been ceaselessly disrupting the even tempo of my life. But every time I've tried to chuck them far, they return full force.

I meet his stony gaze. "Honestly, Ten, I don't want you to leave." My throat feels as dry as cardboard.

He calms, and I sense we've stepped into the eye of the storm. The winds will pick back up soon and they might carry him away, but for now they're gone and have left him standing before me.

"Then why?" he asks huskily.

My heart starts thumping again, its rhythm slow, steady, steadfast. "Because it shouldn't be my choice. It needs to be yours. *Only* yours. If you end up being unhappy here, you'll resent me, and I don't want that."

His hands drop alongside his body. "I could never resent you."

Once you find out I'm entering your mother's contest you will.

"Don't you think I've tried?" he says.

I give him a sad smile.

He doesn't smile back. "I won't go. Even if I get in, I won't go."

I don't want to hope for this. I *shouldn't* hope for this. "Can I still get a ride home?"

Finally, a smile warps his toughened expression. "You think I would leave a girl stranded on a dark street?" As we start back toward the car, he shoves his hands in his pockets. "You're really something else."

I cock an eyebrow. "Something else?"

"Different. Unpredictable. Spirited."

I twist a lock of hair around my finger. "That's a first. I usually get *dazzlingly hot* and *insanely talented.*"

He snorts.

"Fine. I'll admit that only Rae speaks of me that way."

His eyes flash with amusement. "Spend some time in the boys' locker room, and you'll see it isn't just Rae who thinks of you that way."

My pulse turns jumpy, scattering heat through my veins. "Liar."

We're back at the car, and he's drawing my door open. "I might withhold information when need be, but I *never* lie."

Heart still pumping wildly, I climb into the car, and he shuts the door before striding to the driver's side and getting in.

As he pulls out of the lot, he says, "Where's your bike?"

"At home. Can't bike in a mini." I point to my lap, but then regret bringing attention to my legs considering how much skin is on display. I tug on the skirt's frayed hem, but my efforts are wasted. "Besides, Mom doesn't like me to bike at night. Unless my destination's in the neighborhood."

"Your mother's a wise woman."

"Yeah. She is."

"You two are close, huh?"

"She's everything to me." I roll one of the threads on the hem of my skirt between my fingers.

"Did she ever remarry?"

"No. She's never even had a serious relationship since Dad."

"Really? Why?"

"It's a long story." And a personal one.

I'm not *there* with Ten yet . . . at that place I can spill my family's deepest, darkest secrets. I haven't even told Rae. Maybe I'll forever be incapable of speaking about the father who wanted nothing to do with me and who wasn't nice to Mom.

The thread rips.

"What about your dad? Did he ever remarry?"

"Almost. She was only interested in his money. Took him a while to figure it out, but at least he came to his senses before sliding a ring on her finger." Ten eases to a stop at a traffic light.

The taillights of the car in front of us tinge the thread bloodred. I spin it between my fingers.

Ten drums his fingers against the steering wheel. "And before you assume anything, he's never taken a dime from Mona."

The thread slips out of my fingers and vanishes in the darkness of the car. "I—I . . ." I don't finish my sentence, because I don't want to lie to Ten.

He heaves a ragged sigh. "That's what was written up in all the newspapers, so that's what a lot of people think."

I rake my hair back. "I'm sorry for being one of those people."

"You couldn't have known." His long fingers loosen on the wheel.

"I couldn't have known but I also could've *not* jumped to any conclusions." After a quiet minute, I ask, "Did you ever play the piano?"

"When I was a kid."

"First time I saw your hands—after you knocked me off my bike—I thought you had pianist hands."

"That's what crossed your mind?"

A blush creeps over my cheeks. *Among other thoughts.*

"What other thoughts?"

Oh. Crap. *No.* Did I say that last part out loud? "Like I would ever tell you."

He shoots me that stupid crooked grin of his that sends my heart pounding out of control.

"I still can't believe you crashed into me," I say.

"I was distracted."

"By trying to find the fastest route out of Nashville?"

His gaze drops to my lap, to the inches of bare skin, and then he clears his throat and tugs on the collar of his black T-shirt emblazoned with three white block letters: WTF. "Yeah. That." Beneath the block letters, there's a small sentence: WHERE'S THE FOOD?

"I like the shirt," I say.

He looks down at it as though to refresh his memory. "I'd lend it to you, but it would cover up your new skirt."

I smile. "What a shame that would be."

The corners of his lips quirk up.

Not in my wildest dreams did I imagine the night ending like this—me in Ten's car, conversing easily. Where's the animosity that always crackles between us?

Perhaps in the mailbox . . .

A vintage Pat Benatar song spills faintly from the speakers. I know it by heart because my father recorded an acoustic version of it on a practice CD I found in a box the day we moved into our new house. I turn up the volume and start singing the lyrics to "We Belong" but then realize I'm singing in front of someone and crush my lips shut.

"Don't stop," Ten says, eyes on me.

"And this is why you run into poor girls on their bikes . . . because you don't watch the road."

He returns his gaze to the road. "I'll watch where I'm going, but only if you keep on singing."

"What if I refuse?"

"Then I'll keep watching you." As though to prove his point, he angles his face back toward me.

When we almost ram into the back of a white sedan, I open my lips wide. "Stop!"

He brakes. "Do we have a deal?"

"And you call me the crazy one," I mutter.

"I called you spirited, different, and unpredictable. Not crazy." A car honks behind us. "Please sing."

I wring my hands nervously.

Another loud honk, and then car tires squeal as the car goes around us. Ten has stopped in the middle of the road and is making no move to start driving again.

He watches my hands. "It's just me, Angie. Just me. Sing for me."

A marriage proposal would've rendered me less panicky.

Ten must sense I won't do it, because he finally bears down on the gas pedal. We don't talk the rest of the way home.

"Thank you for the ride."

He keeps his gaze leveled on the white columns of my house, tight-lipped, tight-jawed.

I sigh. "I don't even sing in front of Rae, Ten."

He side-eyes me, as though he doesn't believe me.

"I clam up when I feel someone watching me. Which I know is weird considering I want to be a singer, but . . . yeah"—I gulp—"stage fright is real."

"All great artists have stage fright, or so Dad tells me," Ten says. "He hangs out with so many of them. If you don't have stage fright, then you're apparently not as good as you think."

My ego laps that right up.

"You have a really nice voice, by the way."

Hopefully, the darkness camouflages my budding blush. "I bet you say that to all the girls," I joke, because what else am I supposed to do? Thank him? Wouldn't that sound smug?

The strain on his face finally breaks. "I usually comment on their rack."

I smirk because Ten is so not the type of guy to do that. "Didn't think you had anything in common with Brad."

"We're almost the same person."

I shake my head and grin at him as I open the door and get out.

He powers down his window. "Promise you'll sing for me someday?"

Someday. There's no expiration date to that word. I want to write a song to that word. Already lyrics are jostling in my mind.

I nod, and my hair springs out from behind my ears.

He shoots me a smile that for once isn't crooked or brazen, just heartbreakingly sweet.

39

Blinding Dreams

I wake up on Sunday to a message from Lynn to stop by her place. As I throw on some clothes, I wonder if she wants to see me because she's thought of some way to make my song better.

After grabbing a banana and scarfing it down, I bike over to my coaches' house. I find them in the backyard, tending to their lawn and hydrangea bushes.

"Hey. You wanted to see me?" I ask.

Lynn rises from her crouch, rubbing her dirt-stained palms against her jeans. "I did."

She's smiling, which makes my nerves tingle with anticipation.

"A friend of mine owns a recording studio. I called him up and booked you in for Saturday."

I frown, not sure I'm understanding what she's saying. Her wording isn't elaborate, but my brain's telling me this is too good to be true, and before I start doing handsprings, I want to make sure I heard her right. "You booked me—"

"To record your song. I thought a professional recording could really make it stand out. We could've recorded it here, but—"

I pounce on her and hug her so hard her breath whooshes from her lungs. And then she's patting my back, laughing softly.

"*Thankyouthankyouthankyouthankyou!*" I chant before letting her go.

"Does Saturday work for you?"

"Heck, yeah!" Tears pop out. "I'm going to record a song in a studio! A real studio!"

Lynn laughs gently. "It's about time."

She gives me all the details while I try to quiet my emotions. I don't do a good job of it, though. My eyes are as watery and puffy as the time Rae squirted hot sauce into them—long story . . . wasn't her fault.

"You should tell your mom to come," Steffi says.

That blitzes my meltdown. "I'm sure she's busy."

They both scrutinize me.

I look toward the shivering magnolia tree. "But I'll ask her." I won't, though. If I ask her and she comes, it'll ruin the greatest moment of my life. "I don't know how I'll ever be able to pay you back for this."

"You could help us weed," Steffi suggests.

Laughter snaps out of me. "I don't think that would be wise. I'd probably murder your lawn."

Steffi grins. "It was worth a try."

"How about I go make some lemonade? I'm pretty useless in the kitchen but I make a mean lemonade."

Lynn crouches back in front of the hydrangeas. "By all means, squeeze away."

After straining the ligaments in my hands, because Lynn and Steffi don't own a juicer—I make a mental note of getting them one as a thank-you—I return to the backyard with a pitcher and three glasses.

I spend another hour with them, discussing the contest while they clip and till under a sun that seems brighter and warmer than it's ever been before. If I close my eyes and tip my head up, I can almost imagine it's the beam from a stage light.

Not that I've ever felt one, but hopefully . . . soon, I'll be blinded by one.

40

Killing Me Softly with Food

The strange thing about your mom being a decorator is that every space she touches feels like home, even if it doesn't look or smell familiar. She's only worked on the Dylans' mansion for a little over a month, but already the walls have been painted in a broad palette of pastels—Mom loves mixing colors like elephant gray and dawn purple—and the oak floors have been oiled instead of varnished. Where the hallway meets the living room, the hardwood planks are staggered with slabs of beige stone cut in the exact same dimension as the planks. She calls this technique *fade in, fade out*.

"Let's watch the show upstairs." Nev rushes up the swooping wooden staircase, but halts when I don't follow. "Are you coming or what?"

"Give me a second, girl. It's my first time here." I shrug out of my denim jacket and stuff it into my tote. "Can I get a tour before we sit on our butts and inhale popcorn?"

She zips back down the stairs so fast she almost stumbles. "Sure." She starts off down a short hallway. "Over here's the kitchen."

. I follow her, taking in the modern glass sconces that adorn the whitewashed wainscoted wall. Even though it's not yet dark out, the lights are on. In fact, it seems like Nev's turned on every light in the house.

When Ten, who's been extra friendly all week, mentioned he had a track meet tonight, which happens to be the same night his father needs to be in LA to dine with a client, I suggested hanging out with Nev.

"Are you sure?" he'd asked me during art class.

Gnawing on the top of the crayon that should've been sweeping over the vellum sheet before me, I nodded. "I'm so going to fail this class," I muttered, studying the overflowing basket of fruit.

Ten filched my paper and with a few quick strokes corrected some of my shading, creating perspective where there'd been none. I spent the rest of class trying to re-create what he'd done and failing miserably. Right before the bell, he'd lifted my paper again and hurriedly turned my childish sketch into something way better.

The Dylans' kitchen is made up of a wall of bow windows that look onto a garden that's in the process of being landscaped. I run my fingers over the gigantic slab of smooth, midnight-blue granite that glistens like a dark pond at the center of the room. The space smells new, like cement and glue, but also like chocolate and butter.

Nev struts to the stovetop and lifts a piece of foil off a pan. "Ten made blondies for us."

I squeeze my phone between my fingers, applying so much pressure I imagine it bending. "If they're any good, I'm going to kill him."

She grins, then steals a gooey morsel right from the pan and sticks it in her mouth. After she swallows, she says, "Yep. You're definitely going to kill him."

I walk over and scoop out a piece that binds to my fingers and then to my teeth. It's heaven. Like, seriously. Best. Blondies. Ever. "I so am."

Nev hands me a spoon, takes one for herself, and together we put a serious dent in the mushy treat. Bellies full, she finishes giving me a tour of the house. I get to see the downstairs area, which is a mess of bare plaster and tarp-covered furniture.

"The movie theater will be through here, and then the pool table will go there, as well as a less formal living room. Dad calls it the kids' area, even though I keep reminding him we're not kids anymore," she says, as she leads me back upstairs.

She shows me the formal living room, which is composed of structural greige couches and storm-gray leather armchairs arranged beneath a showstopping glass chandelier. Mom loves her artistic light fixtures almost as much as she loves her binders bursting with fabric swatches.

"I'll show you my bedroom," Nev says, tugging on my wrist. "It's not totally done." She tows me up the main staircase toward the bedrooms, gushing about Mom's talent. "Over here is Dad's room."

I dig my sneakers into the hallway runner. "I don't feel comfortable going into his bedroom."

"Do you want to see Ten's room?"

I shake my head. Not that I'm not curious, but I'd rather not barge into his space unannounced, so we head over to her bedroom, which is gray and pink, like her outfit. One of the many finds of our shopping trip.

"You match your room, Nev."

Blushing, she pats her pink blousy tank while I drop my bag by her door, remove my shoes, and sink into a beanbag, which molds around my body.

"I still can't believe you have a TV in your room. You're so lucky."

She grabs the remote control, plops down on the other squiggly patterned beanbag, and rakes her hair back.

After three episodes of our favorite witchy show, we head to the kitchen. There's a Tupperware filled with giant meatballs in tomato sauce. We boil pasta and then mix it with the sauce.

As we slurp down our meal at the gigantic island, I ask Nev about school, about the girls who make fun of her. Apparently nothing has happened since the cafeteria standoff, which is unexpected and comforting.

"Actually. That's not true," she says.

I put down my fork, appetite on hold. "What happened?"

"This boy . . . Charlie . . . he asked if I wanted to go to the movies with him."

Not what I was anticipating at all.

She tucks her hair behind her ears. "He's like the most popular boy in our grade."

I pick my fork back up and twirl some pasta around the tines. "What did you say?"

"I told him I'd think about it."

"Do you like him?"

"A lot, but I'm not sure why he asked me out."

I point my fork at her. "Because he likes you?"

"You don't think it's a"—she sticks her fork in a meatball, crushes it—"a trick?"

"A trick?"

She shrugs. "To embarrass me."

"I don't follow . . ."

"What if Crystal put him up to it? What if I say yes, and it's all a joke? Everyone will think I'm desperate."

"First off, that's crazy, but exceedingly creative of you. Second off, do you want to go out with him?"

"Maybe."

"Maybe yes or maybe no?"

"Maybe yes."

"Then say yes!"

A smile flits over her lips. "Dad will never let me go to the movies unchaperoned."

"I'll go with you. I'll sit in the back."

"That won't be weird at all."

I smile. "What if I drag your brother along?"

"You mean as your date?"

"What? No! As a friend." I stuff a huge meatball in my mouth, feeling like all the radiators in the house have suddenly turned on.

"You're red."

"Shut up."

Nev giggles.

I glare at her.

She just laughs some more.

I pinch her side. "Stop it. It's really not like that between your brother and me."

"Uh-huh."

She finally stops laughing, but her shiny eyes stick to me as we rinse our bowls and slot them into the dishwasher.

"Want another blondie?" Nev asks before we return upstairs.

"Maybe later."

Stomach full of pasta and butterflies, I trail her back to her girlie den. We watch two more hours of TV, and then I play grown-up and tell her she needs to go to bed.

"Can you stay in my room until I fall asleep?" she asks after climbing into her canopy bed.

"Won't budge from the beanbag." I pull out my phone and browse Mona's Instagram feed until I'm all caught up on the happenings in her life, and then I read the millions of messages on the senior WhatsApp.

When Nev's breathing slows, I pry myself out of my seat and stretch, then tuck the comforter around her small body. As I turn to go, my heart lurches into my throat.

A broad figure darkens the doorway.

41

Easy Come, Easy Go

Palm flat against my still-careening heart, I inch toward the door. "I think I just had a stroke," I whisper to Ten, picking up my tote and hoisting it onto my shoulder.

He chuckles softly, moving out of the way so I can pass around him. Then he draws the door closed, but not completely.

"How'd it go?" he asks, pushing the sleeves of his forest-green hoodie up his forearms.

"Oh, you know . . . painfully boring, but hey, we got through it."

"Let me guess. You two watched six hours of Netflix, ate pasta with meatballs, and inhaled half the pan of blondies."

"Did Nev text you a play-by-play of our night or was that a wild guess?"

A corner of his mouth lifts. "Nev texted me."

"How was the competition?"

"Good."

"Did you win?"

"Maybe."

I raise my hand for a high five, which he delivers. His palm lingers on mine. I swallow and take a quick step back, move my hands to my jean pockets but can't get more than my first phalanx in. Albeit stretchy, the denim is a little tight.

"I should go home."

"Right away?"

"Um. Well . . . it's a school night, and it's ten thirty."

"I'll drop you off."

"I biked over."

"Angie—"

"Your sister would totally freak if she woke up to an empty house."

He sighs. "Do you have your earbuds?"

"Please don't tell me not to listen to music while I bike. Rae's always on my case about that."

His lips quirk up. "I just want you to talk to me during your ride home."

"This is Belle Meade . . ."

"If you don't, I'll drive you home."

"Ten—"

"Angie."

"God, you're so freakin' stubborn."

A smug look settles on his face. "Pot calling the kettle black."

"Fine," I mutter, digging my earbuds out of my bag.

He lets me go ahead of him down the stairs.

As I untangle the pink cord, I ask, "What do you think of my mother's taste?"

"It's . . . interesting."

"Whenever someone says *interesting*, it's never good."

He shakes his head, smiling a little. "The reason I said that is because she's managed to make it sleek yet homey. I think it's all the colors she uses. Our house back in New York was gray. Not a single touch of color. Well, except Nev's room, which was pink."

I grin. "Don't doubt it."

He opens the front door, then walks me to my bike, which I parked alongside the Dylans' garage door. As I shrug on my denim jacket to counter the nippiness in the air, Ten runs a hand through his mussed hair.

"I'm not sure how to thank you for babysitting my sister."

"Better not use that term in front of her."

"She'll always be my baby sister. Even at thirty, or fifty."

I think my heart just melted a little. "Believe it or not, I enjoy spending time with her. She's extremely mature, or maybe I'm incredibly immature, but we totally click." I clip on my helmet, stick my earbuds in, then plug them into my phone. "Besides, you made blondies. Consider that payment enough." I wink at him and then roll my bike down the driveway, when my phone rings shrilly.

Ten's name flashes on the screen. I look over my shoulder and pick up the call. He's still standing there, one hand stuffed in his low-riding sweatpants' pocket, the other cradling his cell phone. "You didn't tell me what you thought of the blondies."

"They were awful. Absolutely terrible."

He must hear the smile in my voice because he chuckles softly. "Glad you hated them."

The gate creaks open, and I climb onto my bike's saddle. "So, you really won that track meet?"

"I really won."

"What happened to Bolt?"

"He came in second."

"Cool. And Archie?"

"Sixth. Wasn't his night."

"Happens to the best of us."

We talk about it while I bike, then about the TV show I watched with Nev, about the food he's cooking for himself. God, it's so easy to talk to him. It almost feels like I'm talking with Rae, except when I talk with Rae, my pulse doesn't perform insane sprints.

We keep talking long after I get home, only stopping when I notice it's almost midnight. I dream of Ten that night. He's a warlock in my dream—a darn sexy one—who casts a spell using a magical whisk (no joke) to make himself vanish, and even though I canvass an enchanted forest in search of him, I can't find him.

And he never reappears.

42

My Rae of Sun

I've tried to shake off my dream all morning, but it clings to my subconscious like an earworm, forever on repeat.

"Angie, did you hear a word I just said?" Rae is trying to shove a book into her overstuffed locker.

"I did."

"So you agree that leprechauns are cooler than unicorns?"

"Wait, what?"

"Ha. You were so not listening to me."

"Okay. Fine. I was distracted. I had this weird dream last night, and it just won't go away."

"What about?"

I don't want to tell her about it, not because she'd judge or make fun, but because I'm afraid that voicing it will make me sound pathetic. Plus Mel and Laney are right next to us. Granted, they're discussing the Halloween party at Brad's house, so they're not really paying attention.

Rae shuts her locker door. "Out with it," she says as we walk toward home ec, the only class we have together.

Sighing, I give in and recount my dream but leave out the identity of the warlock.

"Classic fear of abandonment," she says, once I'm done talking. "Not that I'm a shrink or anything."

She might not be a shrink, but she has a point . . . I do fear abandonment. More so now that I'm aware of my parents' history.

After Mel and Laney vanish into their classroom, I tell Rae about Dad turning his back on us. She stares at me, brown eyes wide with shock. At some point, her hand wraps around my arm, as though she might keel over. Or maybe it's to hold me up?

"Please don't tell anyone," I whisper.

"I would never, hon."

I feel a teeny bit lighter after that. Hopefully, it'll last.

We're late for class, but Mrs. Rainlin doesn't comment on it. Probably because she doesn't even realize it. Our one-hundred-year-old teacher can't hear anything. *Okay*, she's not a hundred, but she's half-deaf and seriously old—she taught Rae's grandmother, a Reedwood alum.

Rae and I whisper back and forth during the entire class. About Dad at first, and then about Mona's contest.

"I'm gonna have to forge Mom's signature," I tell her.

"She's still saying no?"

I twist my arrow earring. "Yep."

After the bell rings, Rae asks, "Want me to talk to her?"

I shake my head.

"How about I sign it for you so I get in trouble in case you—I mean, *when* you win?"

I shoot her a grateful smile. For her wording, and for having my back. "I don't want to involve anyone else. But thanks, Rae."

She latches on to my hand. "Always, hon."

I'm not sure what I did to deserve such a good friend, but I must've done something right. I think of Nev then. I hope she finds her Rae. Everyone needs a Rae in their life.

"And in case you were wondering, I'll never abandon you," she says, squeezing my hand.

43

Leaving My Mark

"From the top." Lynn's voice pops into my headset.

This is my fourth take, and I'm starting to sweat through my Mona Stone T-shirt. The piano music, which I recorded earlier, comes on again, and, heart bouncing around like a tennis ball, I snap open my mouth and start singing, and it's okay until I reach the chorus. My neck and face grow hot from a blend of annoyance and humiliation. I may not have a huge audience, but I do have an audience: Steffi, Lynn, the sound engineer, and Mom.

Yep . . . Mom's here.

Lynn phoned her yesterday, because Mom apparently had to sign a waiver form for me to record. I doubt it's true, because I haven't seen any form. Then again, I haven't asked to see it, because neither do I want to put Lynn on the spot, nor do I want to appear ungrateful.

Lynn steps into the vocal booth and readjusts the height of the mic—as though *that* will fix my awry singing. "Forget she's there."

My lids pull up real high.

"I had Pete cut your mic. They can't hear us."

I look at Mom, who's sitting beside Steffi on the brown leather chesterfield covered in Sharpie scribbles—autographs of all the artists who've recorded here.

"Did you know that vocal cords are actually folds that vibrate hundreds of times per second to create sound?" Lynn asks.

I frown. "Um. Yeah."

"And that whispering is terrible for singers because it doesn't require using our vocal folds, so if you only whispered, they could potentially atrophy?"

"Okay . . ." I hadn't heard that, but I can see how it would be alarming.

"Another fun fact for you. A man in Missouri has a vocal range of ten octaves, while Mariah Carey can only sing in five. How astonishing must his voice be?"

"Pretty astonishing."

"Now, forget she's there. Close your eyes if you need to, but forget she's there."

I blink at her. Did she just spout out all those weird facts to distract me?

Lynn pats my shoulder, and that small gesture injects courage into my spine.

As she walks back out and the door shuts with a sucking *whoosh*, I square my shoulders. Roll my neck. Stretch my jaw.

I think of the man with the extraordinary vocal range. Did he ever record a song? Was *his* mother supportive?

The instrumental music clicks on.

I close my eyes, tap the beat out on my thigh, and then I sing. Soon, I'm fording through the chorus. Once. Twice. Three times. The piano begins to decrease in tempo and in volume. And then it fades completely. And I stand there a little dazed because no one interrupted me.

Slowly, I lift my lids and look at Lynn.

She shoots me a thumbs-up.

I am so disbelieving that I don't lower the headset.

Steffi's clapping, effusive as always. Although her appreciation means a lot, I'm looking at Mom, I'm looking for *her* approval. Which is torture . . . Will there ever come a day when I won't yearn for it?

She sits rigidly, hands in her lap. She doesn't clap. Doesn't whistle. Doesn't smile.

My short-lived exhilaration melts into a giant, grim puddle.

Finally, I take off the headset and hook it to the mic. On legs that feel leaden, I tread into the control room.

Mom's studying the tiny silk knots between the white pearls of her lariat necklace.

Lynn grabs me in a quick hug. I plaster on a smile for her sake. I even manage to whisper a pitiful, "Thank you."

While she discusses editing with the sound engineer, I walk toward Mom and Steffi. My dance coach must sense the tension, because she pulls out her phone and steps away.

"Why did you come? You hate my music . . ." My voice catches on a sob. I seal my lips, because I don't want to cry. It would be completely childish and unprofessional.

Mom's hand jerks, and the necklace clinks as it settles back against her white linen blouse. "What?"

"Oh, come on, Mom." I roll my eyes, but that's mostly to get rid of the tears. "Every time I sing, you look bored."

I try to decipher the signature scrawled underneath her skinny jeans. I can't tell vowels from consonants, so I have no clue whom it belongs to.

She shoves her hair back. Twice. "It does pain me to listen to you," she finally murmurs. "Because . . . because you're *good*. Real good."

I blink. Parents are genetically engineered to praise their children, and although Mom has always praised me on other achievements, she has *never* complimented my singing.

She stands up and hugs me. "And that song . . . that song is insanely gorgeous. And I hate that it was so gorgeous."

My eyelashes bat away tears. "Why?"

225

"Because . . . I might lose you to *that* world after all."

"You really think I'm good?" I croak.

"Oh, baby." She presses me away and holds me at arm's length. "How can you doubt that you are?"

"Because you've never told me before."

She looks at me long and hard. "I was afraid that if I did, you'd let everything else—school, college, friendships—slip."

"I would never."

She bites her lower lip and nods, but her crinkled brow and shiny eyes tell me she's still worried.

"I promise I won't."

Steffi digs a pack of tissues from her black leather vest, then hands one to Mom and another to me.

"Your daddy would've been real proud." Mom sniffles.

I look at her, my heart squeezing. What she's just said burnishes my fragile ego like a flame warming metal, hardening it into full-body armor.

"It's for Mona's contest, isn't it?" she asks.

That knocks the smile right off my lips.

"That's what I thought." Her chest rises with a long breath. "You're going to enter it whether I give you my blessing or not, aren't you?"

I don't say a thing, because I don't want to tarnish this moment with a lie.

"When's the deadline?"

"Halloween."

"I'll make you a deal. If you still want to participate on October thirty-first, I'll sign the form."

Even though she's probably agreeing because she senses I won't win, I squeal and throw my arms around her neck and chant, "*IloveyouIloveyouIloveyouIloveyou.*" I say it a hundred times, yet it still doesn't feel like enough.

Lynn catches my eye over Mom's shoulder, and I finally understand why she invited her here today—to show her how much heart and work I've poured into this song. I mouth a thank-you. She answers me with a gentle nod.

The sound engineer hands me a Sharpie. "You can't leave before signin' the couch."

I stare at the pen, then at the man, then back at the pen. I don't reach for it. "But I'm not famous."

He gets off his springy chair and props the marker between my rigid fingers. "Yet. But I got a feeling that's just a matter of time."

I'm so devastatingly happy that I want to cry and yell and laugh and pump my fist in the air. I don't do any of these things. What I do is crouch, uncap the pen, and draw my name in large, wobbly, loopy letters.

My first-ever autograph.

Hopefully, the first of many.

44

The Non-Date Date

My phone chimes with a message on our way home from the Shake Shack, where Mom treated Lynn, Steffi, and me to lunch.

BEAST: You better not have any plans tonight.

Even though there's no tone to text messages, his sounds aggressive. I'm tempted not to answer him, but of course I do. Nothing can ruin my day.

ME: Why?

BEAST: Because Nev has a DATE with a BOY and she's going to the movies with HIM. Apparently you knew all about this and promised to chaperone her.

I smirk at my screen.

ME: Tell her to text me the time and place and I'll be there. And tell her I'll sit in the back.

BEAST: Can't believe you knew!

ME: Can't believe you're freaked out about it.

BEAST: She's twelve.

ME: She's almost thirteen. Besides, it's just a movie.

BEAST: It's a dark room.

I bet he's pacing his bedroom like a wild creature.

ME: They keep it that way so you can see the screen better.

I add a smiley face.

BEAST: Funny.

ME: I try. Anyway, don't worry. I'll make sure it all stays very PG. I'll text you hourly updates.

He doesn't respond, which is a little rude. He could've at least thanked me. He's probably not feeling very thankful.

I debate changing his name in my phone, but don't because it makes me smile. Probably wouldn't make him smile . . .

A couple of minutes later, Nev shoots me a text.

NEV: I have a date!

ME: I heard.

NEV: What should I wear?

I suggest a couple of different outfits. She snaps pics of herself in them. We finally agree on denim shorts paired with a hoodie (so Ten doesn't completely flip). Plus they keep the movie theater at icebox temperatures. After Nev sends me the showtime, I call Rae to ask if she wants to come with me, but she's meeting Harrison's parents. I text Laney next. She's out of town, but tells me she'll be back in the early afternoon on Sunday if I want to wait for her to go then. I explain I have yoga with Mom on Sundays. Laney asks me where and then says she'll try to come with her mother. I feel like I've just organized a Mommy-and-me play-date. But why not? I don't think Mom knows Laney's mother. Maybe she can become a new source of available men for the woman who keeps insisting there are no eligible good men left.

I take a cab to the mall because I forgot to ask Mom for a lift. If I wait for her to return from the gym, I'll miss the opening credits—I plan on watching both Nev and the movie. When I get there, I race up the mall escalator to the Cineplex. I don't see Nev in the ticket line. I text her that I'm here.

"Here," a gruff voice says, shoving a ticket between my phone screen and my eyes.

I look up so fast I give myself whiplash—okay, that's an exaggeration, but my neck definitely creaked. "Ten! What are you doing here?"

A nerve tics in his taut jaw. "Nev needed a ride to her *date*. Since I was here, I decided to stay."

After the shock of seeing him dwindles, I take the ticket from him and then dig out my wallet.

"Angie, please, it's a movie ticket."

I sense he's too on edge for me to argue, so I offer to get popcorn and drinks, which he accepts. "Want butter?"

He shakes his head.

I get him a large bucket and get myself one with extra butter. He eyes the shiny kernels.

"I can sense the chef in you cringing at all the artificial flavor," I tease.

"I didn't say anything."

"You don't have to. It's written all over your face. You have a very expressive face. Probably to make up for not being all that great at expressing yourself with words."

"What?"

"Don't look so shocked. You're not exactly the glibbest person. Unless you're mad. Then you have plenty to say."

"Any more nice stuff to point out about my personality?" he mutters.

I elbow him in the ribs. "You're not hurt, are you?"

He side-eyes me. "It takes way more to hurt my feelings." He opens the door to the theater for me.

As I climb the stairs, I look for Nev. Ten gestures to a bobbing baseball cap in one of the middle rows. I try to get a better look at Nev's date, but all I see is that he's blond and has a swooping lock of hair across his forehead.

I choose the highest row to give them as much privacy as possible.

"Could you have chosen a farther spot?" Ten asks, settling in the seat beside me.

I smile. "I could've chosen a seat in the front row, but I decided to spare your neck a kink."

He tries to get comfortable, which is apparently a feat for someone with long legs.

Sensing he's wound up as tight as my baby grand's strings, I whisper, "Relax."

"Not gonna happen."

"Ten, you're only hurting yourself."

He grumbles something, but since he tossed a handful of popcorn into his mouth, I don't get what he's saying.

A third of the way through the movie, he leans forward. "Are they holding hands?"

When he starts to stand, I yank on the hem of his zip-up hoodie, and he drops back down.

"Stop," I command him in a low voice.

He harrumphs, then rests one ankle on his opposite knee and begins to shake his leg.

I wipe the popcorn crumbs off my fingers, then clap his pulsating leg. That makes him freeze. It also makes me freeze, because I've never touched a boy's thigh, and although this isn't a date, it's Ten. I have weird chemistry with this guy. I snatch my hand away and dig back into my bucket.

He uncrosses his legs and sinks lower into his chair, which makes his legs flop open.

I try to concentrate on the movie, but the side of his knee brushes my leg. I shovel popcorn quicker into my mouth, then try to angle my body away from his, but the boy doesn't have normal-sized limbs.

He shifts again, and again his knee sidles against my thigh. I swipe my water bottle from the armrest and chug most of it down, hoping it will cool me off. It helps a little. That is, until the hero and heroine make out on-screen. Then every inch of skin that Ten is unintentionally touching burns hot.

Ten leans toward me. "Only a dude hoping to score would take a girl to see this piece of crap."

"He's a smart kid, then. I'd totally fall for a guy who'll sit through a chick flick with me," I volley back.

Ten goes rigid, seemingly appalled by my confession.

I go back to watching the movie but have trouble enjoying it what with his unrelenting twitching. Seriously, he's worse than a tweaker.

I lean toward him. "Why don't you go hike around the mall or something? I'll text you when the movie's over."

He stills, looks at me, eyes incandescent in the glow of the screen. "I'm fine."

"Yeah, right."

He rams his hands into his zip-up fleece's pockets and glues his spine to the backrest, doing his best not to move. I can tell it's an effort from the tension crimping his brow. This is torture for him.

For some reason, that makes me grin. And then I'm laughing, and it's really inappropriate, because someone's just died in the movie. I garner many unhappy glares from the people sitting in the row in front of us, but my uncontrollable giggling loosens Ten up, so it's worth it, if just for that.

He slings his arm around the back of my seat. "If you don't calm down, you'll get us kicked out. And I want to know what happens next."

"What happens next? Have you even been following the story line?"

He stares at me so intently that I sober up. "Maybe I'm not talking about the movie."

My stomach feels as though it's been beamed right out of my body to make more room for my expanding heart.

Ten tips his head toward where Nev and her date are sitting.

He wasn't talking about *us*.

My stomach resurfaces, heavy with popcorn and disappointment.

I turn toward the screen and spend the rest of the movie pretending to be absorbed by the plot when I have no clue what the heck's going on anymore. Even though Ten doesn't lean toward me again, his arm stays locked on the back of my seat, radiating warmth and his salt-and-spice scent.

The worst part is that I don't even think he realizes it's there, while I can't think of *anything* else.

45

Humans Aren't Reeds

"I dreamed of spring rolls all night. No joke," Laney says over lunch on Monday.

She and her mother ended up coming to yoga and Golden Dragon with me and Mom yesterday, because Laney's father was out of town at a real estate convention.

"Did your mom join the book club yet?" Rae asks.

Laney mops up the extra oil on her pizza with a paper napkin. "Jade invited her."

"Get ready to hear your mom speak of *only* that." Rae twirls the ends of her blonde hair. "I swear, it's like a cult."

"You think we'll have a book club when we're old, Rae?" I ask her.

"Gonna be hard fitting a book club in between all your tour dates." I shove my shoulder into hers.

Rae grins at me. "Did you send in your recording yet?"

"Not yet."

"What are you waiting for?" Laney asks, up to speed on everything thanks to Mom, who dropped the subject of my musical prowess in between the dumplings and the Peking duck.

To say I was surprised would be the greatest understatement of the year.

"I'm waiting for Mom to sign the form." I twist my straw in my juice box. "She said she would."

"Oh my God! She did?" Rae all but screeches.

Grinning, I nod.

"Your recording for what?" Mel asks, dropping her lunch tray on our table.

Laney looks up from her pizza. "The Mona Stone contest."

I flick my gaze to Ten's table, where now sit Bolt and Archie. For someone who didn't want to fit in, he's fitting in. Which has me thinking about his boarding school application. He said he wouldn't go, but it's easy to say you won't do something until you have the option to do it.

"I'm so happy for you, hon! Yay!" Rae's still sort of screaming. "Hey. Totally unrelated question."

I drain my juice box. "Yeah?"

"Are we too old to go trick-or-treating?"

I give a little snort. "Yes, but when has that stopped us?"

"I *love* trick-or-treating," Laney chirps.

Mel, who looks more tanned than when school started, asks, "Are you guys serious?"

"Deadly serious. Or is it *deathly* serious?" Laney asks.

"It's *deadly*," Rae replies. "Deathly means cadaverous, grim."

"Mel, do you realize how lucky we are? We have a future superstar and valedictorian at our lunch table," Laney says.

"Who's going to be valedictorian?" Jasper drops onto the chair next to Mel and nuzzles her neck, which makes her giggle.

I didn't expect them to last.

Laney points across the table. "Rae, duh."

Rae grins, but then tears her paper napkin into tiny particles. "Maybe not. Ron Wilkins is extremely smart."

"Not as smart as you, Rae." Laney pats her hand. "Hey, Angie, didn't you say you would let us listen to your song?"

I glare at her for tossing me under the bus, which just makes her smile broaden, because she knows my glares are all bark and no bite.

"What song?" Jasper filches the pudding from Mel's tray. "You're not going to eat that, right?"

Mel shakes her head at the same time Laney says, "Angie's entering the Mona Stone contest."

"No friggin' way!" Jasper slurps down the pudding.

My cheeks grow as hot as the cafeteria's plate warmers.

"Conrad, you gotta sing it for us!" Even though Jasper's words are garbled by pudding, people at other tables have turned to see what the commotion's about.

I sink low in my chair because one of those people is Ten.

The cheerleading twins, who were walking toward the jock section, pause by our table in perfect synchronicity. "Are you guys talkin' about Mona Stone's contest?" one of them asks real shrilly.

The other adds, "Our brother and his band are signing up for it."

"Angie, we've been friends for how long now?" Jasper asks. "Ten years? Eleven?"

Mel sits up a little straighter.

"That should earn us first dibs on hearing your tune," he says.

"Uh." I bite my lower lip. "I'm not allowed to let people hear it until after the contest."

"Are you sure? Our brother's band has been performin' their song all over the state," Samantha says. Or maybe it's Valentina. They don't only look the same, they also sound the same.

I long to drag over one of the potted palms and hide behind it for the rest of the day.

One of the twins has pulled out her cell phone. She hits PLAY, and a melody heavy with electric guitar blasts from the speaker. "They're good, aren't they?"

Ten has just slotted his tray on the metal shelves a couple of feet from where I sit. For the briefest of seconds, our eyes connect, and I can swear I see his glimmer with hurt.

Crap. Crap. Crap.

"So? What do you think, Angie?" Sam or Val asks me.

My pulse is strumming too hard inside my ears for me to hear much more than the instrumental twang. The song could be good, like it could be awful. I have no clue.

A hand squeezes my knee. Rae's. *You okay?* she mouths.

I gulp.

Laney's brow furrows as she looks between me and the cafeteria entrance. After a couple of seconds, her forehead smooths as though she's figured it out.

I touch the little arrow speared through the cartilage of my ear. Twist it. Twist it.

"So? What do you think?" the twin asks me again.

"It's good." I press my palm against my stomach, suddenly feeling queasy.

I inhale calming breaths. I'm having a panic attack from the overload of attention. Or am I having a panic attack from Ten's reaction to the news of me entering his mother's contest? Whatever the reason, I'm definitely panicking, and the fact that everyone in a one-mile radius is gaping at me is *not* helping.

Rae pulls me up so suddenly she almost dislocates my shoulder. "Angie, we totally forgot to finish that project for Mrs. Rainlin!"

I blink at her.

"I need to get my notes from my locker," she says.

It takes my frazzled mind a second to comprehend she's giving me an exit. I want to hug her, but instead I breathe in, breathe out, breathe in, breathe out. Once we're in the hallway, I run to the bathroom and reach a toilet just in time to throw up.

Rae holds my hair back, strokes my neck, says soothing things I can't hear over the anxiety whooshing around my skull.

I finally sit back on my heels, and tears leak out of my eyes. I want to tell her about Ten and Mona, but instead I whisper, "How am I supposed to do this, Rae?"

"How long have you wanted this, hon?"

"Forever." Which is way longer than I've wanted Ten's friendship . . . or whatever it is I want from him. If I renege on my dreams for a boy, then I become the sort of girl I despise—the sort willing to fold herself into another person's ideal.

People who bend too far run the risk of breaking. After all, we aren't reeds; we're made of bones and dreams, not chloroplasts and sunlight.

"Look, if I thought you sucked I wouldn't encourage you," Rae says.

"How do you know I don't suck?"

"Because I've heard you sing."

I snap up my neck to look at her. "When?"

"Last year. I was picking you up to go to the mall, and your mom told me to go on up to your room, and you were belting out some P!nk song in the shower. I remember standing beside your stack of records and being floored by what I was hearing, but I knew you'd hate it if you caught me eavesdropping, so I left the minute the water turned off." She crouches beside me, clasps one of my hands in hers. "You got this, Angie."

But she's wrong. I don't have anything yet, besides foul breath and an empty stomach.

Her eyes suddenly get this glint that makes my insides flop.

"What?"

"Nothing," she says, but she's biting back a smile, so I know she's thinking something, and that worries the heck out of me.

"You're not planning on making me sing over the PA system, are you?"

She slaps a hand over her chest. "I would never do such a thing, Angela Conrad."

"You swear?"

"Cross my heart."

And although I trust her not to do that, I don't trust her not to do something equally terrifying. Rae's life philosophy has always been about facing your demons, and what greater demon do I have than singing in public?

46

The Squeak of Bluebirds

"Lynn's singing at the Bluebird tonight," Steffi tells me as she folds a metal chair and rests it against the wall. "It would mean a lot if you came."

The Bluebird sounds like the perfect thing to get my mind off the emotional roller coaster I've been riding since the incident in the cafeteria. At the end of that horrid day, I got up the nerve to corner Ten and tell him, "I'm not doing this to spite you." He barely acknowledged me and hasn't talked to me since.

"I'll be there," I tell Steffi as I clamber up the stairs of the dance studio.

"I'll email you a ticket!"

I pedal home in record time, shower, and change into black combat boots, fake suede shorts, and a white T-shirt with a black, loopy rendering of a guitar. After swiping on mascara and coating my lips in red lipstick, I blow my mom a kiss and get back on my bike to head to the Bluebird.

The place is busy as always. Butterflies swarm my stomach as I take in the lively crowd, the framed celebrity pictures on the walls, the tangle of string lights over the bar. There's something about this place. Maybe it's the floorboards that have been trod upon by some of the biggest music celebrities, or maybe it's the mics that have been filled with some of the greatest voices, or maybe it's because the Bluebird is where Mona Stone got her start. Whatever it is, this place is magic to me.

Steffi and Lynn wait at a table set for five. I wonder who else they've invited. Another couple probably. I walk over and slip into the seat closest to Lynn.

"Thank you for getting me in!"

They each have a glass of wine in front of them. Lynn's is almost empty.

"Don't tell me you're nervous?" I ask her.

She tips her glass of wine to her maroon-tinted lips and chugs the dregs.

"Every time." Steffi rubs her wife's wrist, then links their hands together.

"Who else is coming?" I ask just as the front door bursts open.

Rae and Laney wave to us and then they're sitting down. My gaze whips around the table, not quite understanding what I'm seeing. I keep expecting Lynn to tell them the chairs are saved.

I sit up straighter, my shoulder blades pinching. "How come you— How do you—"

"Steffi invited us," Laney says.

I frown.

"Dance classes," Laney explains. "Believe it or not, I've *never* been here, and we got to talking about it yesterday during my lesson, and Steffi told me to come check it out, that you'd be here, but I'd already made plans with Rae—"

"—so I invited myself along," Rae says.

It sounds like such a tall tale that I look at Steffi for validation. She sips on her wine, exchanges a look with Lynn, then sets her glass down. I think that look's about me, but then she's reaching for Lynn's hand and saying, "Honey, you're amazing. You'll blow them away. Like you always do." Which has me realizing how selfish I am for assuming the look was about me.

"Were you planning on telling me you were coming?" I ask Rae.

A grin overtakes every inch of her face. "We wanted to surprise you."

"Are you surprised?" Laney asks.

My rigid stance finally loosens. "Very."

Laney reaches for one of the menus in the middle of the table. "I'm starving."

"So you're opening, Lynn?" Rae asks, and it's weird because both hold such an important place in my life, but to my knowledge this is the first time they're meeting.

I toy with the edge of the menu, listening in rapt silence as they talk. I don't hang on their every word; I simply observe them. For some odd reason, I'm a little nervous, but as the ice breaks, I begin to relax.

Steffi orders for the table—spinach dip, mozzarella breadsticks, nachos, sweet potato fries, and chicken quesadillas. My stomach rumbles happily at the sound of all that food. And then my heart rumbles too, because I'm in one of my favorite places, with a lot of my favorite people, and it's so unconceivable, yet completely real.

The only person missing is Nev. She would've loved to be here. But then my gaze snags on a framed, autographed Mona Stone picture, and I reconsider. This place is her mother's temple.

"Good evening, folks!" The manager asks for quiet and then: "I'd like to welcome a Bluebird favorite to open up for the Moon Junkies tonight. Please give a warm welcome to *Lynn Landry!*"

The band's name sounds familiar, and yet I'm not sure where I've heard it before.

"Isn't that the band that played at homecoming?" Rae asks.

That's it!

Lynn settles behind the keyboard set up in the middle of the room, then pushes her orange hair back. "How y'all doin' tonight?" Her jazzy voice fills the room.

Great mingles with the scrape of chair legs as diners angle themselves around Lynn.

She smiles at the crowd, and then her fingers glide over the keyboard. "Ever heard of a singer named Roberta Flack?"

Yeses arise as she plays the opening chords of "Killing Me Softly."

"I thought so."

The crowd settles as she begins singing the old hit. Her voice is as thick as syrup, and hazy around the edges like fog. Lynn never became a star. I'm not sure if this was by choice or because she was never in the right place at the right time.

At the bar, I behold a familiar face—a dark-haired boy with made-up blue eyes. The lead singer of the Moon Junkies. Like the rest of the audience, he watches Lynn with rapt attention.

After she finishes, the room erupts in applause. She nods and smiles. "For my next song, I wanted to play you something a student of mine wrote. She's actually here with me tonight."

Heads swivel. There's no spotlight shining on me, and Lynn didn't point me out, yet I feel like *everyone's* staring at me. I sink low in my seat.

Real low.

"Angie, you might hate me for this, but I'd really like it if you joined me out here and performed it with me," Lynn says.

Heat engulfs me. I start shaking my head, but people clap.

Rae pinches my arm. "Surprise!"

I whip my face toward her; she's smiling.

"I'm going to kill you," I hiss.

"Fine, but wait till after you sing. And try to avoid puking." Rae literally shoves me off my chair, so I have no other choice than to stand.

Laney starts clapping, and then more people join in.

Oh my God oh my God oh my God.

Once I'm standing there's no sitting back down.

Crap. Crap. Crap.

I paste on a bright smile even though all I want to do is crawl underneath the table.

The crowd bellows my name.

I'm going to murder Rae. Lynn and Laney, too. *And* Steffi. None of them will get out alive.

I thread through tables, resisting the urge to fan my cheeks.

Lynn makes me sit beside her and squeezes my knee lightly. I swallow and swallow, and yet can't seem to stanch my production of saliva—my glands are in overdrive. What if I open my mouth and drool?

"The song's called 'Made,'" Lynn says. "Ready?"

Even though my heart palpitates from my collarbone down to my toes, I nod.

"You got this, Angie!" Rae's voice cuts across the room.

Trembling, I lock eyes with her. I hate her for doing this to me even though I know her heart is in the right place. This time when I swallow, it doesn't feel like I'm about to drown in my own spit or regurgitate an organ.

"One. Two. Three." The melody rises from underneath Lynn's fingers.

The instrumental opening offers me a couple more seconds of respite. But then, it's time to sing. I open my mouth, and like in my absolute *worst* nightmares, I squeak.

A shrill.

Loud.

Mousy.

Squeak.

Without missing a beat, Lynn repeats the opening.

Tears pool behind my lashes.

At our table, Laney's mouth moves. I think she's trying to offer me silent encouragement. I look into one of the burning spotlights, then open my mouth and my voice springs out.

I don't sound like myself, but I don't halt. Lynn joins her voice to mine. I think of the man with the ten octaves, and then I picture my mother clapping and my nerves begin to quiet, and by the time we reach the chorus, I've managed to harness my nervousness. My voice has grown sturdier, but it's still not as steady as I'd like it to be. My diaphragm pulsates as my voice bursts around me, pools and curls through the air like steam. At some point, I realize Lynn has stopped singing.

I'm on my own.

I almost flounder again, but Rae is swiping at her cheeks, and for some reason, her tears thread confidence through my backbone, lend energy to my lungs. I sit up straighter, loosen my jaw, and make it through the rest of the song without a single mistake. When the last notes fade, Rae, Laney, and Steffi jump to their feet and cheer louder than everyone else in the room.

And there is cheering.

People are clapping.

For me.

Lynn clasps my hand and lifts it as though I've just won a boxing match.

"Can't believe you just did that to me . . ." I whisper.

She winks. "Angela Conrad, folks. Remember that name. You're going to be hearing it. A lot!"

As I return to my seat, two people stop me to say how impressed they were with my performance. Energy crackles through my veins, detonates inside my head, blurs the noise surrounding me. I can barely hear the new tune Lynn is singing.

Rae hugs me hard. "That. Was. Amazing. I am so proud of you, girl." She's choking me with her hug, but I admit, it feels good.

I feel good.

After she releases me and I fall into my chair, Laney leans over and whispers, "Wow."

"Really?" I squeak.

She smiles. "I'm *deadly* serious. Right, Rae? Deadly?"

Rae grins. "Right."

We don't talk again until the end of Lynn's set. As soon as it's over, though, Laney asks me if that was the song I wrote for Mona Stone's contest. I nod. And Rae says that it isn't fair to everyone else competing, because there's no way they can win now, and I roll my eyes.

"How did it feel?" Steffi asks.

I reach for my glass of bubbly water, but my limbs are trembling so much it takes me two attempts to close my fingers around it and lift it to my mouth. "Horrible and amazing."

Steffi sips her wine with a smile.

There's a break between the sets. A waitress brings our food. Lynn and Steffi get up to socialize, while Rae, Laney, and I stuff our faces. Mostly me. The other two are too busy gushing about how cute the lead singer of the Moon Junkies is.

"Setting the bar high for us, Angela Conrad."

I almost choke on my food when I spot the boy in question standing over our table, kohl-lined blue eyes mirroring the smile on his lips.

He extends his hand to me. "I'm Ty."

I shake his hand, and then he extends it to Rae and Laney. Laney tells him how good they sounded at homecoming, while Rae, who's never tongue-tied, doesn't utter a single word. She just stares and shakes his hand.

"How long you been singin'?" he asks.

"Since I was thirteen," I tell him.

"And you wrote that? Music and all?"

"I did."

"Real impressive."

My heart crackles. Ty might not be as famous as Mona Stone, but he's somewhat famous, and he thinks my song was impressive.

Can a person die of bliss?

"I don't think so," he says, and I assume Rae's asked him a question, but he's looking at me.

I raise my palm to my lips.

Not.

Again.

Ty smiles. "After my first performance, I was surfin' on one hell of a high too. Anyway, I'll be lookin' out for your name." He winks at us, black lashes swooping over his ocean-bright eyes, and then makes his way toward his bandmates.

"He's way hotter up close," Rae says.

Laney shakes her head. "Hey, fangirl, we're here for Angie."

"I was just lookin'. No harm in that." Rae gets up. "I'll be right back."

Laney and I both eye her, both expecting her to go ask Ty for an autograph, but she heads to the bathroom instead.

Laney picks up a quesadilla. "He's her son, isn't he?"

"Her son? Whose son?"

"Ten. He's Mona's son, isn't he?" I must turn pale, because Laney nods slowly.

"You can't tell anyone, Laney."

"I won't."

"Does Rae know?"

"No. The only reason I put two and two together is because he got antsy yesterday in the caf when he caught wind of Mona's contest, and back before school started, my father mentioned something about selling a house to the kids and ex-husband of a really famous singer." Laney cuts her quesadilla into bite-sized triangles. "What does he think about you entering the contest?"

"We haven't talked about it." I wince. "He probably hates me."

"I'm sure he doesn't . . ."

I grip my water glass, fingers still unsteady but no longer from my performance. "How could he not? He *hates* her."

"You're not her."

But I want to be her.

For the first time in a while, I hope Ten gets accepted to boarding school. I hope he leaves. I don't think I can take more looks like the ones he leveled at me earlier. Out of all the boys in Nashville, why did I have to fall for him?

47

Cheese Balls and Osso Buco

However much I tried to enjoy the Moon Junkies' set last night, their songs propelled me back to homecoming, and homecoming made me think of Ten.

It was still one heck of a night.

It's been almost twenty-four hours since my big moment, and I still can't get over it.

I text Rae and Laney that. We have a group chat now that Rae's been filling with pictures of Ty Munder, and Laney and me with GIFs of people rolling their eyes. Mel's not part of the chat.

A new message appears on my phone.

NEV: Hey!

ME: Hey back.

NEV: Can you come over?

I don't answer right away, because her house is Ten's, and I doubt he wants me to come hang out.

NEV: I really need to see you. ☹

ME: What happened?!?

She doesn't answer for so long that I dial her number. It goes to voice mail.

ME: Nev?

NEV: I don't want to talk about it over the phone. Please come.

As I type *I'll be right over*, I jolt off my bed like a pole-vaulter, and then I'm careening down the stairs, yelling to Mom, who's working on the layout of a restaurant she's been hired to decorate, that I'm going over to Nev's.

"Everything okay?" she asks.

"Just boy stuff," I say, hoping I'm right, hoping the mean girls aren't after Nev again.

Even though my legs want to carry me in every other direction than toward the Dylans' house, I bike over. When I ease to a stop in front of their gate, there isn't a car in sight. I feel momentarily relieved that Ten isn't home, but then I worry harder for Nev. She's such a sensitive girl . . .

I push the gate's call button and unfasten my helmet. After a couple of rings, the gate swings open. I stride up the path with my bike, thrust out the kickstand, then hurry into the house through the front door that's been left ajar.

"Nev!" I holler into the dimly lit foyer.

She doesn't answer. I'm about to run up the stairs when my white sneaker connects with a piece of balled paper. I pick it up and toss it onto the foyer table, but then I notice more balled-up papers littering the hallway. I seize one and unfold it.

"Nev?" I spot the words *Arcadia Prep* on the top of the page. I scan the rest of the sheet quickly. It's Tennessee's acceptance letter from that New England boarding school.

This must be the source of her glumness. I sigh because at least no one—not the stupid girls in her school or Charlie—has hurt her.

"Nev?" This time when she doesn't answer, I add, "Where are you?"

I follow the trail of balled-up papers all the way to the kitchen. I'm expecting to find Nev at the end of it, eyes puffy with tears because her beloved brother chose to leave. What I'm not expecting to find is her beloved brother.

He stands by the stovetop, stirring something in a big pot. Perfumed steam drifts up, fogging his chiseled profile.

I freeze in the arched entryway.

Why is he here?

"I live here too, remember?"

I slap my palm over my mouth. I should be rendered mute in stress-ful situations.

There's music on in the kitchen. Not just music. Elvis's "Can't Help Falling in Love." Ten is playing one of my favorite love songs—not that he's aware of this—and cooking a meal.

"Are you cooking for someone?" I ask.

I don't say the word *date*, but I obviously don't mean Bolt or Archie. Ten wouldn't be playing sappy love songs for his track buddies. I'm surprised he's even playing sappy love songs in the first place. Besides, there are only two place settings on the granite island.

When he nods, my heart triples in volume. If I don't get out of here fast, it'll balloon right out of me, then pop.

"I'm looking for Nev," I say.

He doesn't tell me where to find her.

I place a hand on the archway, about to turn away to search the rest of the house for her, but because I'm masochistic, I say, "You got into boarding school."

Ten sets down the wooden spatula and walks over to me. He plucks the paper out of my limp fingers. "I did."

There's a lump in my throat the size of Tennessee, and I mean the state. "And Nev's upset."

"Very."

"Is that why she . . . ?" I gesture to the trail of balled papers.

"Wasn't Nev."

"Your dad did this?"

He snorts gently. "No. All me."

"*You*—Why?"

He stares down at me. "Because I'm not going."

"Oh." I bite my lip, look behind me at the paper trail, then back at Ten.

"And you decided to celebrate your decision with a paper-ball fight?"

His lips curve slightly. "Wasn't a fight. Fights need at the very least two participants, and no one else was involved."

Two . . . My gaze darts back to the place settings before lowering to the floor. "I should go. Is Nev in her bedroom?"

Fingers grip my chin, lift my face. "Nev's not here, Angie."

My swollen heart thumps against my ribs. "But she told me—"

"What I asked her to tell you." His amber irises become blurry smears of color as my eyes mist over.

Mini fists squeeze each one of my organs. "Is this your idea of getting back at me for entering your mother's contest, Ten?"

He frowns.

I gesture to the place settings. "Making me witness a date?" Slow tears spill out. I back away from him and wipe my face.

"Angie?" Ten steps toward me. "You *are* my date."

I stop scrubbing the wet trails from my cheeks.

"I assumed you wouldn't come over if I asked you after"—he rubs his earlobe—"after I shut you out, so I told Nev to text you something to make you come over, and since she owed me for her movie date, she agreed."

A rough, masculine voice trickles through the hidden ceiling speakers. *Say that you don't want me, say that you don't need me, tell me I'm the fool.* I close my eyes for a moment and absorb the music, let it center me. When I open them, Ten is staring down at me, worry lancing his jaw.

"I thought you were never going to talk to me again," I croak.

He shifts his gaze to the darkness beyond the window. "Angie, my mother is a moot point for me. She's ruined so much, but I don't want to let her ruin *this*." He points to me, then to himself. "If I step away from you because of her, then I let her win. And I don't want her to win."

"So you want to be with me to one-up your mom?"

He returns his gaze to mine. "I want to be with you because you're like an earworm, Angie. You're *all* I can think about. I might even need to get new friends, because Bolt and Archie are tired of hearing about you."

I let his words sink in, but they don't. They just float there, in the air between us. "I suppose you thought that because I love music I might find your analogy romantic, but it contains the word *worm*, so"—I wrinkle my nose, even though I'm not truly grossed out *or* mad—"yuck."

He laughs, and that gets a grin out of me.

And a confession. "Try as I might, you're always running on a loop inside my brain too."

His laughter transforms into a grin. "Look who's spurting out analogies now."

I smile, but then I don't. Then I cross my arms because I'm suddenly nervous.

Ten scratches the back of his neck, and then he shifts. He's nervous too. "*So* . . . do you want to try this?"

"By *this*, you mean whatever's in that pan?"

His lips quirk up and down and then back up. "Among other things."

"I could eat." Actually, I probably can't. Not with all those butterflies flapping inside me.

He steps a little closer. "I wasn't really talking about food."

My arms loosen, fall to my sides. "I wasn't really either."

His hand rises to the back of my neck, hovers before settling. Slowly, he tilts my face up. And then his eyes are on mine, and his mouth's a breath away. I wrap my arms around his neck and then I press up on tiptoe to bridge the chasm between us.

His lips open mine gently, as though he doesn't want to frighten me, and then one of his arms slides around my waist, presses me closer. All of him is rigid except his mouth.

His mouth is heartbreakingly soft.

His tongue darts out, touches mine, and I tighten my arms around his neck. His teeth clatter against mine, and his stubble chafes my jaw, but he's still not close enough. I'm not the only one thinking this, because he scoops me up. I gasp, but he swallows up my surprise. I hook my legs around his waist as he walks over to the sapphire island, where he deposits me as though I were made of glass and air instead of flesh and songs. I tug him closer, and still he isn't close enough.

After a long, long time, he eases his lips off mine. "I thought you were going to run out on me."

The sound of his hoarse voice sends goose bumps skittering over every inch of my skin. "Whatever you were cooking smelled too good to run from," I whisper. I *totally* considered running.

He chuckles, and it's the sexiest sound anyone on the entire planet has ever made. And then he imprisons my mouth again. If he keeps kissing me, keeps tugging on my lips, tongue, teeth, he's going to drag my heart right out of my chest. After another delicious moment, he rests his forehead against mine, runs his large palms over my jean-clad thighs.

"I was so afraid you'd leave," I whisper.

His jaw is flushed, and his lips swollen. "In all seriousness . . . between Nev and you, how could I?"

Nev! Ten's kisses made me forget other humans walked this earth. I jerk my face toward the kitchen entrance and press my palms into his chest to put a little distance between us. "Where *is* Nev?"

"She went out to dinner with Dad."

"So we're alone?"

His eyes shine as though dipped in glitter. "Yes. I suspect we have another hour before they get home. I told her to keep Dad out of the house as long as possible."

"She had me so worried with that text of hers."

He cups my jaw and just stares at me. Correction. Stares *into* me. His fingers trail down the sides of my throat, gather my hair, and push it off my neck. He kisses a spot below my earlobe, and I shiver. How is he so good at kissing? I wish the answer was that he was born that way, but I'm unfortunately not that naive. He's had training. Can he tell I haven't?

"Where's your car?"

"In the shop." His words are a little muffled.

"You got into an accident?"

"No."

"Did you finally trade it in for a bicycle?" I tease.

He chuckles as he pulls away from my neck. "It's getting outfitted with a bike rack. Don't know if you heard, but Nev got Dad to buy her a bike."

I smile.

"Plus"—his voice is both sweet and coarse—"I can't have my girl-friend turning down rides with me because her bike doesn't fit in my trunk."

My pulse roars in my ears. *Who is this boy?* "Stop. You're going to ruin me for all other men."

He shoots me that perfect, half-tipped grin of his. He thinks it's a joke, but it's not.

My stomach suddenly growls so loudly, it drowns out the music. Ten pulls me down from my perch and tugs me toward the stovetop to stir our meal again. I'm surprised my legs hold me up since they feel like Twizzlers.

"Can't believe you cooked for me. Can't believe you cook period." I sniff the pot's simmering contents.

"Osso buco alla Milanese with homemade fettucine," he announces.

"Are you for real?"

"I can't sing for my life, but I can cook. Or so I'm told."

I smile stupidly up at him. And then I don't smile anymore because I feel like crying all over again. I thread my hands through his spiky hair and drag his head back down to mine. Before my lips touch his, I say, "Thank you for tonight . . . and for staying . . . and for not making me choose."

"Choose?"

"Between your mom and you."

His expression turns a little grave, but then he kisses the corner of my lips. "I like you more than I hate her. Go figure. I just hope that someday, you'll like me better than her."

My heart squeezes and squeezes. What I feel for Ten is so different from what I feel for Mona.

He whispers, "I shouldn't have brought her up."

But he did. And now all I can think about is her. "Ten . . ."

"Here and now. Let's just enjoy the here and now."

"Okay," I whisper, as he drags his lips over mine.

If he can push Mona out of this moment, then so can I.

But I can't.

How can a stranger hold so much power over me?

This perfect evening with Ten becomes bittersweet, because it feels like borrowed time.

Here and now, I remind myself. *Here and now.*

48

The Clashing Stones

As Mom and I walk into the Landmark Hotel the next morning, I check my appearance on my phone's camera app, afraid I might be glowing like a white shirt under blue light. Besides pink cheeks and a hickey that I've camouflaged with concealer, I look normal. Okay, that's a lie. My eyes are so shiny they seem greener, and the dimple on my chin looks more pronounced.

"Sorry I agreed to this brunch without asking you," Mom says softly.

"It's fine, Mom." In truth, I'm crazy nervous. I haven't told her about Ten. Did Ten tell his dad about me?

The Dylans are already seated at a round table when we arrive. I shake Jeff's hand, then casually wave to Nev as I lower myself into the seat next to Ten. When Ten drapes his arm on the back of my chair, my spine locks tight and I lean forward.

Jeff eyes Ten's arm, then eyes me. And so does Mom, but neither says anything. Impulsively, I palm my throat, the spot with the hidden hickey, and keep my hand there.

Ten leans toward me and whispers, "Relax."

I jerk and knock over my water glass.

Ten smirks and so does Nev. As a waiter sops up my mess, I jiggle my knee. Ten clasps it, but his touch has the inverse effect of calming me. I brush his fingers off before my mother, who's sitting next to me, can see them.

A few minutes later, as Jeff tells Mom a story about the naughtiest but cutest thing Nev did when she was three, Ten's hand returns to my leg. I angle my legs away from him, then cross them.

"If you don't stop," I whisper, "my next glass of water will end up in your lap, and it won't be an accident."

Ten has the audacity to chuckle. I'm dying, and he thinks it's funny. I feel hot and tug at the collar of my navy T-shirt.

"So I heard you decided to stay, Ten?" my mother says, as a waiter deposits a bread basket and a pitcher of coffee on the table. "What changed your mind?"

As I pour coffee into my cup, Nev asks her brother sweetly, "Yeah, whatever changed your mind?"

My hands jerk, and coffee splashes onto my lap. "Shoot."

When Ten grabs his napkin and rubs it against my thigh, I bang my knee into the table.

Cheeks on fire, I spring to my feet and mumble, "I'll be right back."

I can feel all four of them watching me as I make my way up the stairs to the bathroom, where I lock myself in a stall and bang my head gently against the door. "Oh, why did I agree to come?"

I should've faked a stomachache.

"You and me both, hon." A loud flush detonates from the stall next to mine.

Water runs in the sink. I flush even though I didn't pee, then walk out of the stall, and freeze.

My jaw drops a little. Okay . . . *a lot*.

The woman stares at me in the mirror without pausing in her application of red lipstick. Satisfied, she smacks her lips together. "Hi."

My mouth hasn't closed yet. I try to force it, but my mandible must be severed from the rest of my face.

The woman turns from the mirror. Her honey-brown hair is so shiny it's almost blinding. It flows in loose curls over a sheer seafoam blouse that makes her eyes look green . . . an illusion. Her eyes are topaz-colored like Ten's.

"Mona Stone," I blurt out breathily.

She cocks her head to the side the exact same way Ten does and observes me with eyes that are shaped like Nev's.

Nev, who's sitting downstairs.

I stare at the floor as though it suddenly became transparent, as though I'm going to find Ten and Nev and Jeff and my mom all peering up at us.

But then I jerk my gaze back up to Mona. Is she aware that her family's in the hotel? Is that why she's here . . . why she's talking to me?

"Didn't mean to startle you, hon." She smiles, her white teeth setting her face aglow.

The bathroom door snicks open, and I swing my attention toward it, terrified it's Nev or Mom, but it's a woman with messy brown curls wedged underneath a headpiece and purple-framed glasses sitting on her nose. "Mona, they're ready for you on set."

"On set?" I find myself asking. I can't believe I just talked.

Mona tucks a lock of hair behind one ear. Shiny rings wink from almost all her fingers. "I'm filmin' a new music video. Want to come watch?"

I blink at Mona. Is she testing the strength of my allegiance to the Dylans, or is she simply *that* kind? "I, uh . . ." I am *dying* to go, but Ten will *never* speak to me again. "I'm in the middle of brunch," I blurt out.

The assistant's eyebrows arch up so high they vanish underneath her mess of curls. I bet no one's ever turned down an invitation from Mona. I don't see why anyone in their right mind would. Or maybe she's surprised by Mona's casual invitation.

"Talkin' 'bout brunch, Mona . . ." The assistant glances at me. "D'you need the bathroom much longer?"

"Um. No. Just have to wash my hands." I lunge to one of the sinks and turn on the water.

"What about brunch, Kara?" Mona asks.

Her assistant lowers her voice, probably imagining I won't be able to hear her over the gushing water. "Your ex and children are here."

Mona's bronzed skin turns the color of wax. "Here?"

"They're having brunch downstairs." Kara glares my way.

I jerk my gaze to my hands, concentrating on creating the thickest layer of foam in the history of handwashing.

Kara says, "Good photo op."

I freeze.

I don't hear Mona's answer, but her thick hair shifts from left to right as she shakes her head no. I'm so relieved by her refusal that I let out a rapid breath. I turn off the tap and dry my hands.

Nev's hair is as thick as her mother's and almost the same shade, perhaps a tint darker than Mona's caramel brown.

Mona.

I still can't believe I'm standing so close to Mona Stone, sharing the same air. After I toss my hand towel in a wicker basket, I pinch myself to make sure I'm not dreaming.

Nope. Not a dream.

I want to stay longer, but unless I feign stomach cramps and rush back into a stall, I have to leave. As I pass by her, I finally find my voice. "Thank you, Mrs. Stone. For inviting me onto your set." *And for not agreeing to a photo op.*

Mona's no longer smiling, but I sense that has everything to do with her family being one floor below where she's standing.

"Bye, now," Kara singsongs as I finally leave.

I've never disliked someone instantly, but it's the case with Kara. As I return to the restaurant, I wonder if the people who work for big stars are all like her—disagreeable and calculating. But then I thrust Kara out of my mind and run through every millisecond of my encounter with Mona.

What stays with me is that she was thoughtful and empathetic, nothing like the uncaring monster Ten paints. But then his portrait of her is biased, and colored by grief.

I slide back into my seat.

"Manage to get the coffee out?" Jeff asks me.

The coffee! I forgot all about it. I stare down at my jeans, then back up at Jeff, and then at my half-full cup.

Ten nudges his elbow into my side.

I look up at him. His features are larger than his mother's, but the resemblance is so striking. How could I have missed it? It's not like he hides his face behind a curtain of hair like his sister.

"Are you feeling okay?"

"Uh." I swallow. "I think I might be coming down with something," I lie, my pulse twitching with guilt.

"Want me to drive you home?" he offers.

I want to say yes, but then I glance at Mom, whose brow is so ridged with concern that I swallow hard and shake my head. I don't want my weird behavior to reflect badly on her and affect her relationship with her client. "It'll pass."

But it doesn't pass.

I'm so quiet and distraught through the rest of the meal that I'm certain once Jeff finds out his son and I are dating, he'll advise Ten to dump me. The thought adds to the edgy energy short-circuiting my system.

Borrowed time.

49

The Devouring Melody

As we wait on the sidewalk for the valet to bring us our respective cars, Nev touches the sleeve of my wraparound sweater and cocks her head to the bloating crowd of rubberneckers on the other side of the street. "You think there's a celebrity staying at the hotel?"

My hands shake, but they're mostly covered by my knit sleeves, so I don't think Nev notices. Still, I inch them even farther up until only my nails are visible.

Ten sidles up next to me. "It's done."

My breath catches. "What's done?"

"Brunch with my dad. You survived."

Of course . . . That's what he thinks put me on edge. "And he'll never invite me after today. I was so spacey and a total klutz."

Ten has his hands stuffed inside his jean pockets, probably to stop himself from reaching for my hand. He tried during brunch.

"Want to go"—he shrugs—"do something?"

My pulse soars at his suggestion and incapacitates my brain from forming a verbal response. Glancing over Ten's shoulder to make sure our parents are not paying attention, I nod.

"Can I come too?" Nev asks. "Please . . . pretty please. I'll do anything." She presses her palms together and bats her eyelashes at her brother.

Ten glances at me over Nev's head as though to check if it's okay. Like I would ever exclude her . . .

"We could go bowling," I suggest.

"I *love* bowling!" Nev gushes.

I smile. "Do you like bowling, Ten?"

A small smile flicks his lips up. "Hope you're not the competitive type, Angie, because I've never lost a game."

"There's always a first time for everything," I answer sweetly.

Like a sunrise, the intensity of his smile turns up and up until it burns away my residual stress.

"Yay!" Nev slings her skinny arms around his waist.

"But after . . ." he murmurs. He points to me and then to himself, and my heart skips a long beat.

I give him a jerky nod.

"Hello. I'm right here," Nev says, body still attached to her brother's.

He pats her shoulder. "I can feel that, you little sloth."

She presses away from him and sticks her hands on her nonexistent hips. "I'm so not a sloth."

"You hang on like one," he says.

She scowls, but I don't think she's offended. "Would you call Angie a sloth if she hugged you all the time too?"

Ten's jaw turns the slightest shade of pink, which is nothing compared to the burgundy hue I'm surely sporting.

"Are you kids ready to—" Jeff's voice dies at the same time as a clamor rises from the opposite sidewalk.

Ten's body turns as stiff as marble.

"Jeff?" Mona gasps.

My shoulders jab together. I have my back to her, so she can't see me. Nev wheels around, eyes growing wider and wider. Even though the excitement on the other sidewalk is deafening, the silence engulfing the Dylans—or should I say, the Stones—is thick and tragic.

"Fancy runnin' into you here." Mona's surprised act has my spine hardening. "Nevada, you look—"

"Don't," Jeff cuts her off.

"Am I not allowed to compliment my children?"

A vein throbs in Jeff's temple. "Not here." He walks up to Nev, who's gazing at her mother as though she's some fantastical creature come to life, and hooks his arm around her bony shoulders, pulling her to his side. "You want to talk to them, you call me and we can arrange a meeting at the house," he says, his voice low and sharp.

Mona's answer doesn't come right away, but when it does, it's charged and vibrates like a scratched record. "I didn't think I was welcome."

Ten's eyes find mine. Every cell in my body is telling me to act startled that his mother's standing inches away from us, but that's not who I am. The leaves on the tree behind him flutter, dappling the concrete with beads of light that dance around his loosely tied royal-blue sneakers.

"Oh, come on. Don't give me that, Mona. We came back so you could see them more often. You haven't visited once!" Jeff spins toward a paparazzo and shoves his palm against the lens just as the shutter clicks.

"My schedule's been crazy, Jeff. I know my career's never meant a thing to you, but I'm loyal to my fans."

Ten's sneakers finally shift, start to back away. "Then go be with them, Mona. You've always preferred them to us anyway." His words punch the air so hard that his mother gasps.

"Ten!" Jeff snaps.

"What? It's the goddamn truth."

The paparazzo raises his camera and snaps a picture of Ten and Nev.

Jeff bumps his chest into the camera, forcing the man back, and growls, "If you sell a single picture of my kids, I will hunt you down and sue you for all you're worth. Now, back off!"

I finally look up. Ten's eyes have gone dark, as though his pupils have leaked into his irises.

"Ten, get in the car," Jeff says. "And take your sister."

Nev's lips begin to tremble. I can't tell if she wants to cry or protest. She does neither.

"You did a mighty fine job of turnin' my kids against me," Mona says, her honeyed voice quivering.

Anger streaks Jeff's face. "I said, *Not here*, Mona."

"Angie," my mother calls out to me softly. I unbind the soles of my boots from the pavement and stride over to her, and then I finally turn around.

Mona's eyes slip over Mom, then over me. There's no recognition. Am I so forgettable? It's such a silly, selfish thought considering the moment. Mom wraps her fingers around my arm and pulls me away.

I look back once and regret it, because Mona has tears in her eyes. My heart cracks for her. The encounter on the sidewalk might've been staged, but those tears look real.

Are they, though?

As I settle into Mom's Volvo, I dig my phone from my bag. There's a text from Ten. *You knew she was there.*

There's no question mark, but I still type back: *Yes.*

BEAST: Why didn't you tell me?

ME: I don't know.

I'm expecting a blameful message from him. Instead I get: *Sorry you had to witness that.*

No blame. I'm confused but relieved. I rub my forehead as I type back: *Are you guys OK?*

BEAST: I'm fine. Nev's . . . emotional.

"Still think she's such a great person, baby?" Mom asks.

I'm not sure what to think.

"I've changed my mind," she says. "I don't want you to enter her contest."

I pale. "You promised!"

My mother gives me a look that makes me want to jump out the passenger window and hike all the way home. "God, Angie, she hasn't visited her kids in the two months they've been here."

"She works a lot." Why am I making excuses for Mona? To sway Mom into letting me compete?

Mom slaps the steering wheel, and it triggers the horn. Thankfully we're no longer in front of the hotel. "I thought you liked Ten and Nev!"

"I do like them! But I also don't hate her. And I'm sorry if that makes you mad, but that's just the way it is."

Mom doesn't speak to me again during the entire drive home; I don't talk either. We'd just say hurtful things. Instead, I focus wholly on my conversation with Ten.

ME: Bowling?

BEAST: I wish. Things are too tense over here. Let me see if I can get away later.

Even though it's probably just my guilt talking, I ask: *You're really not mad at me?*

BEAST: Why would I be?

Because I don't hate your mother. I obviously don't send that. *Because I didn't tell you I saw her.*

BEAST: Did you ask her for an autograph?

ME: WHAT? No.

BEAST: Then I'm not mad. I'll call you later. Promise.

ME: K.

I start typing *Love you*, but erase the words immediately. Most of my conversations with Rae end that way. They're automatic, the same way people say *hey* or *bye*.

Can't believe I almost sent him *Love you*, though.

Once we get home, Mom vanishes into the kitchen while I go sit in front of the piano and play, and play. At some point, I sense Mom's presence, and I look at her. Her face is still pinched, but I can tell she wants to snip the tension between us.

"She's not a good mother," I say. "I acknowledge that."

Mom's fingers tighten around her mug of tea.

"But Jeff makes up for it, the same way you make up for Dad's absence."

I toy with the keys on the piano, creating the beginning of a new melody. Something sad and forlorn inspired by Nev's expression. A bottomless ache that resonates inside my bones.

"She might be my idol, but you're my hero, Mom, because you have it all, a kid and a career."

I add a new chord to my composition.

Hands settle on my shoulders, and then a tear falls onto the F sharp. Not mine. I crane my neck to look up at Mom.

"I'm sorry, baby. I shouldn't have taken out my irritation on you."

"It's okay."

The tremor building in my fingertips converts into a slow melody that possesses me. I'm so absorbed in my creation that I don't notice the moment my mother lets go, I don't notice the sky dimming, I don't notice the blisters forming on my fingertips until they've bubbled up.

When the world comes crashing back around me, I'm out of breath and light-headed. Is this what happened to Mona? She got lost in her music, and once she climbed out of the melodic vortex, there was nothing and no one waiting there for her?

I snap the lid closed on the keys, almost nicking my sore fingers.

"Mom!" I call out, chest tight.

"I'm in the kitchen, baby."

She's still here.

She's still here.

50

Finding Love in Tennessee

While I stack books in my locker on Monday morning, a warm breath lands on the nape of my neck.

"Hey."

I turn around, heart throbbing a little everywhere in my body. Ten's standing so close that I can smell spearmint on his breath and the intoxicating scent of his hair wax.

"Sorry we never got to hang out yesterday," he says. "It was chaos at home. Dad was fuming, and Nev locked herself in her bedroom." He pushes a lock of hair behind my ear, his fingers lingering on my little arrow earring. "He made me color-code books in the library."

"You're kidding."

He shakes his head, then curls his fingers around the nape of my neck and leans over. When his mouth grazes mine, I jolt away, then touch my lips with my fingertips, darting frenzied glances at all the eyes trained on us.

I put some distance between Ten and me. Not much. Like an extra inch, but enough to catch my breath.

"You look like you're about to pass out," Ten says.

"I think I might," I croak.

He rubs the back of his neck. "Are you—Did you want to—"

"You surprised me, that's all." I quickly press up onto my toes and place a kiss on the corner of his mouth.

Someone coughs. "Get a room."

Brad.

Laney, who's walking beside him, smacks his chest and mouths, *I'm sorry.* But she's fighting off a smile, so I don't think she's that sorry. Or maybe she's just happy that Ten and I finally got together. I think it's the latter.

When I told the girls on our WhatsApp chat after I got home from my surprise dinner date, they flooded it with GIFs of people jumping up and down.

"Hey, Ten, you sure she's not with you because of who you're related to?" Mel says. "Angie *really* likes Mona Stone."

Ten's face clenches, while my stomach bottoms out.

A locker door clangs shut—Rae's. "Shut up, Mel."

Mona's fans leaked pictures of the encounter all over social media before we even left the Landmark, so I shouldn't be surprised people are talking about it. Rae saw the pictures, of course, which led to a *long* phone conversation about why I'd kept it a secret.

One of the cheerleading twins asks, "Is that even allowed?"

"Why wouldn't it be?" Rae snaps.

"I'm no lawyer, but hello? Conflict of interest?"

"You think knowing her son gives her some sort of advantage?" It's Laney who comes to my defense. "That's just stupid."

"No, it's not," Mel says.

"Shut up, Mel!" Laney and Rae both snap at the exact same time.

Mel's perma-tanned skin turns a fiery orange. She scowls at me. "You think you're better than everyone else, Angie. Well, news flash, you're not. And dating the son of someone famous isn't going to make you better either!"

"Stop it, Melanie." This time, it's Ten who says it. He doesn't look at her. Just stares at his dark loafers.

"It's *Melody*," she hisses, before stomping off.

Rae glares at her, then at the crowd gawking at us. Most scamper away; others huddle in groups to whisper. As she makes her way to us, her gaze runs over Ten as though it's the first time she's seeing him.

She leans her shoulder into the locker next to mine. "I can't believe you're Mona's son."

Ten finally raises his gaze off his shoes. "That makes two of us," he says quietly.

The bell shrills, and the hallway starts emptying.

"We should . . ." I gesture toward a classroom.

Rae squeezes my hand. "I'll catch you guys later."

As bodies move around us, carving the tense air, I touch Ten's wrist. His arms are crossed so tightly in front of his chest that tendons jut against his tanned skin.

"Ten, I'm sorry—"

"It was just a matter of time until everyone found out."

I'd been about to apologize for participating in his mother's contest, not to offer my condolences for his lost anonymity, but I go with it.

"Are you going to be okay?"

He shrugs. "As long as no one asks me for free tickets to her concerts or backstage passes, I'll be good."

I give him a rueful smile. "Damn. How am I supposed to get backstage passes, then?"

"You've got to pay for them and contribute to the trust fund I plan on donating to charity at some point."

"Which charity?"

"A couple of different ones. Mostly health care. The system sucks so much in this country."

"That's sweet of you."

"Appearances can be deceiving, huh?"

"I always thought you were sweet."

He shoots me that crooked grin of his that without fail gets my heart whirring. "Yeah, right."

"Fine. But I did always find you handsome. That's the truth." Did I just seriously share that? *Filter, Angie.*

Chuckling, he unlocks his arms and catches my hand. As his fingers thread through mine, I stare at our linked hands. I can't believe I'm holding hands with Tennessee Dylan.

As we stroll toward calc, I stare at our hands a dozen or so times to make sure the moment isn't a figment of my imagination.

His knuckles flex as his grip tightens. "What?"

"I've never held hands with anyone before. Well, besides Rae. And Mom."

"Didn't you date someone before me?"

"I went out with a guy named Ron when I was fourteen, but I wouldn't call it dating."

"Ron Wilkins from our art class?"

I look up into his face. "*Ew.* No." Overachieving Ron Wilkins has serious halitosis. "Another Ron. He left last year." This feels like a good time to ask the undesirable questions. "And you? You had a girlfriend back in New York, didn't you?" I bite my lip. "Actually, forget I asked. I don't want to hear about your ex.".

"Good. Because I don't want to talk about my exes either."

Exes. "Were there many?"

"I thought we weren't talking about them."

"I changed my mind when you used the plural."

"Only about"—he screws up one side of his face—"nine."

"Nine?" I squeak. "Did you start dating when you were eight?"

A smile slinks over his lips, which makes me think he's kidding. Or is he? Rae says guys usually double the number of conquests to heighten their playerness.

We've reached Mrs. Dabbs's classroom, so I let go of his hand.

"Nice of you to join us, Miss Conrad and Mr. Dylan."

"Sorry, Mrs. Dabbs," I mumble.

"Just hurry and take your seats." I'm a little stunned by her complacency. When her tiny eyes dart toward Ten, I conclude she must've heard of the dreaded family encounter and pities him. Or maybe she's a huge Mona Stone fan and wants to ingratiate herself with Ten.

At some point during class, I write *9?* in my notebook in huge bold characters and circle the number twice.

Ten grabs my chair legs and drags me closer to him. I glance at Mrs. Dabbs, who's busy writing a lengthy formula on the whiteboard.

He leans over and whispers, "I dated five girls, but only one was serious."

Ha!

"What about you?" he asks softly.

I'm tempted to say three—three would be acceptable, right?—but it would just prove how insecure I am. "I've never had a real boyfriend."

He frowns. "Really?"

He studies me, but so does Mrs. Dabbs, so I don't say anything.

"The formula's on the board, Mr. Dylan, not on Miss Conrad's cheek."

That snaps Ten's attention off me. For the rest of class, even though he glances my way several times, we don't speak again. As soon as the bell shrills, I toss my books into my canvas bag and sling it over my shoulder.

Ten's still looking at me funny.

"If you don't believe me, ask Rae—"

"So your first time was with a stranger?"

"What?" When it dawns on me he's referring to the drunken conversation I had with him after the game of "Never Have I Ever," my body temperature soars. "Not a *complete* stranger." The lie sneaks out of my mouth. I should tell him the truth, but what if my lack of experience scares him off? I don't want to scare Ten off.

"Not a complete stranger, but not a boyfriend?"

I roll my shirtsleeves up to cool my scorching skin. "I thought we weren't talking about our pasts."

He nods, but a shadow falls over his face. Does he sense I'm lying, or is he disgusted that I fake-lost my virginity to a sort-of stranger?

Ten hangs his backpack on one shoulder.

"We should never have talked about exes," I mumble.

"At least it's out of the way now." He sighs, then grabs my hand and drags it away from my tote strap.

Relief floods me at the contact, and I curl my fingers over his.

"Can't wait to see the look on Bolt's and Archie's faces when they hear I finally made my move."

"You haven't told them?"

"I don't kiss and tell."

"No need for telling when the kissing is so public."

"Does that bother you?"

I tip up my face and meet his worried gaze. "No."

"You sure?"

"I'm sure."

"Good. Because I sort of want to do it again."

He backs me into the cafeteria, which is thankfully empty, pulls me behind a potted palm, and flattens me against the wall. I've never been so appreciative of our school's tropical decor.

Bracketing my head with his forearms, Ten kisses me. Hard. And I feel his kiss *everywhere*. And even though it's not a competition, I think this kiss beats all the kisses we shared Saturday night. My arms wrap around his waist and my hands venture up his back, over the knobs of his spine.

Something rings. Probably my heart. Hearts ring when they're happy, right?

But then Ten is tugging me out of our hiding spot, out of the cafeteria. He releases my hand and starts walking down the hallway toward his next class. Before going inside, he pivots around.

"You're going to be late," he says, a brazen lilt to his voice. "You can put the blame on me."

I most definitely won't be putting the blame on him, because that would mean explaining *why* Tennessee Dylan made me late, and that's not a conversation I ever plan on having with a teacher.

51

The Fame Game

Even after a couple of days of long make-out sessions—in stairwells, in the parking lot, against the lockers, in his car—dating Ten feels utterly unreal.

"I can't believe I have a boyfriend," I tell Rae.

We're both sprawled on the bleachers, absorbing the fiery October sun. On the field below, the coach is having the track team run these thirty-second, full-speed drills that look so brutal I wince every time the whistle shrills.

"And not just anyone. *Mona's* son," she says.

I sit up. "*Ugh.* Don't remind me."

"Hon, I know you don't want to hear this, but maybe you *should* reconsider the contest. It might change things between you and Ten."

Blood pounds against my temples. "He told me he's not mad about it."

"Because you haven't entered yet. It's not real. But once you do, it'll get real."

Borrowed time . . .

I don't want to think about it, so I blurt out, "I got another C in math. I think Mrs. Dabbs hates me."

"Well, you are dating her crush."

"What?" I wrinkle my nose. "*Ew.*"

"Remember at the beginning of the year, when she told me I should get Ten to help me out with my calc homework, she kept on gushin' and gushin' about how good he is, and how mature and blah blah blah."

"That's just gross."

Rae smirks. "Not that she ever had a chance. Since that boy stepped into Reedwood, he's been totally infatuated with you, God knows why."

I flick her arm, and she laughs.

After Rae heads back into school, I wait a couple extra minutes for the track coach's briefing to end. The moment it's over, Ten jogs up to me, sweat glistening on his brow and gluing his gym shirt to his chest. How he still has energy to run is beyond me. I'd be pancaked on the lawn.

He kisses me, and I wrinkle my nose. "Sweaty man."

That just makes him step closer. He even wraps his arms around me.

"Ew," I say, between bursts of laughter. I try to push him off, but he holds on tighter. "You're lucky I like you, sweat and all."

"I count my blessings each and every second of the day."

I roll my eyes and swat his arm.

<hr />

AFTER SCHOOL, I stop by the middle school. I haven't seen Nev since Sunday. Ten told me she was still angry with him, but her lack of response to my text messages tells me she's also angry with me.

I roll my bike up to the middle school parking lot and look for her pink backpack in the ocean of backpacks. It takes me a while to locate her, because, unlike in the cafeteria, she isn't alone. She's surrounded by classmates.

Going out to the movies with Charlie has had quite the impact on her social status. Although I'm glad for her, I also worry because I recognize some of the girls she's chatting with—the pests who bullied her.

I hook up my bike, then traipse over to her. "Nev?"

Slowly she turns toward me. Her gray eyes darken, become the color of thunderclouds. "What do you want, Angie?" Her tone is short. I wasn't hallucinating her anger. She really is mad at me.

"What I want is to talk."

"Are you going to try to convince me she's evil too?"

Her little posse has gotten all quiet.

"No."

"Good, because I'm sick of people telling me what a bitch my mother is."

"Nev!" I'm shocked by her language, and even more shocked that she's talking about Mona Stone so publicly.

It hits me then . . . Charlie isn't the cause of her expanding social circle—Mona is.

She hoists her backpack higher onto her bony shoulder. "What?"

"We're not talking here," I tell her.

"Why not?"

I narrow my eyes. Who is this girl? Certainly not the one who crawled into my bed because she was scared of the dark. I tow her away from the others by force, and even though she tries to fight me, I'm stronger.

Charlie jogs after us, attempting to break Nev free, but I whip around on him and bark, "Get lost."

I'm the angry one now. No, not angry . . . *livid*!

I only let go of her once we've circled the brick building and made some headway into the thicket of myrtles.

"What the hell was that?" I bet smoke is curling out of my nostrils.

Nev rubs her wrist. "You didn't have to pull me!"

"Who are you and what did you do to my friend?"

She scowls.

I scowl harder.

"What's gotten into you, Nev? Since when are Jenny and Crystal your friends?" I half shout, half roar. "Since they found out you're Mona's daughter?"

"What's it to you? You told me I should make friends!"

"I told you to make *real* friends, not sycophants!"

"They're not sycophants."

"Really? Since when have they been your friends?"

She shrugs.

"Since when?" I screech. "Let me guess. Since Monday."

"It's *my* life. If I want to be friends with them, it's *my* choice. At least now you don't need to pity-hang with me anymore." Her eyes are pinkening and turning shiny.

My anger shrinks like a popped balloon. "*Pity-hang?* I never hung out with you out of pity. Nor did I do it to get closer to Ten *or* to get an in with your mother," I add, in case those thoughts have crossed her mind.

As tears dribble down her freckled cheeks, Nev knots her arms in front of her chest.

"Oh my God, you really thought all of that?" My shrill voice hangs in the air between us.

She scrubs her cheeks. "I don't know what to think anymore. Who to trust—" A sob lurches out of her.

"Me! Trust *me*."

Her bottom lip wobbles.

"Oh, Nev." The cry that surges up her throat is so pained that I enclose her in a fierce hug. "Never doubt me."

"I'm s-s-sorry, An-Angie."

"Shh. It's okay." I rub her back until her sobs begin to subside.

"Mom was cr-crying on Sunday."

"I know."

"Dad was so m-mean to her. And Ten . . ." She shakes in my arms, so I squeeze her tighter. "That's probably why she never c-came to see us. Because they are s-so awful to her."

I'm tempted to tell her the run-in was staged, but I'm afraid that'll erase the trust she's just given me back.

"I t-told Dad I wanted her ph-phone number, and he said, *n-no way*. I don't even know why we b-bothered coming back here."

I'm rubbing slow, soothing circles against her knobby spine. They seem to be working because she's no longer shaking.

"I want my mother, Angie."

I tuck her head under my chin.

"Maybe *I* sh-should enter her contest."

My heart bounces. I pull away to see if she's serious. "Your dad would never sign off on that. Besides, you're her daughter. There's probably a clause about family members."

She palms her wet cheeks. "Are *you* still going to do it?"

I swallow, my throat feeling raw from all the yelling. "Yes."

"You promise?"

I'm all at once surprised and not surprised she wants me to participate. "Yes." I just need to get Mom on board again.

"Even if Ten tells you"—Nev heaves in a juddering breath—"that he'll break up with you if you do it?"

"We've already discussed it."

"And he really said okay?"

"Nev, your brother understands how much I want this. He understands that if he tries to hold me back, he'll lose me."

Her expression is so strained that I sense she doesn't quite believe me.

"Can we please talk about your new friends now?"

She toes a clump of grass. "I don't want to be an outcast anymore."

"You are aware some of them might be using you for who you are?"

"And I'm using them for who *they* are."

"As long as you realize it."

"I do." She sinks onto the grass and crosses her legs.

I sit down next to her.

She plucks a blade of grass and twirls it. "Maybe one of them will become a real friend."

"Maybe."

"And by the way"—she raises her silvery eyes to me—"they've been nice to me since Charlie asked me out. They're just nicer now."

I snort. "Have they asked you for concert tickets yet?"

She grins in that same crooked way her brother does. "Jenny did."

I sigh, then lie back and stare up at the sky crosshatched by thin branches and glossy green leaves. "Swear you'll never turn into them."

"I swear it."

I stick up my pinky, and she hooks her little finger around it, and then we shake on it. The silly gesture makes Nev crack a grin, and for a moment, I get the girl who hid under a baseball cap back.

52

T-Minus One

The last week of October passes in a flurry of activity and excitement. Butterflies flap inside of me twenty-four seven, but they're not all brought on by Ten. Some of them come from the reminders of Mona's contest plastered over the city buses, trumpeted over the radio channels, and blasted all over social media.

The deadline is tomorrow, and I have neither Mom's signature nor have I uploaded my song to Mona's website. Lynn and Steffi assume I've already sent everything in. I think Ten does, too. The only people who know I haven't entered are Mom, Rae, and Laney. Mom because she hasn't signed the form, and my friends because when they asked, I confessed my hesitation. Neither passed judgment or pressed me one way or another. Both listened as I listed the pros and cons.

As for Nev, I told her that my mom hadn't agreed to sign the form. Which is sort of true. Since the Mona debacle, Mom and I haven't discussed Mona or her contest.

When I get home from Lynn and Steffi's on Friday, I find Mom sitting in the kitchen with Nev.

Grinning, Nev peels a sheet of paper off the emerald stone island and flaps it. "I convinced her!"

My heart pounds harder than during my dance lesson with Steffi.

Mom's forehead is furrowed and her eyes tight. She's either feeling confused or cornered. Neither is good. I want to come clean but can't. Not in front of Nev.

My fingers shake so badly it takes me several attempts to hang up my denim jacket. I tug on the long sleeves of my exercise top, and it droops off one of my shoulders.

"Something smells good," I say, my voice low and slightly croaky.

"I made roast chicken." Mom's inspecting my face. "Want to stay for dinner, Nev?"

"I'd love to, but I need to check with Dad first."

"Why don't you call him?"

Nev taps on her cell phone, which is next to the signed form. After a couple of rings, Jeff's deep voice rumbles out of her phone. "Hey, Dad, can I eat with Jade and Angie? Ten went over to Archie's, so I'm home alone anyway."

"I was on my way home," Jeff says.

Mom leans toward the phone. "You're welcome to come over too, Jeff."

"That's really kind. Are you sure you have enough food?"

Mom smiles. "Only two chickens and a green bean casserole."

Jeff chuckles. "Were you expecting other guests?"

"No. Just my daughter." She grins, and it smooths away some of the tension crimping her brow.

"Then I'll be right over. With dessert."

"Sounds great."

Nev beams after she hangs up.

Mom grabs a stack of plates from a cupboard and hands them to me. Nev lurches off the stool to help. She grabs the leather place mats and sets them on the glass table, and then I add the plates, but my aim is off on the last one, and the ceramic plate teeters and then crashes to the floor, splitting into large gunmetal-colored shards.

The sound is like an explosion in the quiet kitchen. I crouch and pick up the pieces, fingers shaking.

Mom kneels beside me, her army-green silk pants bunching around her legs. "Nev, can you pass me the brush and dustpan? They're under the sink." She takes a chunk of ceramic from my fingers. "Baby, I'm not mad at you." I know she doesn't mean about the plate. She touches my cheek. "Why don't you go upstairs and take a shower?"

I rise from my crouch in slow motion and start toward the stairs, when Nev chirrups, "Don't forget your form."

I take it from the island, and although I want to ball it up, I don't. The second I arrive in my bedroom, I chuck the paper in the drawer that's become a graveyard for forgotten things.

There's no more doubt in my mind about what I will do.

I won't risk my relationship with Ten.

I'll get into the music business some other way—I'll write more songs, get more demos recorded, send my work off to agents. If I break out on my own, it'll be that much more rewarding.

I don't need a contest to make me.

Especially one that could just as easily break me.

Dinner with Jeff and Nev is fun, in part because no one brings up the contest—if Jeff has any inkling I wanted to compete, he doesn't mention it—in part because making up my mind has lifted a huge weight off my chest.

I'm dying to tell Ten, but I don't want to do it over the phone. I settle on telling him tomorrow, before the Halloween party. I can't wait to see the look on his face. Even if we don't speak about the contest, it *has* to be affecting him.

After father and daughter leave, Mom finally asks me why Nev begged her to sign the form. And I tell her everything. Although my mother's face doesn't betray her emotions, a stillness envelops her . . . envelops us.

"Are you sure, baby?" she asks as I climb the stairs toward my bedroom.

"A hundred percent."

Finally, she smiles.

I pause, hand on the balustrade. "But if Nev asks, I sent it in, okay?"

"Won't she find out the truth?"

"No. She'll just assume I lost."

Mom bites her lip. "As long as you're sure."

"I'm sure."

53

The Beds We Make and Lie In

"Your face is all golden." I swipe my thumb over Ten's jaw to dislodge the face paint I plastered over my skin tonight to match my gold unitard. I'm supposed to be a CMA award, and he's supposed to be a vampire.

Ten's been acting a little weird since he walked into my house—he's nervous. I think it has to do with his mother's contest. He keeps staring at the discolored patch of wall in my room where Mona Stone's poster hung until yesterday.

"I have something to tell—"

But I don't get my announcement out, because Ten chooses that exact moment to ask, "Did you really lose your virginity to a stranger?"

My hands tumble away from his face. Heart blasting, I whip my head around to make sure my bedroom door is closed. Finally, I whisper, "What?"

"You said you lost your virginity, but you never had a boyfriend, so I assumed it had to be a random hookup."

I shift my legs off his lap and scoot to the edge of my queen-sized bed. "I—I never . . . I never did anything."

"But—"

"I lied." I study the fibers of my aquamarine rug.

"Why?"

"Because I'm seventeen. All my friends have done *it*. And I didn't think you'd want to date someone"—I shrug—"inexperienced."

"I'll admit, it's a total buzzkill." His delivery is so serious, I have to check his expression to make sure he's joking. The small smile curling up the corners of his lips reassures me that he's teasing me. He twirls the curly end of my gold-painted ponytail and tugs on it until my face is angled toward his. "Angie, promise not to lie to me again? About anything."

I nod. "I promise."

He twines his fingers through my hair and kisses me. Gently and then less gently.

When we break apart, I say, "My turn to ask a question."

His expression turns cautious.

"After tonight, I never want to talk about it again, but"—I chew on my bottom lip—"did you have sex with *all* of your girlfriends?"

His hand drops to my comforter, dimples the striped fabric. "No."

"But with more than one?"

"Yes. But they didn't mean anything to me."

"Then why'd you sleep with them?"

Regret grays his yellow irises. "Because I was angry and stupid. I believed meaningless sex could help make me less angry and less stupid."

"What made you angry?"

"A bunch of things. Mom. Having to repeat a school year. Moving back here." He rubs the back of his head, mussing up his combed, gelled hair. "Little did I know it would turn out this way."

"This way?"

He raises his eyes to mine. "With me being ridiculously happy." He places his hand back on my body—on my thigh this time. "It feels like I found a part of myself that was missing by coming back here."

I cover his hand with mine, interlock our fingers. He lifts our hands and kisses my knuckles.

"I have something to tell you," I say. "It has to do with the contest."

He clenches his jaw. "I told you, Angie, I'm okay—"

"I decided not to enter."

"—with you competing." The hard lines of his face soften as my words sink in. "You decided not to enter?"

"I did."

Surprise ripples over his clean-shaven face.

"I choose you, Ten."

"You don't need to choose."

"But I did. I do."

He doesn't move for so long that he begins to resemble a real vampire—one that's just been staked.

"Angie . . ." he whispers, his lips settling on my neck, on that spot right below my ear that makes me shudder. "I think I'm in love with you."

My breath catches in my throat the same way my heart catches in my rib cage. I twist around until I'm straddling his lap, and my hands are locked behind his neck. "I love you too, Ten."

Except I don't think it . . . I know it. I fell in love with him long before we even started dating, which I'll never admit. Or maybe I will. I'm surprising myself with the number of things I'm doing that I would never have dreamed myself capable of.

He splays his hands on my waist and then dips his face toward mine, touches my lips to his, crushes my heart to his.

54

Win Some, Lose Some

Whoever claimed happiness can't last was right.

After the two greatest weeks of my life, the absolute worst one begins. It's the morning of Mona Stone's contest announcement. Which isn't the reason it's the worst. I'm excited to find out who she picked. It's the worst because of the name that appears on my Twitter feed.

I read it. Blink. Read it again.

Sometimes, the mind can play tricks on you. Show you what you want to see. Or what you don't want to see.

The name of the winner blurs, then sharpens.

I whip my gaze toward Ten, who's leaning against the locker next to mine, the *only* person not clutching a phone, just as the hallway erupts with noise.

And I mean erupts like a volcano erupts—shrieks, claps, and whistles spew and overtake the entire school.

Ten frowns, while I feel like crying.

Wrong. I *am* crying.

The PA system squeals, and then Mrs. Larue's voice blasts through the school, adding to the mounting chaos. "In the words of the Buddha, *One moment can change a day, one day can change a life, and one life can change the world.* Dear Angela, from all the faculty at Reedwood. We. Are. Proud!"

Ten's gaze goes a little wider and his mouth a little softer, but his jaw, like the winner's name—*my* name—sharpens.

He backs up from me, and then his feet eat up the hallway in long strides.

I try to go after him, but he's fast, and people keep coming at me, keep saying *Congrats* or *I knew she'd choose you*, which they couldn't possibly have known, because one, they most likely have never heard me sing, and two, I didn't submit my song.

I try to get through the fence of bodies, but they keep coming. So many of them. My back rams into the cold, hard metal wall of lockers.

"Yo, back the hell up! Don't you see you're freaking her out?" Jasper yells, which gets some people's attention.

Brad gets the others' attention. He shoves them back, and then Laney and Rae are by my side and rescuing me from the mob. They tow me into the girls' bathroom, kicking out two girls fixing their makeup.

"I don't know whether to hug you or scream at you right now." Rae's voice is so shrill it reverberates in my skull.

"Did you tell us you weren't competing so we wouldn't get our hopes up?" Laney asks.

Sobs rack my body, make me crumple to the floor.

Rae crouches in front of me. "Hon, talk to us."

"I d-d-didn't . . ."

"You didn't what?" Laney asks gently. "Submit your song?"

I nod so hard my head feels as though it's going to unscrew itself from my body.

My friends become smudges of color—blonde, black, peach, and sky blue. I can see them talking, but I can't hear them over the buzzing in my ears.

"I want to go home," I croak.

"I'll call Jade," Rae offers, grabbing my phone from my glacial fingers.

What is my mother going to think? The same thing that Ten did? That I lied? Oh, God, Ten . . . the hurt and anger on his face when he walked away from me brings up a new wave of tears. I have to call him. Have to tell him that I have no clue why his mother chose me.

"Um, Angie, Nev just sent you a text."

Rae shows me my phone. My eyesight is so blurry that I have to blink several times to decipher her words, and after I do, I keep blinking.

NEV: *Don't hate me.*

I close my eyes, head pounding as furiously as my heart.

Don't hate her?

Don't hate her for what?

Like a bucket of icy water, understanding washes over me.

I seize my phone from Rae.

ME: *You submitted my application and song?!?*

My phone rings, and Nev's name flashes across the screen, and although I don't want to talk to her, I want to scream at her, which I do, the moment we're connected.

Rae and Laney look on in stunned silence.

Nev's crying so hard by the time I'm done chewing her out that I think I overdid it, but then I remember the look on her brother's face, and it lessens my guilt.

"I d-didn't w-want you to . . . to give up because of T-Ten," she croaks.

My heart bangs so hard I taste metal. "I never gave up, Nev! I just changed directions."

"B-but you m-made me a p-promise."

I swallow, my throat feeling raw and stiff.

"And y-you didn't k-keep it."

"So that makes what you did okay?"

She sobs so wildly that I expect her tears to seep right out of my phone. "I'm s-s-sorry."

"Are you really, though?"

Silence, then, "For the way I d-did it, yes."

I shut my eyes for a millisecond, massage my temples.

"Don't h-hate me. P-p-please d-don't."

I heave a long sigh. "I don't hate you, but I am *real* mad."

"T-T-Ten's going t-t-to hate m-me," she stammers. "He'll n-never forgive m-me."

"He's your brother. He'll forgive you."

"N-no, he won't. He'll n-never forgive me. He'll h-hate me fo-forever. J-just like he hates M-Mom."

"Don't be ridiculous."

"Did he ever f-forgive her?"

"What she and you did isn't the same thing."

"She's our m-mother, Angie."

And then it hits me why Nev did this. She entered me in the contest as a way to get closer to Mona. Or at least I think that's why. "After school, come over to my house."

"O-okay. Will you t-tell T-Ten?"

"Not until you and I talk."

"O-okay."

Rae and Laney are wearing matching expressions of shock.

"*Nev* submitted your song?" Rae says after I hang up. "Whoa . . ."

"That's really screwed up," Laney says.

I rub my wet cheeks and puffy eyes.

"You could probably still drop out," Rae says.

"But she won," Laney says. "I know we're not celebrating right now, but you do realize you've just *won* a nationwide contest? Your song was picked over thousands."

No, I don't realize this. "Did you call my mom, Rae?"

"Yeah. She's probably waiting for you outside."

I push myself off the tiles, wash my hands, and splash cold water over my face. As I leave the bathroom, Laney says, "You want us to come with you, sweetie?"

I shake my head, then dry my face on my sleeves.

"We love you," Rae and Laney tell me in unison.

I trudge over to them and hug them. Ten might hate me, but at least my friends don't. After swearing them to secrecy, I exit into the empty hallway.

I won.

As I walk out of school, it begins to sink in. And even though I'm still mad, I'm also something else. Something between proud and terrified.

55

A Means to an End

"Ten will forgive Nev, right?" I ask Mom, as she smooths back my hair.

I'm lying on our couch with my head in her lap.

"Of course he will, baby."

I stare at the piano I spent hours practicing my song on. A song I now hate. The black and ivory keys bleed into one another, their joints intersecting at wrong angles.

"Are you sure that's what worries you? That he forgives Nev?"

Is my mother a mind reader?

"I know you and Ten are . . . *close*."

I close my eyes and cringe.

"Angie?"

I don't open my eyes.

"I'd be the most unobservant person if I didn't realize you two—"

I press my hands to my ears.

She pulls my hands away. "Angie, I'm okay with it."

"You are?" I croak.

"Look at me."

"In a second."

She snorts. "Don't worry . . . I'm not going to ask you for any details."

I snap my lids open. "Does Jeff know?"

She smiles. "From one day to the next, his son doesn't want to leave Nashville anymore. Of course he knows."

"Does he hate me? I don't mean for dating his son . . . I mean for winning Mona's contest?"

"He may not be a fan of his ex-wife, but he's a huge fan of yours."

I blow out air through my lips. "You're just saying that to make me feel better."

She stops combing my hair. "I'm not. He's never seen his kids happier than since you've come into their lives. Both his kids."

"Neither is real happy today."

"Today will pass."

I stare at the ivory ceiling, which looks white in contrast to the pale gray walls. Appearances can be so deceiving. "Do you think it's possible Mona picked me because she knew who I was and wanted to get back at her family?"

Mom's hand stills in my hair. "How would that benefit her, Angie? It would just make her look petty. Besides, she picked your song, not you. Do you really think she would've picked a song she doesn't want to put on her album?"

"I guess not."

Mom's phone rings. She leans over to scoop it up from the coffee table. "Hey, Jeff."

I sit up, tucking my feet underneath me.

"She cut school? . . . No, she's not here . . . Okay . . . Of course. I'll have Angie try to call her . . . We'll call you right back."

The second Mom hangs up, she asks me to phone Nev, worry darkening her brown irises. I jump to my feet and head to the foyer to dig my phone out of my jacket pocket.

I call Nev's number, feeling colder than when I made snow angels with Rae, colder than when Ten backed away from me. It goes to voice mail. "Nev, call me back right away. I'm not mad, okay? Just call me back."

I hang up, then stare at my screen, which is overflowing with notifications, tags, texts. I look for one from Ten, but he seems to be the only person in all of Belle Meade who hasn't written me. Even the singer from the Moon Junkies DMed me.

Just as I'm trying Nev's number again our doorbell rings. I stride to the door and look through the peephole. When I see who it is, I open the door wide.

"Mom, Nev's here!" I yell, taking in the sliver of reddened face I can see between the ropes of tangled hair.

"Oh thank God!" Mom rushes toward her, her phone already raised to her ear. "She's here, Jeff. She's okay . . . Hold on a sec." She extends the phone toward Nev. "Nev, your father wants to talk to you."

Nev shakes her head, then croaks, "N-not now."

I hear Jeff roar on Mom's cell.

"Tell him she'll call him back once she calms down," I say, and then I pluck one of Nev's limp hands, tug her into the living room, and sit her down in the armchair.

After Mom disconnects, she says, "I'm sorry, sweetie, but he's coming over."

"How long?" Nev's voice sounds as raw as her face looks.

"He was ten minutes away, but he's probably breaking every speed limit."

"Angie"—Nev wrings her hands—"I'm so sorry."

I sigh. "You should be. You just gave us all a heart attack!"

"Uh, not about that."

Nev darts a glance at Mom.

I cross my arms in front of my chest. "I told her everything."

"Everything?" Nev squeaks, before dipping her chin to her neck. "I'm sorry, Jade."

Sighing, Mom sits on the armrest of the couch, folding one leg underneath her. "Why did you do it? I mean the contest entry. Not the class cutting."

"Because I thought . . . I thought Angie wouldn't go through with it—"

"Which you were right about," I say.

"—because my brother was making her not do it."

It would be unjust of me to say that Ten didn't play a part in my decision, albeit passively.

"Sweetheart, when someone doesn't want to do something, you can't force it upon them," my mom says.

Nev hangs her head lower. "I know, Jade."

Mom and I exchange a look.

"But what's done is done. Now you have to face the consequences."

"Dad's going to send me away to boarding school when he finds out," Nev whispers.

"He won't, sweetie," Mom says.

Nev starts sobbing, so my mother stands and walks over to the armchair, and then crouches in front of Nev. "He would *never* send you away."

"Please don't tell him," she whispers.

"It's not up to me. It's up to Angie."

I sigh. "I won't tell him. And I won't make you tell him either, but I do want you to tell Ten, or your brother will never trust me again, let alone speak to me."

Mom glances at me. I can't tell what she's thinking—maybe that I'm wrong in letting Nev get away with this, or maybe that I'm being mature for letting Nev off the hook.

"I'll give Mona the rights to my song, and that'll be the end of it," I say.

Nev looks up, snot and tears marbling her skin.

"Do we have a deal?" I ask.

She nods just as tires squeal outside our door.

Mom stands up. "That must be your dad."

Nev shrinks into the armchair as Mom goes to open the door.

"When you sent in my application," I ask, "did you attach a personal note? Something with your name on it?"

"No!" She shakes her head wildly. "I just uploaded a screenshot of the signed form and the copy of the recording you sent me."

"So Mona has no idea who I am?"

She shakes her head again.

My mom and her dad are still outside. Mom is probably trying to calm Jeff.

"I have an extra demand." I tap my index finger against Nev's knee. "I have to sing my song in front of cameras and Mona on Saturday, and I want you to come with me."

Nev blinks and blinks, and then she nods and nods.

And even though she's about to get into a heap of trouble, happiness streaks her face.

Her expression confirms my suspicion that she used me to reach her mother. She couldn't have known I would win, but hope convinces people the most insane outcome can come true.

At least now Nev will get some answers, and answers are better than questions, even if those answers might dash all of her hopes.

56

Inflatable Hearts

When I enter the cafeteria at lunch the following day, my peers stand and clap so energetically the palm trees sway. I'm desperate for everyone to stop congratulating me, because each show of support nips away at my stoicism.

Ten didn't come to school today, and I'm glad, because witnessing everyone's enthusiasm would just hurt him, but I'm also worried. Worried he believes I made Nev take the blame.

At the end of the school day, I feel as though I've been teleported to Jupiter, where everything weighs two and a half times more. The last bell can't come soon enough. I can't focus on anything our geography teacher is saying. I just sit there, slumped in my chair, chewing on the end of my pen.

The PA system crackles. "Angela Conrad, please come to the principal's office."

Normally, I would blush at my name being called out, but I don't care anymore. I drag myself out of my chair and plod through the aisle of desks toward the door. I bet Principal Larue wants to discuss my slipping grade point average.

As I step out of the classroom, my heel hits something slippery that makes me skid. Instinctively, I reach out and steady myself against the wall, then look down, and my forehead furrows when I notice what made me slip—rose petals. And they aren't just in front of the classroom door. There's a trail of them that leads up the staircase of our basement classroom. Is this Mrs. Larue's doing? If it is, it's a little weird . . . even for her.

I follow the petals up the stairs and then through the door and into the main hallway. More rose petals are strewn over the linoleum, but they don't lead anywhere near our principal's office.

What if the petals aren't for me?

I freeze and am about to double back when I catch where the trail leads: my locker. Legs feeling like damp cotton, I walk up to it and open the metal door with a clank. Petals rain down over my boots, along with a folded note.

MEET ME WHERE YOU ASKED ME TO HOMECOMING.

I read and reread the note. I never asked—

Fighting off a smile, I shake my head, and then I run out the door and round the walls of red bricks toward the bleachers. I slow down when I spot the lone figure standing there.

For a moment, I watch Ten and he watches me.

Then I yell, "I never asked you to homecoming, Tennessee Dylan! You asked me."

In the distance, I see him smile.

Heart derailing, I stride over to him.

"My dad says humor and flowers help fix mistakes," he says.

I stop a foot away from him. "I thought you were never going to talk to me again."

He extends a bouquet of roses as thick as my torso. I take it from him and inhale the sweet fragrance of his remorse.

"I'm sorry I jumped to conclusions."

The edges of his face are all blurry. "I don't blame you for it," I say.

He swallows, which makes his Adam's apple jostle in his throat. "You should blame me . . . I left without asking any questions."

I shake my head. "When it comes to your mom, Ten, I'll never blame you for reacting weirdly."

He reaches for the bouquet and coaxes it out of my fingers, then tosses it on the bleachers. "I don't deserve you." He tugs on my wrist, and I collapse against him. His hands wrap around my back and pin me to his chest. He cocoons my body with his and holds me in silence for a long time, his chest puffing with sighs. "She's just everywhere, Angie. Every time I think I can break free from her—for good—she shows up. On the radio, on billboards, on TV. This morning, I saw her in a shampoo commercial. However long or fast I run, I can't outrun her."

"This isn't a race. You're bound to see her, whether in person or on TV. And not just because she's your mother but because she's Mona Stone." I lay my palm on his neck, feel the play of tendons. "But remember, the only way someone can get under your skin is if you let them."

His jaw is set so tight it feels like metal. "*You* got under my skin."

"Because you let me." I move my face closer to his until our noses touch. "Do you regret it?"

His eyes darken as fast as the Tennessee sky before a thunderstorm. "Don't ever ask me that again."

Even though my pulse now fills my mouth, I manage to say, "That's not an answer."

"Do you regret waking up in the morning?"

I frown.

"Do you regret being able to laugh?" He puts some space between our bodies, but doesn't let go of me. "Even though you drive me insane sometimes, you also make me insanely happy. So asking me if I regret letting you in is like asking if I regret breathing. The answer is no." He rests his forehead against mine. "I love you."

I swallow his words, let them fill the void he left when he ran from me. Slowly he slants his face and fits his lips to mine. The kiss is deliberate and gentle.

Oh so very gentle.

After a minute, or two, or ten, I rip my lips off his. "Oh my God! Mrs. Larue wanted to speak to me! Your petals completely derailed me."

Ten grins. "Mrs. Larue didn't need to see you, Angie. I did."

My cheeks grow hot. "She was in on—"

"Had to get you out of class early."

"So she knows about the rose petals?"

"Yeah, but she made me promise to shovel them up once I was done *making things right with all my heart*." He air-quotes that last part. Probably one of her inspirational sayings.

Even though more heat rises to my face, I smile. "I can't decide whether I'm mortified or relieved."

Ten chuckles. "You're cute when you blush. Almost as cute as when you're mad."

I swat his arm but laugh, and my heart, which has felt as bloated as Rae's outsized inflatable flamingo since I saw my name on my social media feed, finally shrinks back to its normal size.

57

My Last Stand

The days fall like dominoes. Tuesday knocks into Wednesday, which topples over the next two days. Too soon, it's Friday. The day before I'm supposed to meet Mona.

Even though Ten suggested having his father read over the fine print of the contest to see if we could void my entry, I insisted that it was okay. Besides, asking Ten's father to get me out of a situation he still believes I voluntarily signed up for would probably raise red flags. I don't doubt Jeff will find out, but I'd rather it happened once it wasn't all so fresh. I'd rather he keep thinking Nev cut school because she was overwhelmed by the talk of her mother's contest and the attention she got from her peers.

Nev has been dropping by my house almost every day after school. Rae and Laney have also spent the better part of their week with me. If anything, the bonding that ensued from the mess has made the entire thing almost worth it.

As soon as I step through Lynn's parlor door on Friday, she and Steffi shower me with praise and then give me a thin chain with a tiny diamond star for their "rising star." I weep into Lynn's newly purple hair and then against Steffi's knob-of-steel shoulder.

Tomorrow, I will sing my song for the very last time. After that, it will belong to Mona Stone. I'm at once nostalgic and relieved. I don't want this song anymore because it already feels as though it doesn't belong to me.

I practice it with Lynn, and then I ask her if she's been practicing it with Nev like I asked her to, and she nods. She doesn't know why I asked this of her, though, and I don't explain.

Tonight I'm having dinner with Mom. It's the first time all week we've been alone since she came to fetch me from school on Monday. We talk about a lot of things—mostly about what'll happen once I sign on the dotted line and how it'll affect my life.

"I'll have enough money to pay for an entire year of college." I feel dazed by this fact, because even though it was never about the prize money, it's pretty insane how much I'm about to earn.

Mom runs one finger around the rim of her wineglass, creating a vibration that fills our kitchen. "College, huh? Is that back on the table?"

"It was never off the table. It was just shoved under a lot of other things."

Mom smiles. I think it might be the first real smile she's given me all week. She sets down her glass, then leans over and touches my cheek. "I'm real proud of you, baby."

"For considering college?"

"No. I mean, don't get me wrong, I'm incredibly happy to hear you talk about college. What I'm proud about, though, is how you've dealt with everything that's come at you."

If she knew what I have planned for tomorrow, I'm not sure she'd be saying this.

"Now off to bed," she says, sending me off with a kiss on the cheek and a reminder that she loves me more than anything else in the world.

For the first time in forever, I don't take her words for granted, because not everyone gets to hear this from their mother.

58

The First Stage of Stardom

I don't sleep. Not for a second. When dawn creeps through my curtains, I throw the covers off my legs and get up.

I catch my reflection in the mirror—red-rimmed eyes with purple circles, a complexion that's never been paler. I look exactly how I feel—strung out.

My phone's screen is flooded with messages. From Rae and Laney. Notifications from the senior WhatsApp wishing me luck. And then several texts from Ten saying to come over the second it's done. That he's making lunch—all my favorites.

ME: Blondies?

BEAST: There will be blondies.

ME: Is Nev ready?

BEAST: She's ready.

ME: Will your dad hate me for this?

BEAST: No.

Although Ten tried to dissuade me from bringing Nev, I made him see that she needed this. Good or bad, she has to form her own opinion of her mother.

When we get into the car, I tell Mom we need to stop by the Dylans' house. I'm sure she imagines I want to see Ten. I turn on the radio until I hear the host discussing my performance at the Ryman Theater, which they'll broadcast on their channel as well as on their website. I flick the radio off. I don't need any more wasps flapping around inside me. Yes, wasps. I'm reserving butterflies for the good feels.

When the mansion comes into view, I text Ten that we're out front. He comes out with Nev and walks her all the way down the path. Nev donned the little black dress with red hearts we bought during our mall expedition. She wears it with a pair of black cowboy boots and a denim jacket.

No jeans or leggings.

"Hey, kids," Mom says through my open window.

"Hi, Jade." Ten opens the back door.

"Oh. Are you . . . coming with us?" Her eyes zip to the house, as though she's expecting Jeff to come barreling down the path.

"Yeah," Ten says.

I spin as I watch him slide into the backseat beside Nev.

"You're coming too?" I ask breathily.

"I missed your first performance," Ten says. "Wouldn't want to miss your second one." I must look like I'm two seconds away from crying, because he adds, "I promise to be on my best behavior."

I blink, heart all squashed up in my chest. I know how much he despises Mona. I know how much he wishes I had another passion than music. And yet, he's here.

He clips himself in. "Seat belt, Nev."

Nev rolls her eyes but drags on her seat belt.

Mom still hasn't started the car. "Uh. Does Jeff know?"

"Yeah. I told him," Ten says.

"You did?" I squeak.

Ten nods.

"And he's okay with it?" Mom asks.

"He's okay with it."

Mom cocks an eyebrow.

"I promise, Jade," Ten says. "I would never get you in trouble."

"Okay, then." Mom finally puts the car in gear and pulls away from the curb.

After a couple of minutes of air-conditioned silence, Nev asks, "Are you nervous, Angie?"

"Yeah." I don't return the question because I sense how Nev is feeling. She's been joggling her knees and coiling a long lock of hair around her index finger since we left their house.

When the Ryman comes into view, the wasps become more insistent. I press my hand against my stomach. I'm suddenly not sure if I can do this but then remember why I'm doing it. For Nev.

I breathe in through my nose and out through my mouth as Mom slides past a horde of paparazzi corralled in by police barricades. We sent our license plate number ahead of time so they would know to let the car through.

Flashes go off anyway, but hopefully the images will be too grainy to use. At least Ten had the presence of mind to get his sister to duck a block ago.

We park behind a shiny chrome van with Mona Stone's logo. The woman with the curly hair and glasses I ran into back at the hotel approaches the car. When she sees me exit the vehicle, her eyes grow a little wider.

"I know you," she says.

When Ten and Nev get out of the car, the woman turns so pale I worry she might faint.

"I wish you'd informed us . . . that you were being accompanied," she says.

I loop my thumbs through my jeans' belt buckle. Unlike Nev, I didn't doll myself up. I'm wearing a plain white tank top and my favorite pair of skinny denim. "I emailed you I would come with my family."

The woman's nostrils pulse. "*Your* family?" she has the audacity to say. "I'm not sure I can get you all in."

"Maybe our mother can get us all in?" Ten says tauntingly.

The assistant's eyes blaze with annoyance. "I'll see what I can do." She vanishes through the Ryman's heavy doors.

"You think she won't let us in?" Nev murmurs.

I wind an arm around her shoulders. "If you don't go in, I don't go in."

The assistant comes back out, pressing her glasses up the bridge of her nose. She holds the door open and gestures for us to step inside the temple of music.

Mona is standing in the aisle, pointing out something on the stage to a man with a headset, her smooth, honeyed voice trickling like caramel and sunshine through the converted tabernacle.

Nev's shoulders stiffen as her mom looms larger and larger. When Mona turns, Nev stops walking. And then she starts trembling.

59

Ad Lib

Mona Stone's golden eyes flash over her daughter and then her son. My heart holds perfectly still. I barely dare to breathe, afraid to taint the air with my apprehension.

Ten leans toward me and whispers, "I'll go find a seat somewhere in the back."

As he walks away, Mona's gaze follows him, before settling back on me. Finally she steps forward. "It's a mighty small world." She extends her hand toward my mother first. "It's a pleasure to meet the woman who managed to produce such talent."

Mom's stiff jaw tells me the compliment is lost on her. Thankfully, though, she shakes Mona's hand. "Jade," she offers politely.

Mona's berry-red lips curve into the smile that has blinded her fans for the past two decades. "Nevada." She makes her daughter's name sound like the opening of a song.

Did she ever write songs for her children? I've never heard her sing one about motherhood, but that doesn't mean she hasn't locked one up inside a drawer.

Nev responds in a voice as light as morning fog, "Mom."

A camera surges up behind Mona, disrupting the intimacy of the reunion. I swivel my head and come nose-to-lens with a second camera.

Mona lifts her palm in front of the camera next to her. "No filming," she says. "My kids are off-limits."

Mom blinks and so do I. Here I was expecting she'd milk the moment.

"We'll blur their faces," the cameraman says.

"No." Mona shakes her head, her mass of curls gleaming as they settle over her red silk button-down, from which a rhinestone-encrusted bra peeks out. "Can I ask how y'all met?"

"Angie's mother is our interior decorator," Nev explains.

Mona nods slowly.

"And we go to the same school," Nev adds.

"And Jeff knows y'all are here?"

Nev nods, her combed hair quivering from the intensity.

"Okay, then." Mona tips her head toward the stage. "Let's get you set up, Angie. I wanted you to sing the song first, and then we'll go somewhere quieter to discuss the terms of the contract."

I gulp as I take in the stage set up with a gleaming black baby grand. Like in the Bluebird, some of the world's most magnificent voices have filled this place, have resonated among the pews and against the red and blue windowpanes.

As Mona leads us down the aisle, she says, "Kara will get you and your momma the form authorizin' filming and broadcast of your performance. You'll need to sign that one before you go onstage."

Nev's head keeps swiveling around as she takes in the place and then her mom and then the people milling around. There are *a lot* of them . . .

When we reach the front row, the curly-haired assistant arrives with a clipboard, which she passes to Mom. My mother squints at it, reading it over carefully. Once she's signed, she hands me the clipboard, and I append the autograph I left on the recording studio's couch.

"Nevada, Jade, why don't you two take a seat over here while I set Angela up onstage." Mona points to the front row. After Mom takes

Nev's hand and leads her toward the curved pew, Mona says, "I'm surprised my kids wanted to come."

I find Ten sitting all by himself in the back row, watching me like a hawk. I hope this isn't too painful for him. "Why? They're your kids. Kids want to see their parents."

An almost imperceptible groove appears between Mona's eyebrows. If I hadn't been standing so close, I would've missed it.

"Mrs. Stone, I have a request to make." I say this softly so that no one else can hear me.

She cocks a perfectly plucked eyebrow. "I'm listenin'."

Weeks ago, being the object of Mona's attention would've been the highlight of my life. But that was weeks ago. "I'd like to sing my song as a duet."

Her arms slide back along her sides, her rings sparkling wildly. "I suppose we could do that."

"I want to sing it with your daughter."

"With my"—she lowers her voice—"with *Nevada*?"

"Yes."

She peers in Nev's direction. Nev flushes as scarlet as her mother's blouse.

"Is this some sort of practical joke?" Mona asks.

"No."

Mona's looking at her son now.

"That's one of the reasons I asked her to come today, although she's not aware of it. I didn't want to get her hopes up in case it wasn't a possibility."

"Can she sing?"

I smile. "Better than I can."

Mona scrutinizes my face for a long second, her pupils pulsing in time with my heart. "The only way for her to sing is if her legal guardian—Jeff—signs off on it."

"Not if it isn't filmed, right?"

She bites her lips. It doesn't ruin her lipstick. "I suppose."

"Can we start with that? It'll allow my voice time to warm up before my segment."

For an interminable moment, Mona is quiet and still.

"Please? You won't regret it."

"Will my son be performing too?"

"Ten? No. He's here for his little sister." And for me. "That's all."

An expression—I can't tell whether it's sadness or frustration—mars her perfect face. "Kara!" she calls out, the intensity of her voice startling. "All cameras off. Phones too. Now!"

The few conversations buzzing around us die out.

"Thank you, Mrs. Stone," I tell her as she goes to find a seat.

She gives me a tight nod, and I climb onto the stage. Once seated on the bench, I move the mic around until it's at the right height. And then I say, "Nevada Dylan, get your skinny butt up here."

Nev's eyes bulge. Mom's too.

"You owe me, remember?" I add.

Nev sinks lower into the wooden pew.

I start playing the opening chords of my song. "I wouldn't be here today if it weren't for you."

That makes her jolt out of her seat. Perhaps because she's afraid of what more I might confess. She looks at Mom and then at Mona. When Mona tips her head toward the stage, Nev scampers forward as though propelled by an invisible force. And then she's scaling the stairs, knees quaking, eyelashes batting.

I tip my head to the bench, and she rushes to take a seat.

"It's not being filmed, don't worry," I tell her.

Nev's complexion has turned the waxen gray of someone about to face their greatest fear. I knock my shoulder into hers.

She raises her eyes to mine. "Is that why Lynn—"

"Made you practice my song?" I nod, then, without taking my eyes off hers, I whisper, "Ready?"

She shakes her head no.

I lean in and whisper, "Well, I wasn't either, but you didn't give me a choice, so here I am returning the favor."

60

Hear Us Roar

I press down on the piano keys, so focused on Nev that the theater and everyone in it melts away. "One, two, three," I say, marking the beat with a slight nod of my head.

And then I begin playing the song that led me onto this stage.

As I reach the end of the intro, Nev's lips are still sealed shut.

I elbow her, and she jumps. "Now," I murmur, right before launching into the opening verse. But she doesn't sing.

People say take it slow but they forget it's a race.
So I run, and run, and run, I give chase.

"You know this song. Come on," I murmur.

She still doesn't unbolt her lips.

"What does your bracelet say?" I whisper.

She frowns, then stops twisting her fingers long enough to read the words on it. She needs to trust in them.

Gotta leave behind my demons, to go after my dreams,
Gotta forsake my inhibitions, to step under the beams.
But I run so fast, I stumble and fall,
Collapse against pavement and crash into walls.

My fingers rush over the keys, warm up to the chorus. This time, instead of singing alone, I repeat the bars, willing Nev to accompany me. Her lips remain immobile.

Playing the chorus over, I murmur, "I'll stop and walk out of here if you don't sing."

Her head jerks, and then her eyes finally unglue themselves from the keys and focus on me. I bob my head in time to the beat, grounding her with my gaze, forcing her to forget that her mother is in the audience.

My fingers roll into the chorus again. This time, the cage of Nev's lips opens to release a mesmerizing sound that flocks into the void around us.

> *I'm a dreamer made of love. A dreamer made of thoughts.*
> *An arrow made of feathers, and a rope made of knots.*
> *I'm a girl made of dreams. A girl made of hopes.*
> *A story made of rhythm, and a song made of notes.*

Her voice thunders out of her, spreading like velvet and ink through the old theater, coating everything and everyone in its wondrous, raucous darkness.

> *My chest is on fire. Electric, a live wire.*
> *Stand and dust myself off. Get back on the road.*
> *I blink, I breathe. Adjust my aim, reload.*
> *To run or to walk? Or to shout or to talk?*
> *Oh . . .*
> *I will get there, fast or slow,*
> *'Cause I know where I need to go.*
> *I'm a dreamer made of love. A dreamer made of thoughts.*
> *An arrow made of feathers, and a rope made of knots.*
> *I'm a girl made of dreams. A girl made of hopes.*
> *A story made of rhythm, and a song made of notes.*

I feel like we're back in my living room, singing together for the very first time, our voices overlapping and plaiting.

> *No one's ever caught a dream sitting down.*
> *No one's ever sang a song without a sound.*
> *I keep going,*
> *Stop at nothing,*
> *I will make it.*

I breathe in deeply, greedily. My fingers dance over the smooth keys, moving toward the last chorus, which rises like a storm—slow, steady, powerful. I look at Nev and feel something fierce. She is so young, yet so brave. So tiny, yet everywhere. Her fingers are balled into tight fists, but her spine is straight and her jaw soft. I loosen my own jaw.

Together we deliver the ending.

> *I'm a dreamer made of love. A dreamer made of thoughts.*
> *An arrow made of feathers, and a rope made of knots.*
> *I'm a girl made of dreams. A girl made of hopes.*
> *A story made of rhythm, and a song made of notes.*
> *Oh . . . a song made of notes.*
> *And a song made of notes.*

Like in a game of red light, green light, the world holds still around us. And then Mona, shaking her head, stands and claps. And then Mom, too, stands. She claps but keeps having to stop to knuckle tears from her cheeks.

I shade my eyes to see Ten. He doesn't clap, but nods to me, and that subtle show of approval is more meaningful than any clap.

Nev's hand wraps around mine. Devastating delight spreads over her face and falls in streaks over me. This is all she's ever wanted . . . to be heard by the one person who'd never even tried to listen.

61

My Time

Nev walks off the stage, her head held so high and straight that her hair flutters off her face. I don't follow her. I wait on the piano bench. When she reaches our moms, it's mine who hugs her first.

But then Mona extends her arms, and Nev walks into her mother's embrace. Mona's red mouth moves, glinting in the stage lights. I hope she's telling Nev that she's proud; I hope she's making plans to see her again now that they have something in common.

Ten hasn't moved from his pew in the back, features tight. He's worried, but will he ever not be? He raised his sister. He cares for her in a way that no one, not even his father, let alone his mother, does.

After another moment, Nev and Mona pull apart, and then Kara is tapping Mona's shoulder, gesturing to the camera crew. Mona tips her head to the bench she was occupying, an invitation for Nev to sit, but Nev springs down the aisle before flouncing into the seat next to Ten. He seems as surprised as Mona that Nev decided to sit back there.

I'm not.

Their heads come together, and then he slings an arm around her shoulders and pulls her against him, and the tension blighting his beautiful features finally slackens.

I hope he realizes that Nev will *always* choose him.

A calmness envelops me, as though the buildup of adrenaline is finally draining away, drip by slow drip. I play my song again, pouring everything I have into it this time.

I play it for all the young dreamers out there, those who dare to want something out of reach.

I play it for Lynn, and for my mom, the two women who got me to where I am.

I play it for Nev, to thank her for propelling me forward when I'd stopped moving.

And I play it for Ten.

Especially for Ten.

To prove to him that music can bring about emotions other than rancor and spite.

62

The Dotted Line

While Mom ushers Ten and Nev toward the buffet set up in the back, Mona and I take a seat to discuss the contract. I've already read through it with Jeff and Mom, so there are no surprises, just fancy, frightening words that make it sound as though I'm selling my soul instead of just words and an accompanying melody.

After I append my signature, my song will belong to her. I'll receive a lump sum as an advance on royalties. If it does well, I'll earn more. A couple of cents on the dollar for each listen.

"I'm jealous." Mona crosses her legs. Like me, she wears jeans, but her jeans are adorned with grommets and mine are as plain as they come.

"Jealous?"

She hooks her hands around her knee, her plethora of rings spangling the contract before me. "I choked during my first performance. I was the openin' act for Shania and got so nervous I forgot the lyrics. I ended up hummin' the rest of that song. I thought that would be the end of my career. My agent was furious, but Jeff said it was the best darn hummin' he'd ever heard."

A smile bends her lips—not for long, but long enough for me to see affection existed once between Mona and her ex. I'm not sure why I find this surprising. After all, they had children together. Two of them. One could've been a mistake or an accident, but not two.

"You're a very passionate girl, Angela." She glances over at the buffet, at Ten and Nev and my mother. "Passions can be devastating. Especially when you're a woman. While men are forgiven for not tuckin' their kids in at night, women aren't. Just like we aren't always thanked for bringin' home the bigger paycheck."

Is that what happened between Jeff and Mona? He resented her for prioritizing work and earning more than him?

"A few weeks before I gave birth to Nevada, I was offered my own show in Vegas. I couldn't turn it down. So I signed on the dotted line, and then her daddy signed on another dotted line, decreeing I was unfit to be a mother and took both my kids away."

I'm utterly confused. I can't pick apart the lies from the truths. Mona makes herself sound like the victim, but is she?

"Did you fight for them?" I find myself asking.

She returns her gaze to me. Although her face glows from the rose-gold powder dusted on her lids and cheeks, her eyes are somber. "Divorces are messy and painful. Fightin' means makin' it all harder and more painful. For everyone. Besides, Jeff was right in a way. I preferred being on a stage in front of thousands than sittin' at a dinner table with my babies and husband." She gazes around the auditorium. "So I let them go, and it tore me apart, but at least it kept them together."

Her sincerity thrusts me back to that deserted, dusky classroom where Ten cracked the pedestal on which I'd placed Mona. "Do you regret it?"

"I could never have gotten to where I wanted to go if I'd stayed."

"But do you regret it?"

She tows a hand through her hair, rings sailing over the golden-brown waves like twinkling ships. "You want me to say yes, but I'd be lyin'. Just like you said in your song, I chased my dreams. And people tried to pull me back. Some even made me stumble. *One* made me fall." She glances at Ten, though I doubt she means her son. I think she's talking about the man who looks so much like him. But maybe I'm wrong. Maybe it was Ten who made her fall. "But I got back on my feet. Fallin' hurts, Angela, as does lookin' back, but only stoppin' will truly harm you. I'm very curious to see what you'll do. You have what it takes. Talent. Looks. Presence. You owned that stage."

I hate how deep her praise reaches within me.

"You need a little more trainin' and a lot more opportunities, which are two things I can provide."

Weeks ago, I would've squealed, but that was weeks ago.

"You don't have to give me an answer now. Take some time to think it over."

"What about Nev?"

She frowns. "What *about* Nev?"

"Are you going to offer to train her?"

Mona stares at her daughter. "No." Her answer is short, devoid of doubt. "My daughter doesn't need a mentor; she needs a mother. And I'll never be that for her. If I offer to mentor her, lines will blur and hearts will break, because she'll expect more than I can give her."

"Will you give her *something*?"

"My time. I can give her some of my time. If Jeff will allow it."

"She'd like that."

"You think so?"

How could she doubt her daughter's hunger for her attention? "I know so."

Mona nods.

Ten shifts, flicks his eyes to me, then to his sister, then back to me. I sense he's getting antsy. I lower the pen to the paper and etch my name on the line, then off the line, the letters taking up more room than they're given.

This is as much as I'm willing to give Mona for now, but perhaps someday . . . one day, I'll be able to give her more. I put the pen down and stand, extending a hand.

"Thank you, Mrs. Stone."

"Mona." She takes my hand and shakes it. "So you know what to call me the next time we meet."

When our fingers disconnect, she walks away first. She doesn't head toward Nevada and Tennessee. Doesn't even spare them a backward glance. And it saddens me. Not for myself, but for them.

I don't move for a long time, but then Mom calls my name, and I start back toward her. Ten holds out his hand, and even though Mom's standing right there, I take it.

On our way out, Nev tosses one last, longing look behind her.

I don't.

I keep going.

I keep staring ahead.

No, that isn't true. I keep staring around me, at the people who are moving in the same direction as I am, because unlike Mona, I don't want to lose sight of them.

Outro

A month and a half later

I'm sleeping over at Rae's tonight, because the adults are heading out of town for a friend's wedding—one of the women from the book club who divorced a couple of years back. I vaguely remember her because of her makeup: she always wore this orangey foundation. Not only was it the wrong shade, but she also never seemed to blend it in. I never got why no one told her it looked awful. I mean, I wouldn't let Rae step out of the house with clown makeup on.

As I unstrap my seat belt, Mom says, "Have fun, baby. Not too much, though . . ."

Rolling my eyes, I grab my overnight bag and race toward my friend's house. Before I can even ring, Nora swings the door open, impatient and ready to go. After dropping a kiss on my cheek, she reminds Rae to be good, then yells for her husband.

He comes out of his study, shaking his salt-and-pepper head and muttering, "Do I *have* to go to this wedding?"

"Because you think the girls want to have you at home?" Nora asks with an eloquent smile.

"Fine, fine." He gives me a one-armed hug. "Rae, honey, no parties, okay?"

"Of course, Daddy." As soon as the front door shuts, she says, "So we're having a party."

"What? But—"

"Didn't you check WhatsApp? I sent everyone a memo."

She loops her arm through mine and leads me up to her bedroom, where she heaves out two huge cardboard boxes from under her bed. They're filled with snowflake-print cups, striped paper straws that look like candy canes, garlands of glittery stars, packs of white and red balloons, and spools of shimmery ribbon.

"Where's the mistletoe?" I ask.

"In the box with the helium tank." Rae bends over and pulls another box from under her bed.

"You're serious?"

"Deadly." She opens the flaps and pushes the box across the carpet toward me. "You blow up the balloons while I set up the garlands."

I heave the helium tank out and rip open a packet of balloons. "I didn't bring anything to wear."

"Good thing I have a closet full of incredible stuff."

The doorbell shrills a couple of minutes later.

"That must be Laney. Can you get it?"

Does *she* know about the party? Given her sparkly red dress, I take it she does.

I text Ten on my way back up the stairs.

ME: Party at Rae's tonight. You knew about it?

BEAST: Party, huh? I had other plans.

I still haven't changed his name in my phone. I don't want to. He's still in the dark about it, which amuses me to no end, God knows why.

ME: Cancel them.

ME: Please.

BEAST: I don't want to cancel them.

ME: Please. Please. Please.

BEAST: I'll delay them, but I'm not canceling them.

I'm relieved, albeit a little bummed he has plans. Then again, it's selfish of me considering I jumped on a sleepover at Rae's when we learned our parents were going out of town.

People start pouring in at seven o'clock sharp. None of them are Ten. I keep hoping he'll show up any minute, but lots of minutes pass, and he still isn't here.

"Yo, Conrad!" Jasper yells from the makeshift DJ booth he set up on the mother-of-pearl console Mom helped Rae's parents pick out when she redid their place. "This song's for you!"

My heart snaps to attention. At the first drumbeat, at the first violin stroke, I recognize my song. It's different from the original, better I think. Ten and Nev disagree, but I think their love for me clouds their judgment.

Mona Stone's voice overpowers the instruments.

A group of girls start singing along to the chorus, and then one whips her hands in the air, and beer splashes all over my borrowed dress. She doesn't apologize. In her defense, I don't think she noticed.

It's crazy how popular Mona has made my song. Not everyone likes it, of course . . . Nothing in this world is universally liked. I got my share of hate tweets proclaiming "Made" is "sappy," "the worst song ever," "grating." But I also received an outpouring of love from strangers. A couple of my new fans even started calling out the haters using the hashtag #Harshville.

I think the hashtag deserves a song.

The twins pop up around me and snap a selfie. I barely have time to look at the camera before they're captioning the shot: *The Next Mona Stone*.

They're wrong, though. I don't want to be the next Mona Stone anymore. I want to write the music that artists *like* Mona Stone will play. I'm about to correct them when Ten steps into the living room.

His gaze roams over the room before settling on me, and then he's fording across the room, elbowing people out of his way.

"You came," I whisper, feeling overwhelmed by the sight of him.

It's been two months, and my reaction to him hasn't lessened.

He shakes his head, then encloses me in his arms. "Never doubt it."

He presses his mouth against my nose, my eyelids, my jaw, my forehead, not leaving a single millimeter on my face untouched. "But I really do have other plans."

My heart sinks like a stone. "You said you'd delay them."

"I decided I didn't want to."

I rest my cheek against his chest, heat slickening my eyes. I don't speak for a while, just listen to his heartbeats melt into one another. When Mona's song ends—yes, he can now stand the sound of his mother's voice—he presses me away.

His eyes widen, then narrow. "Are you crying?"

"You just got here. I don't want you to leave yet."

"Angie." His voice is low, serious. So very serious. He clasps my hands tighter. "I'm leaving *with* you."

I blink.

"The plans I made. They're for us."

He gathers me back in his arms and holds me until he senses I'm not about to break apart. Then he kisses my temple. "Now, let's go find Rae, so you can wish her a good night." A sly grin overtakes his face. "And don't worry. She's aware you have another sleepover to attend."

It takes me almost a minute to manage the very eloquent response of: "Oh."

We've discussed sex, come close once, so I'm not surprised, and yet I'm surprised. It's the same emotion that gripped me the day I learned I'd won the contest. An emotion I still have no name for.

His hooded eyes spark in the dimly lit room. "Unless you'd rather your first time be with a stranger."

Even though nerves crackle and sizzle inside of me, I swat his arm. "Will you ever let me live that down?"

He shoots me that crooked smile of his I love so damn much. "Most definitely not."

A new song comes on. I hear the words *girl crush*, but not much else over the earsplitting beat Jasper has layered over Little Big Town's song. I slot my fingers through Ten's and lead him through the swaying clusters until we come upon Rae. She's sitting on her kitchen counter, head thrown back in laughter, legs swinging around Harrison.

The second she spots me, she squeals and hops off the island, then ties me up in a big hug. "Have *soooo* much fun," she whispers.

I blush. "Shut up."

It just makes her smirk. "Get out of here already."

"Night, Rae. Night, Harrison."

After I climb into Ten's car, I ask, "So where are we going?"

He reaches for my hand. "You'll see."

When we pull up in front of my house, my heart starts thundering so hard I fear for the safety of my ribs. Ten jumps out of the car, circles the front, then opens my door before I've even unhooked the seat belt. I let him pull me out, then pull me into the house, because my pulse has short-circuited my brain's ability to control my muscles.

LED candles flicker on almost every surface.

And there are rose petals again.

Everywhere.

"I think you secretly watch chick flicks," I tell him.

He laughs, then spins me so that I'm facing him. He gazes down at me and tucks a loose strand of hair behind my ear.

"But it's missing something," I say.

His fingers are still on the shell of my ear. "It is?"

I draw him toward the piano, which glitters with tea lights, and sit on the bench, pulling him down next to me. "Remember when you asked me if I would sing for you someday?"

He frowns. "And you did."

"I sang 'Made' for a lot of people. Not just for you. Tonight, I want to sing you something I've never sung in front of anyone."

He lifts my palm to his mouth, kisses it, then places my hand delicately back on the piano keys. And I begin playing the song I wrote for him.

A song titled "Someday."

A song about first love.

A song about him and me.

ACKNOWLEDGMENTS

NOT ANOTHER LOVE SONG has been a labor of great love. My first and greatest thanks goes to Kat Brzozowski, who tirelessly went through version after version (there were *oh so many*) of my book to help me shape it into the one you've just read. Thank you, Kat, for your vision, your enthusiasm, and your support throughout this musical journey.

A great big thank-you to the entire Swoon Reads team that worked on *Not Another Love Song*. Your efforts and hours honed my story into a book I'm extremely proud to call my own, even though it's just as much yours as it is mine: Starr Baer, Sophie Erb, Holly Ingraham, Heather Hughes, and Lauren Scobell.

Thank you to Jean Feiwel for making all of this possible. You've created such a wonderful community, which I'm so proud to be a part of.

To the Swoon Squad: Your support system and friendship have blown me away. To many more years of having each other's backs.

Thank you to all my first readers on Swoon, who praised and voted for this book when it was still just a one-woman show named *Harshville*. You made this happen.

To my author besties and beta readers *extraordinaire*—Katie Hayoz, Theresea Barrett, Astrid Arditi—I love you girls and value your opinions so darn much (even when they completely diverge from my own).

To my sister Vanessa, who would've made one heck of a singer, a huge thank-you for all your musical knowledge.

To my parents and other two siblings, thank you for listening with unwavering enthusiasm to all the canine novellas I wrote as a kid and would read you during family meals.

To my husband and three crazy kids, thank you for being the best cheerleaders in the world. And no, I don't love my computer more than you . . . ;)

And last but not least, thank *you* for joining me on my foray into country music.

Check out more books chosen for publication by readers like you.

DID YOU KNOW...

readers like you helped to get this book published?

Join our book-obsessed community and help us discover awesome new writing talent.

1 Write it.
Share your original YA manuscript.

2 Read it.
Discover bright new bookish talent.

3 Share it.
Discuss, rate, and share your faves.

4 Love it.
Help us publish the books you love.

Share your own manuscript or dive between the pages at **swoonreads.com** or by downloading the **Swoon Reads app.**